HIDDEN
IN THE
STARS

HIDDEN
IN THE
STARS

BOOK ONE OF THE
STAR STITCH CHRONICLES

Hazel Vale

HAZEL VALE BOOKS

First published by Hazel Vale Books

Ontario, CA

hazelvalebooks.com

Copyright © 2022 Hazel Vale

Book cover design by moorbooksdesign.com

Inside formatting by hazelvalebooks.com

Edited by Skye Horn

ISBN: 978-1-7780882-0-9 (paperback)
ISBN: 978-1-7780882-1-6 (ebook)

For Leah
because writers need readers
and Wynter needed you.

One

Wynter yawned, fumbling with the yellow apron strings, her arms still shaking off the heaviness of sleep.

Henris didn't want her to keep the apron. He thought the yellow flowers drew far too much attention. Unless it was baggy; he'd always said baggy was best. So she left an extra gap around the middle.

"We need to leave," Henris said, putting a bowl of porridge into her hands. Henris was thin, his hair grey and fluffy like a baby goose. He was always so perfectly attired; she was surprised he didn't notice the apron.

"Go? Go where?" she asked, staring at the porridge. They rarely went out and never on a workday.

The tailor shop was eerily quiet. The wide-mouthed copper vat was usually full of boiling, sudsy water. There were no morning steamy clouds of citrus freshness. The irons hung in a row of silver triangles, and the cutting tables were still tucked away.

Certainly there was work to do; they always started before

sunrise. The mending basket was full, each item tagged with names and numbers. The torn seams and loose buttons were her responsibility now. A big honour, according to Henris. She was only thirteen but had a better stitch than the best dressmakers on Orion.

Wynter spooned the still warm bites into her mouth as quickly as she could. The blunut syrup stuck to the side and slopped onto her fingers.

She carefully set the bowl into the sink and washed her hands, making sure they were clean.

Last week, a lady had noticed how clean her hands were. She'd also commented on Wynter's green eyes and high cheek bones, nodding and assuring Henris that Wynter would grow into her features. Henris hadn't liked the compliment.

It wasn't safe to be noticed.

Wynter tugged out her braids and ran her fingers through her tangled hair, looping the dark brown strands back into a knot, and hurried back out to Henris.

"Let's go," he said. A small laundry bag leaned against his leg. Her ugly mauve apron poked out. Stuffing it back in, he cinched it closed.

"We're not working today." He looked at his feet. She looked at his feet too. They were more or less normal, with shiny black shoes and blue rolled cuffs at the bottom. She wondered if his toes had the same fluffy white hairs as his knuckles did. It probably wasn't something she should ask about.

"Are we going to the cobbler? I know you said it wasn't a good idea, but he wouldn't even look twice at me," she said. The feeling she was missing something tugged at her heart like apron strings.

"No, not the cobbler." Henris looked toward the back of the

store, out the front window, then back again. She wanted to tell him he'd already looked there, but kept her mouth closed.

He frowned at the yellow apron, finally noticing it. Wynter pulled at the middle fabric to make it hang a little more.

"Is it a surprise? You said one day I'd get to see the festival booths."

"I'm sorry, Wynter. We can't go to the festival." He picked up the laundry sack, slung it over his shoulder and started for the front door.

"Wait, I made a new list." It was in her room on the desk, a scrap piece of receipt the machine had printed wrong, but last night she'd dreamed up more questions and had jotted them down for when the ladies arrived.

"No time." His eyes darted to the back of the shop again.

It must be important, this trip they were going on. He never said no to her lists.

He always let her listen in when the fancy dresses were being picked up or altered.

The ladies always paid too much for dresses—even if they didn't fit right—then Henris would fix them. Wynter loved watching and listening as she pressed and tidied. Henris must have been bored of it all, but he'd ask the ladies her questions anyway. One after the other. He'd inquire about the details of parties, what colours were in season and who they had danced with. His glasses would slip down his nose, threaders on his fingers as he kept a steady pace, while Wynter dreamed of the day she'd be able to dance at a ball like the ones they described.

Henris didn't like it when she dreamed out loud.

"But where are we going?" she asked, following him out of the shop. The door chime played her favourite of the rotating jingles, and she smiled.

He locked it behind them as they stepped out through the solid brick doorway and onto the street.

The shop's narrow arch was squeezed between the watchmaker on one side and the cheese house on the other. They rarely saw the watchmaker, but Wynter was sure the noises coming from the building next door had little to do with clockwork. Wynter often asked Henris about the noises but was told her to mind her own.

The cheese shop was owned by a woman with wrinkles in her cheeks. Wynter thought she looked a lot like a round ball of cheese. She smelled even worse, but Henris was always happy to see her. Wynter minded her own without having to be told.

Early morning shop lights blinked on around them. Like his tailor shop, Henris had taught her that guilds on Orion were always up before the sun.

Wynter counted ten blocks before the sun crept over the edges of the shops. A few more blocks and she wondered why she couldn't wear yellow more often. No one cared a grape if she was walking down the street, even with her yellow apron on.

The streets looked different in the morning light; the sun cast glitter across the shop windows. She smiled at the colourful peaked roof tops she'd only seen as shadows in the dark.

Block after block they walked. The edges of her eyes soon felt sore from squinting. The morning traffic hurt her ears, and her feet ached.

"Are we almost there?" she asked.

"Almost." He took her hand, helping her along.

She watched the trollies fly past with their shiny flat fronts and floor to ceiling windows. She wished they could sit on one of those plush purple chairs for a moment. But Henris wasn't watching the trollies. Instead, he was looking back toward where they'd come from and forward again to wherever they were going.

They reached the white stone space hub in the centre of town. Streets sprang from it like spokes on a wheel. Court ivy crisscrossed up the sides in perfect squares. The dome was open, and shuttles were flying out at regular intervals, gliding over the village, past the mountains behind them and into the puffy clouds to deliver goods and passengers to the larger ships in orbit above Orion.

The blunut syrup from breakfast turned a little in her stomach.

They didn't go through the large scan archways where lines spilled into the streets. Instead, they walked around to one side of the building. Henris opened a door in the paneling using a small card and ushered her through.

The automatic lock clanked behind them.

Crates, conveyor belts, boxes, and workers bustled around like a hive. Three workers in bland uniforms glided past, controlling floating carts with luggage and crates. They didn't pay them any attention.

Wynter scrunched her nose. The room smelled clean, but not the good soapy kind of clean from the laundry. This clean burned her nose.

"It's the fuel," Henris stated.

They walked past the back ends of the shuttles docked in rows. A metal skirt hung from the ceilings and closed around them, shielding boarding passengers from view.

Henris consulted a small scrap of paper. He appeared to be counting the docks, the lines in his weathered face deeper than usual.

At the end of the row was a shuttle, its back end open for

loading. He wiped his forehead, took a quick look around, and walked up the ramp into the cargo bay. Wynter followed. Once inside, the hull muffled the noise of the loading docks, leaving only a dim rumble in her ears.

"Where are we going?" she asked. She'd never been on a trolly let alone a shuttle, and the back of a shuttle couldn't be a good way to travel. "Henris?"

He was checking the sides of crates and stopped in front of a long wooden box. 927 HELIX had been stamped in neon pink on top of an arrow that pointed up. He unclipped the metal latches. Inside were rows of bolted fabric.

Was this why he couldn't say anything? Were they here to steal material? Henris had always talked about honest business, but Wynter didn't have a problem with stealing if he said he needed to. She looked at the rolled bolts, then back at Henris.

But Henris took nothing out of the crate. Instead, he tucked the little bag inside.

"I've kept you longer than I should have. I can't hide you forever." He looked as though he was biting at the inside of his chin, the way it squished and rumpled. "Madame Helix has a spot on a ship. She's proper, and she's talented. You do what she says and don't cause trouble." His voice was shaking a little.

"Who's Madame Helix? You're sending me away?" Her breath felt stuck, like the air was already being sucked out of the cargo hold.

If she was going somewhere, shouldn't there be a seat and a harness?

"I need you to get in," he said. He gave her a little lift until she sat on the edge with her feet barely touching the floor. There would be just enough room for her to lie down.

"Madame Helix will meet you on the ship once her items are unloaded and safe in her rooms. The ship is big. They carry cargo for the guilds as well as passengers. But don't get too curious." His voice caught. "She'll keep you safe, I promise."

Safe? On a ship? "I like space as well as anyone. Doesn't mean I want to live there," Wynter said, feeling her chin shake.

He ignored her plea and made sure the bag was tucked inside so the lid of the crate could close.

"There's a little panel here," he said, showing her the little latch that opened from the inside. "You'll be able to open it once they take off, so you won't feel so closed in, but the crates aren't airtight, you'll be able to breathe fine either way."

"How long will I be gone? Will you come find me?"

Taking the long gold chain which held his guild pendant from around his neck, he held it in his hands for a moment, then pressed the pendant to his weathered lips.

"I'll come get you when it's safe," he said, placing it around her neck. "Stay ugly, stay hidden, stay alive."

She held the metal in her hand, feeling the lingering warmth. He loved his pendant. She knew because he'd told her many times. He'd earned it when he was only twenty, and the guild had designed it specially for him. Like all Tailor guilds, it had the crossed needles, but this one had a strand of blue inlaid through the eye, joined with black and silver and braided around the outside. She'd never touched it. She'd stared at it in awe when he spoke respectfully about guild law. Like a ghost story, it sent shivers up her spine, only better. And now she was wearing it; but she didn't want it, not if it meant leaving.

Questions tumbled around on the tip of her tongue. How long would she be in the crate? How long would she be gone? If they left Orion, it could take months to return. New cargo always took months. How long would it be before she saw Henris again?

He held the lid. His hands were shaking. Despite the growing panic, she laid back onto the rolls of smooth fabric; her chest squeezed tight. She wished she could tell him she didn't want to go. She'd promise to stay hidden in the shop. No one ever noticed her. She'd do better so she could stay with him.

The lid closed. She felt the brush of the wood against her nose when she tried to lift her head. There was a soft click as the latch caught, and then the sound of his black shoes as he walked away.

She tried not to rumple the bolts of fabric as she wiggled, hoping her salty tears wouldn't leave marks on the beautiful material. There was the sound of muffled voices, the thud of something being dropped, more crates being loaded, cargo being slid across the metal grated floor. All the time she was trying not to panic or scream or make anyone aware of where she was. She was good at hiding, but Henris had always been with her. What would happen if they caught her? Henris had always kept her hidden.

The bing of the intercom startled her. Instinctively she sat up a little, banging her forehead on the wood. She lowered her head back down slowly, face aching.

"This is your captain for your quad-shuttle to the Obsidian," the voice boomed through the shuttle speakers. It echoed around the room and came through the fabric and wood like a muffled stranger.

Wynter felt a rumble and deafening bang as the cargo bay door sealed and locked. The surrounding air changed, thickened, then evened out.

"We have a special passenger on board today—Lord Isaac

Ward…" the voice continued in a chipper and annoying way.

The crate swayed a little, pulling gently at the edges of the tie downs.

"He'll be your new first mate on the Obsidian. We wish him all the best."

Stay ugly, stay hidden, stay alive. She said it over and over, blocking out the shuttle speakers.

The crate rattled and shook as the shuttle pod rocketed into space.

Two

The large black panels of the Obsidian opened, reverberating through the ship's guild-level work rooms. Wynter held the ball gown to her chest, refusing to let go.

"I'm taking it with me," Madame Helix said sternly, looking at herself in the studio mirror. Wynter stared, hoping she'd be more concerned with her own apparel than the dress they'd been fighting about.

Helix was tall and straight like a stick. She must have been at least thirty, but Wynter never asked. Helix ran her hands over her brown travelling suit and then frowned at her reflection.

Wynter had told her the brown was flattering.

It wasn't.

If she could convince Helix to put a green hat on, she'd look like a tree. But right now, she was fighting to keep the dress.

Helix turned back to Wynter, stepped over the piles of fabric on the floor, and held out her hands expectantly.

"Can't we hold on to this one? You've already packed every

dress we've made. You never sell them all," Wynter said. Her heart was pounding as she tried one last defence. She'd designed the dress for Orion. It was Orion fashion, and more importantly, she'd stitched Henris's crest into the bottom row. She always stitched it into the design, but this one he'd recognize. It was an unreasonable hope, but if the dress came by his shop, he'd know it was her who'd made it. If Helix took it to Valtine, that would never happen.

"I have a request for this dress from a lady. She will pay triple what we'd get on Orion," Helix replied, unmoving.

"It's not possible; she's never seen it."

"You can make another one," Helix said as she reached out and yanked the dress from Wynter's hands. She should have kept it hidden and unfinished.

Wynter suppressed a scream as Helix pressed the treasured gown into the crate between the others.

"I expect the work room and display areas to be clean when I get back." She picked up her small bag with one hand and waved the other around, as if Wynter didn't know what she was talking about.

Bolts of fabric lined every wall, shelving stacked double high. At the end of the workroom there were storage compartments, a door to their private bathroom, and beside that, Helix's room. Above the personal rooms was a loft for storage. She'd lined the front of it with crates, and behind them was a bed where Wynter slept, and storage for her few belongings.

Everything, from the front of the room to the back, was a disaster.

The large table in the middle of the room was piled with half-sewn dresses Helix hadn't finished and a dozen more Wynter had started. Fast trims, pins, and papers littered the floor, indistinguishable from packaging, embellishments, and bits of everything else one might imagine was necessary for a seamstress to have.

"Don't be seen when the crates are being picked up," Helix warned.

"Of course not," Wynter said. Picking up a roll of lace off the floor. She ran it through her fingers before rewinding it.

"And don't get caught doing anything."

"Of course not," Wynter said again, as if she hadn't heard the same speech on every planet that they orbited for the past seven years. Spying a green ribbed cap with little jade feathers, she plucked it off the pile of accessories and handed it to Helix.

"Don't forget your hat." Wynter smiled. It made her feel a little better.

Helix fluffed the little feathers, then fixed it on her head, patted the crates, and left.

Wynter waited a minute, then two, then tossed the lace back onto the floor. She quickly changed into a stolen cleaning crew uniform; two long braids fell down her back, matching the standard crew style. The fitted black pants went longer than was usual, so the hem would cover her not-so-standard slippers. She tucked in the slate top, then puffed it out around the middle and let it hang loose over her frame.

She waited an extra minute. When she was certain Helix wasn't coming back, Wynter stepped into the hall. Some guilds had specially designed rooms for sleep, wares, cargo, and a small shop front, like the one she lived in. Other guilds commissioned the Obsidian to carry goods and cargo from one planet to another.

The guild level had smooth polished wood floors, crystalline ceilings, and well-lit alcoves. So unlike the passenger floors with plush carpets and vibrant walls.

The Helix suite was at the end, tucked around the corner and buttressing the stairwell. It was cozy, like a small cocoon nestled at the edge of the massive luxury cargo ship.

Passing through the empty guild floor, Wynter made her way to the bustling mid floors. She hoped the change of pace on the ship would lighten her mood. It wasn't only the dress that upset her; she wanted to be there, on the planet, at the ball. She wanted to be a guild Madame who fit her creations perfectly and then watched her gowns spin around the dance floor.

Another shudder went through the ship as the first shuttle pods were dropped into space.

Wynter walked past passengers getting ready to disembark. A large group, dressed in brightly coloured travelling clothes, had congested at the gallery windows. Bags and luggage tightly clutched, coos and sighs of excitement bubbled out of them as they watched Valtine come into view.

She fixed her gaze past the group and kept her head up, not too high, not too low, her smile polite and unenthusiastic.

She resisted the pull inside her stomach, drawing her toward the lookout point. There would be lots of chances once the passengers were all off the ship, but there was something about having a planet so close after weeks in the darkness.

People stopped to look out before heading to the shuttle bay, jamming the hallways. Along with them, four crew members were coming toward her. They guided float carts loaded with boxes, luggage, and crates. She took a quick turn down a secondary hallway toward what she knew were recently abandoned rooms and disappeared.

Emerging on the other side, she grabbed a lunch basket off one of the meal carts and made her way slowly up three floors to Dr Moss's empty medical bay.

This part of the ship was large and almost always empty. The clinical black floors and silver-lined hallways were gloomy and naturally kept passengers away.

There was always a small stack of books left sitting on the instrument tables of the medical bay. She grabbed one with a red spine and tucked it under her arm without checking the title, then kept moving. She wondered if the doctor had an entire library tucked away in his room.

The medical bay melted into rows with tall doorways leading to cargo holds and safety pods. It was the long route to the upper pool decks, but it was the easiest way to avoid the crowds.

She trailed her hand along the walls, letting her fingers dip in at every soft glow pot.

The silence, the empty halls, it would be hers for the next three weeks. Valtine was the largest planet in the hex-system, which also made it the longest stop.

After Valtine, they'd go to Orion.

Maybe Henris would contact her this time. Maybe he'd say it was safe.

Three

Eucalyptus steam curled out when Wynter opened the door. The waterfall feature along the far wall splashed into the deep oval pool. Folding chairs, sunlight lamps, and exotic plants made it look like an oasis, or as close to one as she could imagine.

She took off her slippers, rolled up the bottom of her pants and sat down on the edge of the pool. Her toes tingled as she dipped them in and out of the water, letting them make little swirls as coloured lights changed the waves.

The edge of Valtine spanned the corner of the dome window, picking up bits of the planet's sun as it cast a rose-glow over the surface. Wynter watched the imperceptible rotation of the world below, longing for the warmth of a real sun and not just the heated day lamps.

Her solitude was brief. A gust of steam from the door jets went off heralding another visitor to the misty decks.

The young man was wearing a crisp white shirt tucked into fitted navy pants. His hair was cut to the side, and she recognized him even without his typical, formal jacket. Of all the people she'd done her best to avoid, Captain Isaac Ward was at the top of her list.

She knew his routine, and visiting the pools after docking wasn't on the captain's typical agenda. Pulling her toes out of the water, she stood, arms at her side.

Captain Ward looked like perfection as always with not a mutinous hair on his head. He nodded at her, and she let her arms hang a little less stiff as she'd seen crew members do a hundred times.

"I'm looking for my necktie, shoes, or cufflinks. Are they in here?" He smiled, as if it was completely normal for a captain to be looking in the pool area for articles of clothing. He checked under the chairs and around the base of the waterfall. She held her breath and tucked her wet feet back into her slippers, wondering how she was going to sneak out.

She'd never gotten this close to Captain Ward before and didn't plan on sticking around. His brown eyes narrowed on her. They were flecked with amber, but she quickly looked away, flattening her uniform.

"I don't know," she said, her heart picking up an extra beat.

"You must have been sent to report my frustrations back to the others. You can tell them stringing my formal attire all over the ship is the least ghostly thing they could have done. It's a terrible prank." He walked to the back of the room and looked behind the potted plants.

"Oh no, I'm just up from Valtine for the day," she lied. It was at least believable. An influx of cleaners would be on board. She just needed to make him believe she was one of them.

"Well, then forget I said anything about a prank. Forget I was here at all."

Of course, she knew about the pranks. Crew were good at

keeping secrets, but everyone who wasn't a casual passenger would know about the pranks that the late Captain Holt had instituted. Captain Ward never looked very bothered by it all, which had probably angered the old captain. Everything had angered the old captain, and if he was still alive, she wouldn't have risked being at the pools. The last two years since his death had been pleasant, and not only for her. She could tell in the way the rest of the crew carried themselves around the ship; it all felt lighter somehow.

"Of course, sir," she said as confidently as she could. His focus drifted away from her and back to searching the room.

Even without his formal attire, searching for missing clothing, Captain Ward looked so put together.

She wished she could have that type of confidence, especially with Helix. Maybe if she did, she would have been able to hold onto the dress. She liked that the captain was clean shaven, and lacking the long beard his uncle had worn. But perhaps he should have one to make him look older. There was always talk in the halls; they said he was young, far too young to own his own ship.

Looking out across the water, Wynter spotted the tie dangling from the ceiling over the centre of the pool.

Captain Ward saw it at the same time. He'd found what he was looking for and so she really should try to make her escape. Picking up the book and lunch might draw too much attention. She didn't want him questioning why a day crew member was relaxing at the pools and not working. Abandoning them was her only option, but when she went to make her retreat, he stopped her.

"Oh no. You should stay and watch my victory. Let them know this was easy. Day crew or not, you all talk." His feet were on the edge of the pool now. He leaned forward, but the suspended tie still dangled an arm's length away.

Wynter stood frozen between the need to run and not wanting to draw more attention. She pressed her arms into her sides.

"Yes, sir," she said, having nothing better to say.

He was balancing on the lip of the pool, leaning over, but he remained too far off no matter what angle he tried. Wynter looked up at the tie, wondering how any member of the crew had managed to place it there.

"Not to worry, I have another idea," he said, and winked at her. The Captain of the Obsidian winking… she hoped the flush she felt in her cheeks didn't show.

Dragging one of the white chairs from the deck over to the edge, he punched the button to let it lie flat, then balanced the chair on the edge of the pool and looked at Wynter.

He hadn't said it, but it was clear what he was thinking. He grabbed the far end of the white lounge chair, thumped it down a few times on the edge to make sure it was sturdy.

It didn't look sturdy.

"I'm going to hold this here. Then you walk out on it. My weight will easily offset yours, and you'll be close enough to yank the tie off the string." There were a dozen things wrong with this plan, but he was staring at her, smiling, waiting.

She didn't like the idea. She'd never done more than dip her toes in the water. Swimming wasn't something Helix could teach her—that would require being seen together—and it wasn't like she'd had a chance to swim back on Orion.

"You must have other ties," she stated, staring at the rickety chair. "I think that tie makes a nice decoration up there."

"No, it has to be that one."

"Why?"

"Because it's the one the ghost took. Don't look so afraid, it's not a real ghost, and the whole thing was never my idea," he explained. She wasn't afraid of the ridiculous pranks, what she was afraid of was the water.

"You're the captain, can't you tell this ghost no?" The idea sounded better than getting on the chair.

"I can't. There are rules to these pranks."

Wynter really wanted to know what those rules were. She'd only been able to catch bits and pieces here and there.

"As captain, can't you change the rules?" She pushed a little, seeing if he'd give her anything back. It was probably not something a crew member would say, but she felt a light bubbling in her chest talking to him, overruling the desire to run away.

His eyes narrowed, but the smile still played on his lips.

"As your captain, I could order you to help."

"I think ordering a crew to help would be against the rules," she said, biting back the urge to say he wasn't really her captain.

"I'd owe you?" he suggested instead.

"I'm only here for the day," she said, knowing she'd better not be seen by him again after this.

His grin reached up to his eyes. Clearly enjoying himself, he thumped the chair legs on the deck again to prove how sturdy it was. "I've got it. You'll be fine."

What other choice did she have? She stepped over him, finding her balance by holding onto his broad shoulders, and took a deep breath in as the chair creaked. To her surprise, he smelled like soft citrus, like the soaps Henris used. Like home.

She stood up straight and balanced. Without lifting a foot, she slowly shuffled to the end of the chair, looking down at the colour changing lights in the water below.

At the edge, she reached out and caught the top of the tie, giving it a tug. It didn't come down. A second tug and still nothing. Pulling down hard, she felt the wire give way, freeing the cravat.

At the same time the chair snapped, plunging her and the bit of fabric into the water.

The cool water gave her a momentary shock. Her feet reached for the bottom, searching for something to push off.

Wynter tried to pump her legs back and forth but the pants weighed her down, pulling her under. She closed her eyes tight and tried flapping her arms, but they felt stuck in glue, the heavy uniform sucking onto her.

A muscular arm wrapped under her, and she felt her body being dragged toward the surface. She gasped for air, kicking her legs wildly.

"Stop squirming! I've got—" His head went under for a moment then bobbed back up.

Taking another breath, she propelled herself to the edge of the pool, placed her arms on the edge, and dragged herself out. Lying on her stomach on the cold tiles, Wynter pinched the tie between her fingers, motionless as Captain Ward pulled himself out of the pool beside her.

A few moments later, a fluffy towel hit her back and then another.

Rolling her soaked body over, she sat up. Rubbing her face with one towel, she put the other one over her shoulders.

Captain Ward jumped back into the pool to retrieve the broken bits of chair and tossed them onto the deck.

Wynter stood. Her tight braids had come loose, and her hair

was a tangled mess. She tucked the tie into her pocket, puffed out the bottom of her shirt. Squeezing handfuls of fabric, little rivers of water dripped out and slunk back into the pool.

Captain Ward started doing the same, bunching up the bottom of his shirt and wringing it out. She tried not to stare. The white shirt was plastered to his body, and he looked completely unkempt and unbelievably handsome. A crew member wouldn't be staring like she was. Averting her eyes, her fingers untangled her braids and pulled her hair back into a knot.

"Are you okay?" he asked, using his captain's voice, but his eyes roamed over her, looking for any damage.

Wynter pulled at her uniform, trying to make it baggy, but it slurped right back against her skin.

"I'm fine," she said, knowing that not even the best crew member would know what to do in this situation. "Are the pranks always so dangerous?"

"Dangerous? There was no danger—" he smiled again.

She raised a brow, looking at the mess around them.

"Maybe we don't mention this part either? I don't suppose you have my tie?" he asked. He adverted his attention from her long enough to look around the discarded towels and bits of broken chair for his missing tie.

Taking it out of her pocket, she held it out to him.

After this, he'd remember her. After this, she was going to have to be careful, to be invisible, to disappear.

He flattened his hair and tucked the wet shirt into his pants. Towel around his neck like a glorified scarf he looked completely in control again, not like he'd just taken an unplanned dunk in the pool.

Her heart was fluttering like she'd run the length of the ship.

She reminded herself one last time she was crew and composed herself.

"I should probably go change my uniform," she said.

"If you have any trouble, you can send a message through Platt." His brow drew together, as if he was thinking he should do something else for her.

"Don't worry," she said quickly, "I'm fine, and I won't have trouble keeping your secret."

"Well then, thank you for the swim," he said, giving the slightest bow, which a captain probably shouldn't do, and then left.

It might not have been a ballroom, but it felt as though she'd danced with the captain and gotten away with it.

Four

Captain Isaac Ward squared his opal cravat and adjusted the set of silver clasps that ran the length of the navy formal jacket he wore. His white cuffs poked out at the sleeves, and he gave them a final tug before stepping onto the ship's bridge.

The bridge was the crown of the Obsidian, with arched ceilings and long beams that curved up and met in the middle. Two main control desks faced each other from either side of the room, a wide walkway ran between them. Toward the front of the ship, a narrow window looked over the top and down the front. Once docked, the large shutters swept back to reveal panes of glass stretching from the floor up to the centre peak.

The bridge was quiet. Two of his engineering crew manned the basic orbit controls while another two sat hunched over the internal system screens.

Toward the back of the bridge was a long desk of panels and control areas where Rane, his chief engineer, was working.

Ward stepped over a bundle of cables, taking a moment to assess the opened panels and exposed main system circuits.

"That you, Captain?" Rane poked his head up from under the

desk where he was working and stood. The silver desk matched the shade of grey in the old man's hair. Rane could have easily retired years ago, but Ward needed him. Rane knew it, and the crew knew it too.

Rane's left hand held a full bouquet of wires. Putting the pliers in his mouth, he let the tool dangle from his teeth while he split the cables in half.

"I'm looking for my cufflinks. Have you seen them?" Ward asked, then waited for the chuckles from the front of the room to die down. He'd recognized one of the crew as Claire and the other as Haynes, the two most likely to be involved in executing the prank.

They looked a little too pleased with their efforts, considering they hadn't done anything exceptional, but Ward didn't let his annoyance show. Maybe laziness had settled into the Valtine pranks, or perhaps they were finally bored with it. He was hoping for bored.

Rane dusted off his red engineering shirt and put down the pliers. "You're two hours early."

"Of course I'm two hours early. It was a terrible prank." He would have been earlier if he hadn't gone for an unexpected swim. After drying off and changing, he'd resisted the urge to have Rane locate the woman from the pool. She'd looked so terrified of him, and clearly knew who he was, but he didn't want to embarrass her anymore. At the same time, he felt the need to apologize. Then he'd been stuck listening to Dr Moss rant over Ward's lack of control of the ship's crew, which was an ironic conversation since Dr Moss always did whatever he wanted regardless of ship rules.

Stepping over another conduit of wires, Ward inspected the

screens displaying all ten floors and the lower engine rooms of the ship. The secondary control rooms would be sealed and fluxed to clear any human contaminants from the systems. He wished there was a way he could use the flux gases on the rest of the ship, but cleaners would have to do. He flicked through the timing logs and plans.

"Did you know the ghost put my shoes in the sick bay?" Ward asked loud enough for everyone in the room to hear.

"Ghosts aren't dumb enough to go into the sick bay," Rane stated as he fished a long yellow wire through one of the open holes in the control panel and passed it to Ward to hold while he yanked it from the other end.

"Dr Moss wasn't happy about the ghost spilling into his territory."

"Dr Moss is never happy," Rane said. He attached the final wire and crawled out from under the desk, giving him an approving look. "You look handsome enough to get any lady's offer."

Ward frowned. Rane had brought the idea up every time they docked. If Ward could tie the Obsidian to land through marriage, the backing and security would open doors into higher paying cargo. They might even be able to downsize the passenger decks. It was something his uncle had refused to do, but as a young captain it might be the best choice for the future of his ship. At least that was what everyone continued to tell him. Especially Rane.

"I need my cufflinks," Ward said, ignoring Rane's comment about marriage.

Rane nodded to the front of the ship.

In the middle of the doubled row of clear panes, his cufflinks were suspended.

Ward walked between the control desks to the dangling silver bobbles. He grabbed them from midair and snapped the thin clear cord they hung from.

"You wouldn't know how these got here?" he asked Claire and Haynes.

"No, sir," they both echoed.

He pushed the rescued cufflinks through the loops and walked back to Rane.

Rane fed another long line through the back of one panel and popped it out the front, passing it to Ward before scooting under the desk again.

"Your uncle would have had the ghost charged with mutiny," he said from below, his loud voice echoing into the large room.

The chuckles from the front of the bridge stopped. Ward passed Rane the roll of thin blue electrical wire. He wondered what his first few years would have been like if his uncle hadn't encouraged the crew to play a trick on him the first time that they had reached Valtine, or the second time, or the time after that. What if his uncle had just treated him like an heir to the Obsidian and demanded the respect of the crew? Ward shook his head. It wasn't horrible, and as long as he kept an even temper throughout the whole thing, the crew forgot about it even before the ship departed for Orion. The pranks also provided the opportunity for him to show everyone he was nothing like his uncle.

"Now that I'm fully attired for tonight, and I've put the ghost to bed for another year, I'm handing the bridge and the repairs over to you. How are we doing?" Ward asked, handing the last grouping of wires to Rane.

"We're right on track, as always. Prep is done. I already started venting the flux gasses. After that's cleared, we have a few more system upgrades to run but nothing major. We'll finish within the week; lots of time to load cargo and make adjustments."

Ward surveyed the large screens again. The two hundred passenger rooms, entertainment decks, guilds, and storage spaces, plus the massive cargo hull. His ship. He looked down at where Rane was working and resisted the urge to thank him. A captain shouldn't thank anyone, but there were worse habits. Rane had been everything his uncle hadn't. Gratitude didn't cover half of how Ward felt about his chief engineer.

Satisfied with the progress, he gave one last tug on his cuffs and turned to leave.

"Wait, sir!" Haynes called after him. Claire and Haynes stood from their control desks, side by side in matching uniforms.

Ward glared at the two of them. He needed to get down to Valtine where lateness was not acceptable.

Both had clenched jaws like they were holding in marbles.

"Is there something else? Because I believe I'm done here." Ward tried to hide his annoyance, keeping his voice calm and controlled.

"You have to wait." Haynes took in a big gulp of air, squeezed his lips back together, and looked out the windows down toward the front of the ship.

Rane stood, equally annoyed, and followed their gaze. Nothing. And then all at once, the outer shell of the Obsidian lit up in a flash of purple bursts of colour.

Finding his clothing had been slightly annoying, but this was useless. Maybe it *was* time for the pranks to end. Was this even considered a prank at this point? Even though the display of lights would be seen from the other ships or the docking stations, anyone would assume they were running tests or upgrades.

Claire and Haynes burst into a fit of laughter. Rane looked cross.

"Very well—you can turn it off," Rane said from across the room.

Claire dialled the call on her arm and rolled her eyes at Haynes. "Okay, Turk. You can turn it off."

But the lights didn't stop.

Ward looked down to the front panel where they should have been operating the outer beacon lights from.

"You're not controlling it from here?" he asked.

"No, we can't. Rane has the panel disconnected, so Turk's in the secondary control room."

Ward sifted through the screens bringing up the secondary control rooms. Turk was in the room Rane had started filling with flux gasses.

"Rane, can we stop the decontamination?" Ward asked clearing the bridge in only a few long strides.

Rane was already ducking under the desk while Haynes stood stunned and immobile. Claire was frantically trying to reach Turk on her comm to no avail.

"Working on it, but it's going to take time, and it won't be enough." The ice in Rane's tone was felt through the bridge.

"Can we open the door to get oxygen flowing from the hallways?"

"Manual only. The system won't let me open it if there's gas present."

"Let me know when you have access. Get Dr Moss down there *now*."

Ward took off at a sprint and brought up the ship's

announcement system as he hit the first stairwell.

"This is your captain," his voice boomed through the massive ship as he ran down the hall. "Medical in the secondary control rooms. Venting flux, requesting Dr Moss on site." Switching the link, he brought up Rane's call.

"Is he moving?"

"No access yet." Neither said anything for a few minutes as Ward sprinted through the halls of his ship, taking every shortcut he knew to reach Turk. "Captain, I got Idex scans back up. He's alone. There's no way you can get there in time."

Ward was well aware that the flux gases were highly effective and deadly.

Rane had been right. His uncle never would have let this happen. Dr Moss had also been right. He had no control over his own damn ship.

"I don't know how but the doors have been opened. I've got the filtration system in the hallway going, but the air's going to be toxic by the time you get there." Rane's warning came over his comm.

Ward didn't heed the warning as he ran through the halls, his breathing heavy. All thoughts of pranks being harmless fled from his mind. No one had ever broken actual protocols before. There was always foolishness, but it was never dangerous. Everyone knew better.

He should have known something like this could happen. These crew members hadn't even had the common sense to stay out of Dr Moss's rooms.

His chest pounded and he could already feel the weight of the blood on his hands dragging him down.

Ward opened the manual hatch, then rounded the final

hallway. It was wide; the vents rumbled as Rane pushed the filtration system to its limit, but the smell of the flux gasses wafted around him, filling his nose, and making it hard to breathe.

Turk would have known. What could have possibly made him stay to do the prank when he knew how dangerous flux gasses were?

The walls bent and swayed as Ward tried to keep his breathing shallow, but the run had him gasping for more air.

Turk was lying outside the door, face down.

From the corner of his eye, behind the tall vent stacks, a bit of blue waved in his periphery. Ignoring the movement, he knelt beside Turk. Relief settled into his chest as he found a pulse.

Dr Moss arrived behind him, and without warning jabbed Ward in the arm with a needle, then bent over Turk and did the same.

"You could have warned me," Ward said, feeling a hot sting where the needle had gone in.

"It's toxic down here. He should be dead," Dr Moss replied.

"I'm aware."

"You'll be fine now," Dr Moss grumbled. Ward tried to focus on the man beside him. Like Rane, Dr Moss had been on the ship since Ward was a boy, maybe longer. His black hair was peppered grey with age. Soft lines at the edges of his eyes revealed he must have smiled at some point in his life, although Ward had never seen it. He was average height but well-toned for a man who spent most of his days in a medical wing.

Dr Moss refused to wear standard medical uniforms, he refused to see patients he didn't believe were unwell, and he had just jabbed Ward in the arm with a very long needle. But right now, Ward was simply thankful Dr Moss was there.

Turk's chest was already rising and falling at a more even rate. Ward helped Dr Moss roll him onto the lowered float gurney that the doctor had thankfully brought along.

As he stood, Ward's head finally cleared. His eyes fixed on the locked door. How had Turk gotten away from this with no significant injuries?

Ward noticed a trail of bright red blood from the door to Turk's body. He was splashed all over with large droplets. Ward patted him down, trying to find the source.

"I can't tell where he's bleeding from," Ward said, running his hands faster over the body, trying to find the source of the blood. Not even a seam was torn, no punctures.

"Probably a nosebleed. Happens all the time," Dr Moss stated dryly. He mumbled something akin to curses, then gave Ward a sour look.

"You should change before your party."

Not waiting for a response, Dr Moss brought the lift to waist height, turned and floated Turk down the hall without a backwards glance.

Ward looked down at his rumpled, blood-spotted suit, frowning.

He rubbed his eyes and took a few deep breaths as the air cleared before calling Rane.

"He's alive. Dr Moss is on his way to medical," he said, and then dialled into the primary system, giving the rest of the ship an all clear.

He looked at the locked door again. There was blood leading from the door all the way to where Turk had been laying. He had no idea how Turk had gotten out of that room alive.

He rubbed his arm where Dr Moss had jabbed him, already

feeling the start of a bruise.

"Rane, can you run a systems scan?"

"Levels have returned to normal in the hallways. We'll have to re-vent for repairs once the sealed off rooms have been cleared. No other personnel in the area."

"Thank you," he said, even though he shouldn't have.

"What happened?"

"I don't know. We'll have to ask Turk when he wakes up," Ward replied. There was no one else down there to ask.

He'd almost lost a crew member today because he'd allowed these pranks to go on. He should have put an end to them as soon as he had taken over being captain. But ending them would have been admitting his uncle's treatment of him bothered him. Ending them would have meant giving up on the promise he'd made to himself—the promise he still hoped to keep.

His pride had almost cost someone their life, something his uncle never would have allowed.

He gave a final look at the floor and rubbed his jaw. There was a lot of blood for just a nosebleed.

Five

Wynter held the thin needle between her finger and thumb and pressed it above the outside of her knee. The needle wobbled and slipped like silk on her blood. At least, she thought, it was her own blood.

The small storage box in the bathroom held her weight. Her leg was bent and hanging into the shower. The discarded crew uniform, that was still wet from the pools, was draped over the folds of the glittering light blue dress she was still wearing.

She wished she hadn't put the dress on.

Now it was a mess. Just like the ribbons on the floor. Like the rest of the room. Chaos spun in colours.

She took a few deep breaths, waiting for whatever the toxins had done to stop, willing her mind to clear. It didn't. The layers of blue material were now decorated with spots of blood. She didn't like the spots. They didn't match. What had happened?

Closing her eyes, she leaned back.

After her unplanned swim with Captain Ward, she'd felt light and happy and a little reckless. Cleaning didn't feel like the right choice when all she could think about was the way his shirt had clung to his chest. She remembered knowing she needed to be careful. But Captain Ward would head to Valtine—he always did. And so she'd dried her hair and swept it into a curled knot at the back of her neck, with pins and a glittery clip. Then she'd put on the blue dress she'd been working on. The one now ruined with blood. Helix was going to *kill* her.

There should have been more fear, caution at the very least. But she couldn't get the fluttering feelings out of her chest.

The empty control panel bays were quiet. There was a small room off the main hall; it held spare parts and electrical equipment. It was all tucked behind silver lined doors which reflected perfectly.

It was important to see how the dress looked when she spun in it, to see if the sequins would catch the light the right way. But now they couldn't because they were splattered with red.

Opening her eyes just a little, she steadied her hands as best she could, not wanting to look.

Perhaps… if she just lined up the needle and then pushed it straight across… but what if she didn't catch the skin on the other side? Should she push through both quickly? Or bring thread through one side before the other? It should probably be disinfected—did she have anything to disinfect with?

Mopping up the cut with a clean cloth and she took another look. There was a small white line deep in the gaping wound. Was it bone or a bit of material? Hoping for both and neither, she watched the blood as it pooled and filled and dripped onto the floor, narrowly missing the white crinoline.

She needed to wash out the cloth. Reaching from where she was sitting on the crate, she turned on the curved golden tap. The water was chilly. Perhaps cold would stop the bleeding, but she couldn't bring herself to put her leg under the flow—she might get the dress wet and if the spots ran, she'd never be able to fix it.

She had to slow down; she needed to breathe and to think.

Air in and air back out. Taking a sip from the white jug she'd grabbed from the front room, she rested her back on the wall. It didn't taste like anything. She couldn't smell anything either, not since the acidic air burned her nose and lungs.

Her thoughts drifted back. She'd heard a group coming toward the small room and had climbed up to the second-floor rafters. One was explaining to the other how to set the relay to change the lights. They said they'd signal once when it was time to start. It was supposed to be super easy, just input b784a7. The other crew member hadn't wanted to do it, but the woman with them had been mean. Wynter remembered b784a7 like a song. The combination had danced in front of her.

At one point, all they would have had to do was look up to see her on one of the exposed beams, like a ghost floating in blue silk right over their heads.

But they'd continued on, and Wynter had been free again to enjoy the silence. She'd been down there awhile when Captain Ward's voice boomed over the comms and through the empty storage room.

Ignoring the voice would have been a better choice.

She should have waited until someone else showed up, but there was no one else. She knew there wasn't. She was alone.

If she hadn't needed to manually open the stupid door, she never would have cut her leg. If she'd just stayed in her room, the cut wouldn't have bled all over while she pulled the mammoth sized man out of a closed-off section. If only she hadn't put the dress on in the first place.

She lifted the balled-up fabric again, hoping to see only spots, hoping the bleeding had slowed. But the flimsy, gauzy material was soaked in red.

Pulling the edge of the blue, she closed her eyes and winced as she tore off the bottom hem an inch around. It was ruined anyway. Wrapping it tighter around the leg, she got up, steadied herself, and rummaged through the little drawers, looking for some kind of pain relief. The drawers were full of make-up, lotions, and hair pins. Underneath, there was a little compartment with a silver box she was hoping was useful, but all it contained were little vials of greenish-blue fluid.

Defeated, she sat back down, untying the mess, and went in for another try. The needle again pressed against her skin. It was sharp and thin.

Sucking in a breath, she told herself it would be like sewing leather. Just push through to the other side. She could do this. Stay alive. She needed to stay alive.

Wynter pressed in a little harder. Jaw clenched, she felt it sting as she made a small hole.

The needle now halfway through, she muffled a scream as she pulled it the rest of the way, leaving a thread strung between the open place in her leg. What was she thinking? She'd just added two more holes. She couldn't do this.

Hands shaking, she pressed the cloth back against her leg. With one more steadying breath, she tied the thin strips of fabric around her leg and knotted it, then took another long drink. Leaning back, she let herself close her eyes. Maybe if she rested. Maybe it would heal on its own. Maybe it wasn't so bad.

Stay alive.

Six

Ward was late. After three additional scans, Rane had confirmed no one else had passed the Idex checkpoints within half an hour of the incident. The blood must have been Turk's. He'd changed for the third time that day and checked in with Dr Moss, who assured him that Turk was fine and that he could question him after the ball.

Leaving the Obsidian, Ward took his own private shuttle pod off his ship to reach the planet as quickly as possible.

Aurora Palace sat on the edge of a cliff in Valtine's capital city of Dawn. Ward glided over the dark water and swung up around the white towered turrets. Once he was cleared to dock his ship, he was escorted up to the main house. He was stopped at three check points. Each guard greeted him as Lord Isaac Ward and confirmed his Idex clearance. Each time, he corrected them with Captain Ward and requested the files be updated.

There was a lot of frowning and 'of course sir', but none of them did what was asked. He was a Valtine lord, but only because his mother was a well-titled landowner, which outranked his status as captain.

The ballroom was enclosed with eight closed double doors. Two men, dressed in all white with burgundy gloves, opened the first pair of doors when he approached.

Lady Daye was an heiress and one of the largest landowners on Valtine. Her Idex went back further than anyone in the hex-system. To be invited to one of her parties was an honour. Lord Daye was a fashionable man, at least twenty years her senior.

She wouldn't be happy he was late. He knew he needed to find her as quickly as possible and make his apologies.

White marbled floors were interspersed with white pillars; tables were covered with white linens and pale decor. Like paint thrown at a blank canvas, guests wore vibrant gowns and formal attire. They stood out against the white luxury, dancing and swirling, talking, and laughing. There were flashing colours and glittering jewels, like a rainbow of decadence.

Lady Daye, the hostess, was easy to spot in the cascade of colour. Her form fitting black lace gown fluttered around her ankles. Ward crossed the room of dancers quickly and made his way to her side.

Taking a deep bow, he took her hand in his. Standing, he turned her hand palm up and raised it to his lips to kiss the inside of her gloved wrist.

"If you wanted to kiss my wife, you should arrive on time," Lord Daye said as he snatched his wife's hand back. The Lord's deep purple jacket flattered his height. "Ah, Ward, it's you. Not like *you* to be late."

"My apologies to you both. I couldn't find my cufflinks, sir."

"Men can never find their cufflinks," Lady Daye said. Then, pulling her hand out of her husband's grasp, she flicked out her charcoal feathered fan and let it glide in front of her face.

"My cufflinks have been known to go missing a time or two. What does a woman say when her cufflinks are missing?" Lord Daye asked.

"She can't find her gloves," she answered.

"Ah right. Many missing gloves over the years." He winked at Ward then turned his back to them both, rejoining the group of men he'd been entertaining when Ward had arrived.

Lady Daye slipped her arm in Ward's and let her gaze wander up toward the ceiling, tilting her chin delicately.

He followed her gaze. Chandeliers hung between each of the open crystal shutters, which let in an ocean breeze. Garlands fanned like white peacock feathers from the chandeliers and fluttered with every breeze, sending down a heavy floral scent. The smell was overwhelming. He grimaced. Lady Daye had a very subtle way of making her guests feel uncomfortable.

"What do you think of the song-bird flowers? They grow only on Valtine you know."

Mixed with the roses, it was like being bathed in perfume. He chose not to answer.

She smiled at him, flicked her fan again, and guided him around the edge of the ballroom, closer to the open windows.

"You look exceptional this evening," she said.

He nodded his thanks. It was often best not to answer Lady Daye.

"Are the rumours true?" she asked. "You've given up your uncle's ideologies of leaving your ship without land ties and could be looking for a proposal?"

He wasn't sure where she could have possibly heard those rumours or if she had suggested it to see what he would say. But it wasn't untrue. He had been talking to Rane, trying to figure out if marriage was the best option for the Obsidian's future. His uncle had refused to marry and tie the ship to land. He hadn't realized that when his uncle brought him on it was so prospective merchants would think one day it might have land ties. Ward was sure his uncle had planned to drop him if he ever married—he just hadn't expected to die at such a young age, leaving the ship to Ward.

"I'm not in a hurry, but it would be the best thing for my ship and crew," he said carefully.

They walked outside into the warm evening where guests were catching the fresh air. When they saw Lady Daye coming, most smiled politely at their hostess and retreated inside. He hoped the over-scented flowers was the only discomfort Lady Daye had planned for the evening.

"Don't look so terrified," she said, her lace glove tightened a little on his arm, but her smile never wavered. "I've chosen Lady Cristelle for you. She's young and pretty. Her land could secure any cargo you'd like, the type of cargo your uncle never would have gotten his hands on."

"How do you benefit?" he asked. He should have been grateful but sensed there must be something in it for Lady Daye.

"I didn't like your uncle. No one cared when he died. Just like no one will care when I die. But I like you. I have so few pleasures and so you must allow me the intrusion into your business."

It wasn't a very compelling reason, there was something Lady Daye wasn't sharing, but on Valtine everyone had secrets.

Despite the grand way she carried herself, he knew she'd grown up in the same world he had. If your Idex was perfect, one wrong step could mar it for future generations, but no one was perfect. Secrets were essential.

"There is a small thing," she added. "I would like to introduce you to my niece. She hasn't taken to Valtine society since she's been here. Dancing with you might improve general approval before she leaves and ensure more success on future visits."

"You're flattering me. I'm only a captain," he said, not trusting her reasons.

"By now, all my guests have noticed our closeness. You're a wealthy captain with an ancient Idex of good bloodlines. It's not flattery; it's usefulness."

"And what if she suits me more than Lady Cristelle?"

She stopped short, her eyes narrowing slightly. "A mere lord with a solid-blooded mother doesn't make you a prospect for *my* niece."

"I inherited a ship." He shrugged and smiled down at the Lady.

"Ah yes, a captain." Pursing her lips, she continued. "You wouldn't suit. She's far too... *free* for your tastes. She is, however, dear to me. Be kind and I'll forget you arrived late." Lady Daye led him back to the main ballroom.

They walked around the large table of sweets and glasses full of white fizzy bubbles, then past more tables covered with vases of tall songbird flowers arranged between all the overly sweet cakes.

"Lucy dear, this is Lord Isaac," Lady Daye said. Lucy appeared to be the only guest not bothered by the heavily perfumed dessert tables she lingered beside.

Lady Daye released Ward's arm and then turned from them both without another word, heading back to her husband's side.

"Captain Ward," he reintroduced himself, bowing slightly.

Lucy was drowning in an intense gown. Pink and orange flowers cascaded over her shoulder, dipped daringly low; they bunched there, hanging in multiple layered strands around her legs. Her blond hair was curled with equal exuberance on top of her head; it waved and bobbed and had a life of its own.

He gently tugged at his cufflinks and smiled as if the rose tragedy was the most natural thing in the world.

"Would you care to dance?" he asked politely.

"Oh, I'd love to!" she exclaimed, trying a coy smile. "How'd my aunt rope you into dancing with me?"

"I was late," he responded with equal frankness, making her laugh.

He led her onto the floor. The orchestra started a set of all strings, a favourite on Valtine, with a smooth, low key. The simple footwork allowed for more quiet conversation and fewer twirls and spins. He'd hoped for something where he wasn't required to talk much. Thankfully, Lucy talked enough for the both of them.

"... she was supposed to be an expert seamstress," she continued. "Cristelle recommended her out of spite. I just know it, because I could carry on a full conversation with Lord Kent, and she couldn't even get him to smile at her."

"Lord Kent?" he asked as he half lifted her and turned them both to avoid her leading them into another couple.

"You must know him. Everyone knows Lord Kent. It's not like she could be seriously interested. He's so old!"

"That Lord Kent?" he asked, watching the young man swing by them. "He's barely thirty."

"Old—boring—same thing." She frowned at him, seeming annoyed that she had to explain. He took the hint and stopped talking, letting her continue. "Cristelle said her seamstress had an opening because her mother got a Helix for her, but I swear she paid off the old witch to kill her own career by draping me in roses."

"It's very fresh," he offered. They drifted across the floor. Her dress didn't look very well constructed. He worried what would happen if they spun fast, so he kept it to slower turns around the outside of the dance floor.

"It's hideous, and I wore it anyway. I look ten times as good as she does even if she is wearing a Helix. And I could get any man in this room if I wanted—oh don't worry I don't want you. I'm not interested in living on a ship."

"Too boring?"

"Oh, worse. But I am looking forward to getting home. It's quite a group of us coming, you know. My aunt secured passage. I wanted to go on the Verity—no offence. But I think she's trying to push me toward Lord Kent. He's frightfully jealous of you, you know, which is why she made you dance with me."

It was unlikely Lord Kent would be concerned at all about him, but he didn't point it out. He tried to hold a smile when he realized what she was saying.

"You're coming aboard the Obsidian? Back to Orion?" Ward asked, something else Lady Daye had failed to mention.

"Yes, all of us are, you know. I wanted to be on the Verity, but this way I'll at least have a chance to talk to Madame Helix. My aunt won't let me near her, but there's not much she will be able to do about it when she's down here and I'm up there."

It was the second time Lucy had mentioned the Helix gowns. He knew they'd been growing in popularity but hadn't realized they'd reached Lady Daye's ballroom.

Lucy's chatter continued about the other gowns and women and plans for gatherings while sailing. Ward let his mind wander, smiling and nodding, waiting for the dance to be over.

"I don't even think she knows she's wearing a shuttle engine."

"What did you say?" He mis-stepped and almost spun them into a tall vase of songbirds. Recovering, he composed himself.

"They've been talking about it all night." She pushed her hip a little to the left, leading him into a turn that brought him in line with a group of six other gentlemen. "Apparently, it's a shuttle engine. I can't see how. Lady Lyska said it was like wearing a cascading waterfall, but I said Cristelle may as well be wearing the design for a toilet. How would she know the difference?"

The music stopped. Ward picked a few loose silk petals that had snagged on his buttons and pressed them into Lucy's hands. She gave a hearty chuckle.

"If I drop a few every dance maybe my dress will become more popular than Cristelle's." She gave a delicate bow then left Ward on the dance floor.

The group of men along the east wall were getting more and more animated, fixating on the woman wearing a silvery dress, whom Lucy had identified as Lady Cristelle.

He hadn't been introduced to her yet and so he joined the gathered men, shaking hands with the few he knew well. He was introduced to the other two, but chatter was intense. They were all watching the movement on the floor as the next dance started.

Lucy hadn't been wrong. The dress was covered in a pattern of silver and plum crystals. It looked almost organic, the way it flowed with Lady Cristelle's movement; the design was unmistakable. It was haunting, the way the beads rippled with each move like an engine slowly turning, the tiny complex parts in beautiful symmetry.

"Are you sure it's a shuttle?" one of the gentlemen asked, trying to keep his voice low. Ward thought it unlikely any of these men spent much time looking at the underside of a shuttle. He wondered how much time Helix had spent with his shuttle in order to pull off such an exceptional design. A ball was not the place to make such inquiries, but it certainly piqued his curiosity.

He studied the dress for a few more minutes, and as Lady Cristelle turned, his eye caught what could be a crest woven in among the moving parts. It really was extraordinary. When the music stopped, he excused himself from the group to speak with Helix.

Lady Daye kept her invitations as tight as possible, but even she couldn't stem the tide of celebrity that must have fallen on Helix.

Helix was draped in an elegant green dress. She turned her back on the gathering of young ladies when Ward approached.

"Madame Helix, I want to congratulate you on your success this evening," he said.

She smiled and tapped her fan three times on his arm before snapping it closed. "Nonsense, I've just been raving about your ship."

"Yes, quite extraordinary what you did with the engine design. I'd love to know how you did it."

"What?" Her composure faltered for a moment. She looked genuinely confused. Helix looked at Lady Cristelle and the growing gathering of men watching her dance. Helix opened her fan back up and batted away the flush in her cheeks. "I'm so glad you like it," she said, flicking the fan closed. "I'm just still not used to all the fuss you know, I'm just a seamstress."

Ward raised a brow. Helix had never been known to be modest before. He nodded politely as an incoming gathering of giggling ladies vied for Helix's attention, excusing himself.

Ward turned to saunter through the heavily perfumed ball

room, looking for Lady Daye. He couldn't spend all night staring at a dress of his potential future bride without even being introduced to her.

Seven

Wynter rubbed her eyes and stood, at once feeling a sharp pain shoot up her right leg. It forced her to balance on her left foot, then sit back down. In the small bathroom, she tried to focus on the black-rimmed, square sink or the smooth white walls.

Grabbing a handful of fluffy blue skirts, she lifted them a bit. The need to get the dress off gripped her as her fingers slipped on the buttons. No, she needed to get the fever under control.

She couldn't die alone in this room with a thread dangling from her leg. Helix wouldn't be up for weeks, not when there were balls and parties and dresses to sell. No one would be in the guild halls, not until they started to reload the ship.

Wynter would be there, alone and dead. What would Helix do when she found her? Or worse, what if Captain Ward had seen her? She thought she'd snuck away quickly enough, but everything had turned so fuzzy so fast. There was no way she could be sure.

Sweat pooled along her neck and down her back. She hoped the medical bay would be empty—maybe, just maybe there would be something there to stop the bleeding. She refused to try stitching herself together again, but bleeding out on the bathroom floor was not an option either. Dr Moss was usually out of his offices and enjoying the quiet lounges. He was predictable, easy to stay away from. She'd always liked that. But she'd only ever taken books from the medical bay, not actual medical supplies. Could she find something for the effects of the flux gasses or fever?

Wynter limped to the door, trying to come up with an excuse in case she ran into someone. She'd tell them she was fine, just had too much haze. She'd seen plenty of passengers stumbling around after drinking too much.

She stepped into the hall only to bang her thighs directly into a float gurney. The impact forced her over and half onto it, her cut burning from the movement, worse than when she'd originally injured it.

Trying to steady herself, she felt a firm hand guiding her to lie down.

"It's about time." He sounded angry.

"Dr Moss?" she asked, trying to focus. He was easy to recognize anywhere on the ship; everyone wanted to stay away from him. But he didn't know who she was. Why he was here? He shouldn't be. She needed to stay hidden. Grabbing the side of the gurney, she pushed herself up to flee back into the room.

"No, you don't," he said. "On you get."

"No thank you," she responded. Dr Moss lowered the gurney until it sat at her shins and pulled her onto it before raising it back up.

She tried sitting up, but he tossed a heavy grey blanket over her, plunging everything into darkness. She felt the movement of being raised, and a steady hand rested on her shoulder. Then there was a sharp jab as he stuck something in her arm.

"You won't get far until I patch your leg up." Dr Moss's voice was guff. The smell of cleaners and mint clung to the heavy blanket. Wynter let herself lie back.

It wasn't as if she could disappear now. How had he found her?

They slid down the hall and around multiple corners. It was nothing like the cargo carts she'd ridden on occasionally, but perhaps it was because she wasn't controlling the remote.

She peeked out from under the blanket, watching the floor pass beneath her and realized she never would have made it to Dr Moss's office on her own.

They moved through what she could tell were the front rooms of the medical bay, then down a small hallway. She heard the soft click of a security lock releasing and finally they reached a brightly lit room somewhere behind the rest. The books she'd stolen were always left in the front rooms; she'd never been back this far before.

Dr Moss pulled the blanket off and tossed it into a bin. She sat up slowly and looked around. Whatever he'd given her in the injection was already working. She felt her head begin to clear. The doctor handed her a bucket. She held it, glanced into the empty bottom wondering why she was holding it, and promptly threw up what looked like black tar.

Dr Moss moved quickly around her.

"First Turk and now stitches," he swore as he grabbed supplies. "Let's see it."

Wynter hesitated. She hadn't eaten much, and she wasn't sure why he'd want to see what she'd just thrown up.

"Not the bucket, your leg," he said, taking the bucket out of her hands.

She leaned back on her forearms and stretched her right leg in front of her. The cut ran from her knee halfway up her thigh and moving hurt almost as bad as walking had. The blue layers of silk still covered most of her wound at the high point. She was grimy, sweating, and the bits of fabric clung to her bloodied leg.

"Stitches are easier with freezing, crazy girl," he said, catching sight of the bloody needle and thread. Grabbing another blanket, he draped it over her other leg and up around her waist then put a warm cloth over the mess of material and blood. She expected him to rip it off with the same efficiency he'd stuck the syringe in her, but he gently peeled it back.

He covered the gash with another cloth. It smelled like the pools after they'd been cleaned. It stung a little but was cool, like it was pulling the heat through her skin. He rummaged around in his cupboards for a minute, then came back. She noted absently how Dr Moss was older than she'd thought; his grey hairs were hiding between the black, and the stubble around his jawline was most definitely grey.

"Should be frozen," he said, lifting off the cooling cloth. She wished he'd left it on. Her entire leg was going numb, the pain was draining out of her. He poked at the edge of the cut.

Dr Moss yanked the stray thread out of the needle hole she'd made. The sting brought a quick gasp, but she clamped her lips together before anything else could escape.

"I guess it's not quite frozen," he said, instead of an apology.

"How did you know I needed help?" she asked, looking around the office. Wynter felt the freezing go to her toes. If she tried to leave, she didn't think her leg would hold her weight.

He raised an eyebrow in response, pulling a chair up toward the bed. He sat down on it, so he had a better angle for stitching up her leg.

"A-are you g-going to tell Captain Ward?" she asked, even though he hadn't answered her first question. She didn't know what would be worse, dying in her room or facing stowaway charges. She had no idea what they could be, but Helix assured her on a regular basis it would be bad.

He pulled out a stitch kit and set everything on the little table beside him.

"For the record," he said finally. "I never saw you. You were never here. I don't know who you are."

"My name is Wynter," she said softly. He ignored her.

Wynter looked at all the instruments on his tray and noticed the small Idex scanner. Her heart beat out of rhythm, and she tried to keep her hands from shaking. Henris had told her enough to know she needed to stay away from any situation where someone could scan her. It was something only Henris and Helix knew.

Dr Moss stopped what he was doing, following her gaze to the scanner. He picked it up and tossed it onto the counter behind him, out of sight.

Wynter focused on the needle as it hovered over her leg. Dr Moss gave something resembling a smile. It was thin and came from the centre of his jaw instead of his eyes. It was the kind of smile Helix gave when she doubled a contract on a dress for no reason and the client paid it.

He pulled the silver thread through, closing the skin like she would a torn seam. The questions were ready to burst from her.

"There's nothing you need from me other than to stitch you up," he said gruffly, reading her thoughts and squashing any idea of her getting more information from him. He frowned, put another compress over the stitches, and wrapped it.

"If you're trying to stay hidden, maybe don't run through the halls dressed like a cake," he said as he finished.

She'd been good at hiding. For seven years no one had noticed her, except Dr Moss apparently. She looked at her leg all patched up and felt a little guilty she'd never returned any of the books she'd taken.

"I'm good at hiding," she said in her defence. He helped her back to the float gurney. She laid down, and he tossed a fresh blanket over her. She wanted to stay. She wanted to ask him questions but didn't know how.

"No, you're not," he said, taking her hand; his felt large and worn. "They just aren't good at seeing you."

Eight

Ward had a nagging feeling he was missing something and returned to his ship instead of staying on Valtine for the duration of the docking. He needed to oversee the rest of the repairs. He wanted to be there even though Rane assured him multiple times that everything was fine. He also wanted to take steps to end the pranks, which he couldn't do from Valtine.

He had a file tucked under his arm. A file his uncle had ignored and he had avoided for too long. But it was the key to putting the ghost pranks to rest. Unfortunately, after a brief review, it was clear the whole file was a mess. Everything had been either input incorrectly or not submitted at all. It wasn't only his uncle. Dr Moss had also failed. Ward had updated the information as clearly as he could, but the bulk of his investigation would have to wait until Orion.

After reviewing the file, Ward went to the medical bay to debrief with Turk only to find he'd already been discharged. He wouldn't be able to talk to Turk about what had happened without drawing more attention to it than he'd like. But Dr Moss had assured him it was all in a report he'd get to when he wasn't busy.

Dr Moss had also kindly informed him the anti-serum for the flux gases could cause hallucinations, night terrors, loss of bladder function, impulse control issues, and nervous twitches. Every time Ward asked another question, Dr Moss added to the list of possible side effects. Ward was certain Dr Moss was making it all up to get rid of him, but it was still unnerving. Especially given the upcoming evening's choice of formal attire.

After giving up on getting any information out of the doctor, Ward changed into his white suit, the silver buckles and triple decked star distinguishing him as a captain, and headed back for Valtine without answers.

All the guests wore white to stand out against the colourful background. Like every other event on Valtine, each evening was designed to highlight the guests, if they played the part.

The small group of exactly one hundred met in the ocean view dining room. A long glass tube stretched out into the sea, only partially submerged in the water surging under and gently cresting over it. Turquoise and plum crystal chandeliers created a soft glow like the fading dusk.

Unlike her guests, Lady Daye's gown was deep blue. It shimmered and picked up the turquoise, making her look like she had stepped out of the ocean. The music changed, signalling dinner was to start, and they all sat down in their predetermined places.

He'd expected to be placed beside Lady Cristelle, but instead he was seated between two elderly lords.

"I heard you landed three of your crew," Lord Matthews said as he dangled his soup spoon in the air.

"Reassigned, not landed," Ward replied. It was the first time he'd removed anyone from his ship, but the pranks had put someone's life in danger, and they'd ignored standard protocol.

"Must have been something noteworthy," Lord Bundren, who sat across from him, said, angling for more of the story. "Was it all three at once?"

"Should we be talking about such unpleasantries at dinner?" The lady across from him took her white gloves off, picked up her spoon, put her spoon down, and put the gloves back on. Ward took pity on her. No, they probably shouldn't be talking about his crew at dinner.

"I noticed the lavenders were in bloom today," Ward said, changing the subject.

She relaxed and smiled. "I love lavenders. Songbird flowers are this planet's pride, but, if I'm allowed, I would say there is nothing as exquisite as lavenders." She sighed decidedly.

He nodded. Everything on Valtine was beautiful, flaws were unacceptable. Every inch of the surface had been cultivated and tamed. Stunning ancient architecture, flower fields blooming in rotation. Beauty and perfection.

Stifling perfection.

He could have easily settled in any of the major cities or taken up life in a country village; the options were endless for him. But feigned perfection wasn't something he enjoyed. He wondered if anyone truly did.

His decision to take his uncle's offer to join the Obsidian had shocked his family, but he'd loved the ship from the first time he'd seen it. Named for its sleek black exterior, it shone with deep crimson and blues, and boasted of a luxurious and decadent interior. His uncle had offered him an adventure off-world, and he'd found a home.

Ward looked down toward the far end of the table where Lady Cristelle was and wondered if she'd feel the same, or if she'd long for Valtine and solid ground beneath her feet. She fit in well in this world. She was beautiful and cultured. He also noted that she was the only other person at the table aside from Lady Daye who was drinking the champagne.

The wine glasses were long and thin, the sides had scooped edges with rounded dips. Full of blue bubbled champagne, the shape of the cup made it impossible to drink. With the points and scoops, it either dribbled over the top or out the scooped sides.

He half expected Lady Daye to dare a toast, forcing everyone to take at least a sip.

Ward didn't even try to drink his and looked sympathetically at the young woman across from him who had picked hers up and set it down at least three times.

He noted Lady Lucy at the end of the table; she had finished her soup, dumped the contents of her wineglass into the bowl and was using her spoon. Lady Daye was glaring at her niece.

Ward answered a few other questions regarding his ship and its capacities. He was a novelty at a dinner like this, and he knew it had to be because of Lady Daye's desire to see his ship land tied to Lady Cristelle's estates.

News that Lady Cristelle, Lucy, and an entourage of women would be on his ship must have travelled fast. There was not only an increase in lords and ladies filling out his regular passenger list, but he was also being honoured with the presence of an ambassador.

His uncle had never welcomed an ambassador on board. Ward felt a little pride in achieving the honour.

He smiled at his dinner companions. They were now discussing the damaging winds from the north and what preventative measures could be taken. The rest of the meal was filled with polite and pointless conversation. All he could think about was getting back to his ship.

After dinner, the gathering moved to the adjoining room. Like the dining hall, it was a large glass dome, its acoustics were perfectly designed for light music. Lady Daye took a moment to introduce Ward to Lady Cristelle then retreated back to her husband's side.

"Lady Cristelle," he said, offering his arm, finally able to have a word with her. She wore an all-white gown like the others, perfectly fit with little swirls like the crest of a wave. Lady Cristelle smiled with her teeth and looked irritated, but she accepted his arm and they walked around the room together. He asked polite questions, receiving minimal answers for his efforts.

"Have you sailed before?" he asked, hoping to glean more than a *yes* or *no* response.

"Of course. I've been to all the hex-system planets. Although there's none like Valtine," she answered, trailing her fingers lightly along the glass as the moonlight crossed through the gentle waves.

"What brings you to Orion?"

"Inktons—the family business. Someone in your position must be acquainted with the company."

He was. He'd been down to their shops earlier in the day.

"We've had success bringing vials to the other planets from Valtine," she continued, "but manufacturing on Valtine is costly."

"You take an interest in the family business then?" he asked, taking a moment to observe her. Everything about her was perfect, from the soft shaped smile, the arched nose and high cheek bones to her curled hair and designer gown. Valtine perfection was something to be admired, but the icy glare she gave him made him wonder.

"My father doesn't call it a business. It's a lucrative hobby—but he allows me to be involved so long as I pursue *other* things." She smiled. "I heard you have family here. Do they travel on your little ship?"

He thought he heard a sneer in the way she said little, but he ignored it. "Once, a few years ago, I brought my younger brother on a tour, but they prefer to stay on Valtine."

"Will you see them?"

Ward paused to watch a fin-sale swim by, its rainbow colours flashing through the water.

"They know I'm here," he replied.

"I'm sure. I never miss my family when travelling."

"I miss them enough, but they have other obligations."

They'd made a full circle of the tunnel without saying much else and then returned to the group.

"You'll have to take time to show me the pools when I'm on board. Assuming you have those," she said.

Her smiled broadened as she rejoined the larger group before he could respond.

He wasn't sure why Lady Daye had suggested the match for him. Lady Cristelle sounded unenthused about travelling. The benefits would be entirely on his part. If she offered for him, his ship would be tied to one of the largest landowners on Valtine with an Idex stretching back in perfection almost as far as Lady Daye's.

He watched her mingle with the others, and was looking for an introduction with the ambassador who would board his ship, when Lucy spotted him from where she leaned against a large harp.

"My turn!" she said decidedly, taking the arm he'd quickly held out.

"What a bore this all is. Did you see Lord Cage's suit? Little blue drips everywhere! Oh, and the white—you look quite dashing in white, all the men do—but it washes me out. This was my aunt's idea to turn me into a lady like her; she spent more on this gown than I would on anything, and I still look dreadful in it. I don't know what was wrong with my dresses from Orion, or why my aunt won't let me wear a Helix. Cristelle is wearing ANOTHER Helix. I bet you noticed. I still say I look better even if I have fish fins flying out of my hips." As if to emphasize her point she pressed the fabric down letting it bounce right back into place when she lifted her hands. He tried not to chuckle and scanned the room. Lucy did the same pointing out bits of blue on everyone's white attire.

Lady Cristelle was talking to Lord Kent with animated attention. Lady Daye was tethered to Lord Daye's side and hadn't left it all evening, but she gave him a nod as they walked by. He had no idea why she disliked Helix so much. Whatever it was, it hadn't stopped her from sending Lucy on the same ship as her.

"No matter, we'll be sailing for Orion soon enough," Lucy continued. "Then I'll get my chance. Although, I talked to Helix at the ball. Wouldn't you know my aunt didn't let me get ten words in before she hurried me off. Helix is quite nice, so I don't understand the problem. There's a whole group of us travelling together, you know? We keep adding more. For every one Cristelle invites along I'm obliged to invite one as well. If your ship wasn't so large, we'd have run out of rooms, but as it is, we've all been cleared. Do you know who else will come along? Is there anyone we'll be able to socialize with I mean?"

He'd received hourly updates from Rane on the passenger list. It was the fullest they'd ever been, and extra space was being made to accommodate more.

"Yes, we have at least a dozen who would be acceptable company and I've been informed we'll be welcoming an ambassador on board. I was hoping to meet him tonight."

"An ambassador. How boring. I was so hoping you'd have someone fun. At least Lady Cristelle will be there."

He raised a brow and almost asked how *that* would be fun, but she answered before he could get a word out.

"Oh, we don't get along at all, which is precisely why it's fun!" she said, leaving his arm to follow the waiter who carried a tray of bubbled champagne.

He sensed the journey to Orion might not be the kind of fun he and his crew were used to. If ever there was a time to make sure he was the captain he needed to be, it was now.

Nine

Wynter planned on hiding in the Helix suites for the rest of her life. She'd be safe from Captain Ward and safe from Dr Moss, except Dr Moss knew where to find her.

The day after her stitches, a small bottle of pills had shown up through the delivery hatch at the front of the room with a note from Dr Moss.

For pain only, it said.

Hiding was useless. Wynter wanted to know—needed to know—how Dr Moss knew her. Squashing her curiosity, she focused on sewing. She took apart the blue tulle dress, carefully cropping away any damaged fabric, and was surprised at how well it washed up.

She'd rescued, sweat in, and then bled all over it. But it wasn't like anyone would know. She felt a moment of guilt because she'd now be passing off a very used dress as new.

It wasn't like she was selling it, she told herself. Helix was.

Wynter imagined the dress gliding across a dance floor on some faceless body, the colour changing as the fabric rippled.

She did not try it on again.

Taking a small piece of the cleaned blue silk, she cut a square. Climbing up to her loft, she opened her small trunk where she kept her meagre belongings and pulled out the patchwork dress she'd been adding to for seven years. She let her hand wander over the pieced fabric. The bits of grey from the dress she'd arrived in, the yellow apron she'd used to let out the sides and add length as she grew, then the small coloured pieces that were no bigger than her palm, from each dress she'd sewn. The ones she'd designed after engines or things she'd seen in books, the ones she'd dreamed of—places she'd never been. Bits of glittery green chiffon, crimson threads, purple velvet, and blue silk, stitched along with every dress she'd worked on, every dress she'd designed. Fitting the square into the bottom, Wynter stitched it around the edge, like a canvas of her time in space. She imagined the day when she'd finally be done with it—when she'd show Henris how far she'd come. She folded it back up carefully and tucked it into the box beside her bed, then went back down to clean up the sewing room and bathroom, making sure to erase any signs of her injury.

***

The next day, when she was trying not to wonder how Dr Moss knew about her, she organized the work room. She rolled, folded, and stacked the shelves. Once the job was finished, there were empty sections for new materials Helix would bring up from Valtine.

Wynter hung the ribbons, trying not to think about everything that had happened, then swept up the threads and other scraps littering the floor.

She was quite proud of herself for distracting her mind as long as she had, but eventually her curiosity won. The need to talk to Dr Moss again overwhelmed the fears she had about leaving the safety of the Helix suites.

Putting down her needle, she dressed in her crew uniform, and quickly double braided her hair. The moment her feet left the guild halls her resolve wavered, and she found herself meeting up with a dining cart. Helix always made sure there was plenty to eat in their rooms and had cleared a corner to use as a small kitchenette, but options were few and no one paid any attention to a crew member taking their lunch break.

Sitting on a bench in one of the alcoves, she ate the small container of nuts and poked at the greenhouse fruits. Enjoying the rolled meat stuff with cheese, she watched the ships and shuttles that were docked around them. So many people out there, and how many more on the planet? The moments of reflection helped build courage, and she knew she had to at least try to talk with Dr Moss. So she made her way up to the medical bay.

The curtained windows were closed, lights dim, but the main door was open. Thin beds, long tables, glass cases, and shelves ran the length of the empty room.

Passing the outer rooms, she went down the narrow hall. Two doors were open, they looked like private medical rooms. Dr Moss wasn't in either of them. She knew she should go back, but at the very end was a closed door. Before she could lose her nerve, she curled her fingers into a fist and knocked on the door.

There was a rustling from inside, and it swished open. Dr Moss took one look at her, peered behind her for a moment, and then grabbed her arm, pulling her in.

Instead of another medical room, she found herself in a small living space. She should have realized his living area was attached to the medical bay just like the guild suites.

Dark green walls were almost completely covered by closed case shelving. Books were lined up perfectly behind the glass: red spines, then black spines. A few empty spaces. Empty, probably because she still had those books tucked up in her loft. She was incredibly uncomfortable to be in his personal rooms, but at least it wasn't his sleeping quarters.

A small slide out table extended from the far wall with two cushioned chairs on either side.

Grabbing a black bottle, he flipped the top and poured two large glasses before sitting down. She took the gesture as a sign and sat down across from him, back straight, feet pressed together. He frowned, and she thought maybe she wasn't supposed to sit, but he passed her the second glass.

"You could bring them back when you're done with them you know," Dr Moss said.

"The books?" she asked, taking the offered glass.

"Was there something else you stole?"

"No. Just the books." She looked down at the dark liquid as it swirled around her glass. If he knew she was taking them, he shouldn't have left them out, she thought. Then she realized he'd continued to leave them out because she was taking them. The questions she wanted to ask doubled.

"I'm not giving you more pills. There should have been enough," he stated.

"I didn't need them all…." Her voice trailed off. All the confidence she'd had moments ago was slipping away.

Taking a drink, she tried to keep it down. It was thick and harsh and burned. She held her lips together and put the cup down.

He was sitting less straight, drinking much too quickly, and staring toward nothing at the other end of the room.

She wondered if he was going to say something or pretend that she wasn't there until she left. She thought of all the times she'd heard people engaging in long conversations. It looked so easy. She talked with Helix easily enough. However, that was because Helix did a good deal of the talking, and Wynter did very little. She thought of pretending to be old friends the way she'd watched passengers in the alcoves. But Dr Moss wasn't an old friend, or even a friend.

"You know who I am?" she ventured slowly.

"No."

"Oh." Picking up the cup she tried another drink, smaller this time. He stood, took the cup out of her hand, poured in fizzy blue liquid, and mixed it until it was a sludgy grey. Then he passed it back. It was still thick but sweeter. She took a big gulp and let it settle into her stomach.

"How did you know where to find me? How did you know I needed help? And how did you know the Idex scanner wouldn't say anything?"

His scowl deepened, and he glared at her to keep her from asking anything else.

"I didn't figure you'd be stupid enough to come back this way. I don't have any answers for you."

"But you knew the scanner wouldn't say anything."

"Don't," he murmured.

Wynter knew she should be afraid—everyone was afraid of Dr Moss—but his stitches were in her leg, which proved something. She just didn't know what yet.

"Thank you," she said as she finished the drink and put the glass down.

He nodded, then passed her a book.

"I had this one picked out for you next," he said, passing it to her. He was still frowning at her, or maybe he was frowning at the wall. She couldn't quite tell but she took the book and held it to her chest.

"I'll return the others."

"Don't bother, and don't come this way again. I don't have any answers for you."

"You don't have any? Or you won't give them to me?" She felt herself shrink back the moment she said it. He didn't respond, and she couldn't stand there forever.

Wynter left with more questions than she had before. They flooded around her, filling her chest, and made her hands shake.

When dusk hit the following day and the hall lights turned to a softer glow, she grabbed the pile of books from under her storage. She dusted them off and made sure the corners weren't bent. She didn't even try to stop herself from going back to Dr Moss's rooms.

When he opened the door this time, annoyance rolled off him like smoke, but he took the books out of her hands and let her in. Opening the glass cabinet doors one at a time, he placed the books back on the shelves, red spines and black spines, locking them as he went.

After putting the books back, he stood with his arms crossed over his chest.

Not allowing the silence to pass, Wynter asked about her stitches. Dr Moss said they should be dissolved by now—which they had.

She didn't ask anything else and left as quickly as she'd come.

The following morning was spent in the greenhouses sketching another dress design and making progress on a few new pattern ideas. Afterwards, she made her way to Dr Moss's office with a plan.

If he really wanted to avoid her, he didn't have to answer the door when she knocked.

He didn't look surprised to see her back this time.

"I was wondering if you had any books on the history of the hex-system?" she asked before he could say anything. She smiled innocently. He scowled in a way she was beginning to find familiar, and went to his shelves, picking out a large volume to hand her. She took it and sat down opening it to the first page. After a few minutes, he sat down in the chair across from her and opened his own book. He was making a very bad show of reading. She wasn't doing any better, she tried to make her eyes look like they were moving across the words, but she'd read the same sentence three times and didn't know what it said.

"This isn't going to work," he said.

Wynter nodded, as if she'd conceded she wouldn't try to ask questions, then finished her drink and left. Her plan was going to work, it had to work.

* * *

Wynter kept going back each evening. Dr Moss would scowl, but two glasses always waited on the table when she got there.

She sat down in the now familiar chair. Even if he wasn't answering her questions, she liked being there, sitting in the same room as someone else, reading, or at least pretending to read.

She'd had so little real interaction with anyone other than Helix that it felt like a step, a huge step, into the real world. A place she couldn't go but at least for a few minutes at the end of the day, she was feeling a little more a part of.

By the end of the second week, she knew she was running out of time. Repairs were finished, and the ship would soon fill with passengers, returning crew, and cargo. She could still slink around unnoticed, but regular visits to Dr Moss would be suspect.

Helix had always loved the little things Wynter would make for her, so she brought a gift to Dr Moss, hoping he'd be willing to share the information he'd been holding onto. The information she'd been hoping he'd somehow just give her if she kept showing up.

She'd made a small black pouch with a rusted gold trim. It was perhaps a little ornate for Dr Moss, but she hoped he would like it.

However, he'd looked almost angry when she'd showed up at his door and handed the present to him.

"Ship's going to be filling tomorrow," he said as he tossed the small pouch into the trash bin without even looking at the intricate design. He could have at least handed it back to her, she thought bitterly.

If he could get angry about a little gift, then she was allowed to be angry over his secrets. It wasn't the way she wanted to get the truth out of him, but she needed to know.

"How did you know I wouldn't come up on the Idex scanner?" she asked.

He sighed and rubbed his forehead. "What do you even think an Idex is?"

"Well, the Idex is recorded at every security scan point. It includes family history, medical information, ancestry going back thousands of years, land inheritance…." She rattled off everything she knew from the books, everything everyone knew.

"No. An Idex is an inescapable curse. Every move you make, every mistake, every legal change can be added to the record. It's a history of dirty secrets—one most people will never shake." His words were ice. He stared into his glass, as if he was deciding her fate from the sludgy bottom.

"How did you know about me? I was told no one could know I don't have an Idex."

"Anyone with half a brain, which is no one on this tankin' ship, would recognize there's someone moving about undetected."

Wynter folded her arms across her chest.

"Not good enough," she said, ready to demand more.

His eyes met hers, unwaveringly cold, but she didn't back down.

"You aren't the first person I've known without an Idex code," he said finally.

There were more? More people like her? She smiled because if she wasn't the only one, then it couldn't be as unsafe as Henris had always said.

"There's more people like me?" she said, trying not to sound too excited by the idea.

"No, I don't expect there is." He sighed. Her excitement shattered.

"Why don't I have an Idex?" she asked. It was something Henris said he'd explain one day, and never had. She'd asked Helix before but was always told no one would care why she didn't have an Idex, people would only see her as lesser in a society of extraordinary histories. She was told she should be thankful Helix had taken her in.

"You weren't born with one." He paused long enough for her to keep talking.

"But everyone is born with one."

"I think it's time to go." He was closing down on her, but she was so close. She could feel there was more below the surface, more he wasn't telling her.

"Is it really so bad… not having an Idex code?" She felt like she was nine years old all over again, asking Henris the same thing. So what if she didn't have lineage or clearance or whatever? So what if she was 'nothing' like Helix had said?

Dr Moss refilled both glasses to the brim, passed hers back, and sat back down in his chair.

She'd won. He was going to tell her. She didn't sit but leaned against the shelves. Her fingers trembled over the smooth cut glass.

"Think for a minute. You've been on this ship seven, maybe eight years? Undetected. You can put on any uniform you like and sneak into any room. It doesn't matter if it's off limits to passengers or guild; you can go there. Let's say someone wanted you to steal cargo, or sabotage a ship, or even kill someone. You could do it and no one would know."

"I would never do those things!" Wynter defended herself, although maybe she'd steal, but only if she needed to.

"If someone found out who you are they could take you off this ship, change your appearance and your name. You are untraceable."

"Except I'm the only one without an Idex, so I'd be pretty obvious don't you think?"

"Only if you're caught." Dr Moss grinned and took a long

drink.

Only if she was caught.

Instead of answering her questions he'd opened a floodgate of new ones.

"If someone found me, without an Idex code…." She hesitated. "They'd make me steal for them?"

He took a moment to answer, choosing his words carefully.

"There's plenty of people wanting to be born something other than what they are, and plenty of people need to erase what they've become." He was getting agitated. She knew she should accept what he said and leave, but she had to know. She looked him in the eyes, begging him silently to continue. "There's not so nice people out there, and they'd experiment on you. Idex coding isn't only in a person's blood; it is impossible to take it out, remove it, or change it. But you don't have it. And they'd do anything they could to create something to reverse their own coding."

He picked up the blue bottle and drank straight from it before putting the cap back on and locking it in his cupboard. "I don't have any intentions against you, but it's probably best you stayed away from me after this."

The lights chimed and dimmed, signalling dusk setting into night. The hallways would be lit with constellations along the walls and foot lights soon.

"Don't let anyone see you leave and don't come back this way again." He got up, went to his own room, and closed the door, leaving her standing and staring at the space where he'd been.

After a moment, she downed her still-full glass and left the medical bay, mind reeling with everything she'd learned— everything he'd let her learn.

Once she was safely back in the Helix suites, she took the

finished blue dress off the form. It looked too soft, too delicate.

She'd been waiting for years for Henris to tell her it was safe to come home. She was hiding, always hiding. Henris feared someone would find her, Helix said no one would want to associate with her, Dr Moss had all kinds of terrifying theories.

But was she really going to hide forever?

Picking up long sheers, she held the dress in her hands. It looked wrong, the way she'd put it together. The lines and curves were soft and billowy. It didn't match the fabric she'd chosen. She ran the blades two inches in, and then again and again until the floor was strung with long streaming bits of blue. She liked the way the material sliced apart under the sharp blade.

She'd remake it in the morning, she thought. It would be fixed before Helix returned.

Ten

Ward forced a reassuring smile on his face, making sure none of the boarding passengers would notice how tired their captain was. The days above Valtine were ending. He'd travelled up to the Obsidian over a dozen times, and now he was back on his ship to stay.

Ward hired extra crew to lavish attention on arriving passengers, including the Ambassador from Corva. The passenger list had grown exponentially. With each name added, five more wanted to be enrolled. Rumours of a potential match between himself and Lady Cristelle had doubled his cargo contracts.

However unlikely the match looked to Ward, everyone else viewed it with great promise.

"The Ambassador's shuttle should arrive in bay seven in three minutes. It entered orbit and is lining up for docking," Rane said, looking at his scans as they walked. The clear glass of the encased corridor surrounding the loading docks gave a good view of the arriving passengers.

The smell of fired fuel came in waves as it vented through the many filtered ducts. Halo lights shone as they stood watching the shuttle pods fly in and out.

Ward tugged at the bottom of his crisp jacket.

"You completed the second scan?" Ward asked.

"Yes, I accounted for all crew members, including temporary changes. Everyone is where they're supposed to be."

Another shuttle docked with more passengers. Ward rubbed his jaw, glancing over Rane's shoulder to see how many more shuttles were still to come.

"I realize the passenger compartments are full, including the newly refurbished ones, but I wasn't expecting so much stuff," Ward said, watching the procession. Hats toppled over hastily removed travelling coats, boxes piled on top of each other, and his crew were being weighed down by bags—so many bags.

"I'm sure they were told the limits for personal cargo," Ward mused.

"Yes, but I'm uncertain you can tell these lords anything," Rane said.

The baggage kept coming. Even with all the space they'd opened, it was going to be tight in the smaller rooms.

"Let's open the long-term storage rooms. Passengers need to be aware they cannot go down to retrieve items. I don't want anyone down there until we reach Orion. Coats, hats, anything not needed in a climate-controlled ship."

"Yes, sir."

The next shuttle unloaded another group of ladies who looked a little unsettled from the transport. Dr Moss entered the loading dock and looked miserable as a second medic with a float gurney arrived in the shuttle bay. One of the ladies had a conveniently timed swoon and was gently lifted onto the waiting gurney. A few women who appeared fine at first changed their minds and leaned unnecessarily on willing crew members.

"What happened to mandatory screening for shuttle travel?" Ward asked.

"Some people can't handle it. I have a feeling some of the regular checks may have been skipped." Rane looked back at his cargo list.

Ward rubbed his eyes and put the smile back in place. It wasn't just the constant back and forth between the planet and his ship, or the balls and parties, or the changes to his ship. He'd been thinking of the long list of side effects Dr Moss had told him could follow the intake of flux gasses. He was fine, everything was fine, but with the increase of guests he couldn't afford to not be in perfect health.

Arriving passengers looked up to the corridor and waved. They would be on the same vessel for a little over a month and needed to feel confident in his command.

The Ambassador's shuttle finally pulled in. The air lock closed, sending a vibration through the shuttle decks.

The Ambassador from Corva was middle aged and solidly built. He wore a finely tailored travelling jacket with folded pleats to his knees. Green tassels dusted the floor at the end of a vibrant blue shawl. True to Corva's style, he flattened his brown hair and let it curl onto his shoulders. He was the first off the shuttle, followed by a few other dignitaries who Ward recognized from his meetings on Valtine.

Without hesitating, the Ambassador ignored the crew who were standing with the door open and proceeded up to the closed off area where Ward and Rane were standing.

The Ambassador took Ward's outstretched hand, shook it briefly, then tapped the stars across Ward's left lapel.

"Did you know the stars to identify a captain were first used as a concealed weapon? If removed, the bar could be thrown, and some added poison to their pin. They abandoned the poison when a certain Captain Hargravers, not the one who famously charted Corva to Koka, but the one who sailed on the Winch, well he stuck himself with poison during a rendezvous with—"

"Ambassador, this is my chief engineer Rane," Ward interrupted.

The Ambassador grinned politely.

"And it looks like Lady Cristelle is also joining us," Rane added.

The narrow hallway was feeling snug as Lady Cristelle was escorted up. It was a little presumptuous on her part, but Rane looked pleased with the development.

The Ambassador stepped forward, bowing slightly, took Lady Cristelle's outstretched hand and kissed the inside of her wrist. "Lady Cristelle, the stars will shine brighter because you are sailing among them."

She smiled, letting her hand rest on the Ambassador's for a moment longer than Ward believed was necessary. That only seemed to delight the Ambassador more.

Ward looked down at his screen, flicking through the cargo listings to make sure they'd all docked and were on schedule.

"I wouldn't dream of disturbing your work, I just wanted to inform you we'd arrived," the Ambassador stated.

"Thank you," said Rane, offering his hand as well, putting the Ambassador in a position to release Lady Cristelle's and take it. "Welcome to the Obsidian."

Eleven

Wynter watched from the attic storage space as cargo from Valtine was delivered to the Helix suites. She could see the thin line of movement from where her face was concealed behind small bins and boxes.

Delivery crew dumped the crates from the lift one at a time. Wynter counted each time another thud hit her ears. Six, seven, EIGHT... how much had Helix purchased? Old stock was out of the way, but space was tight. She waited for the soft click of the security slide before climbing down the metal loft ladder and pushing her way through the tall crates.

She was desperate to finish the reassembled dress before Helix returned. Between longs strips of the blue that she'd cut, she wove a charming line of black netting decorated with onyx pearls. Thankfully, the delivery crew hadn't knocked it over, but they cocooned it between three of the massive boxes.

Wynter sucked in her stomach and flattened as much as she could to fit between the crates, then let out the air she'd trapped in her lungs and frowned. She couldn't get the dress out without compressing it but couldn't finish the hem without more space.

She thought of unloading the crates, but Helix would throw a fit.

Squatting down, she rested on her heels and balanced the hem over her knees, threaders on her fingers she rolled the fabric under. The clambering noise coming from the hall was more than crew bringing up cargo.

The door opened again, this time to a flustered Helix who was talking excitedly to a group of women in the hall.

"I promise to meet with each of you. We have four weeks, no need to fret," Helix said to the crowd in the hall. The door closed. "Not a chance I'm meeting with half of those brainless socialites—Wynter, where are you? We need to get to work!"

Wynter thought about staying where she was and not answering, but it would only delay the inevitable.

"Here," she called out.

"What are you doing back there?"

"Sewing."

Helix poked at one of the large crates. "I don't suppose they could have left us a lift. You wouldn't believe the luggage boarding. Dr Moss was even there."

Wynter went still at the mention of Dr. Moss. She hadn't gone to see him again. She wondered if he put out two cups every night anyway, or if he had locked his doors.

Wynter stood and looked over the boxes. There was hardly any space to move.

"If we put them all against the door, we can unload them from there," Wynter suggested

"If we do, then we won't be able to get out," Helix replied. She unbuttoned and threw off her travelling coat.

"I wasn't planning on going anywhere."

"No, I don't suppose you were. Alright, let's push all the crates against the door, unload everything, and then toss the empty containers out into the hall. If we lose all the packaging, we'll have room to breathe."

Wynter went to push the one closest to the door from her hiding place. It didn't budge.

"You lose some strength while I was gone? This crate isn't moving a bit." Helix complained.

"It's because I'm over here." Wynter replied, realizing she was pushing the wrong one.

Coordinating their efforts, they finally got the boxes moved against the door. Instead of putting things away as they unloaded them, they took bolts out and stacked them high on the tables. The unpacking was the fun part. Wynter was certain she'd be putting everything away on her own later. There were piles of rich bolts, an array of buttery smooth silk with swirls and waves, a bold pink lace, sea foam satin with matching net for jewels, and dozens more.

"Did you ever see such fine fabrics?" Helix gushed. Wynter hadn't. They'd purchased high-quality materials from Valtine before, but never this expensive. Once everything was unloaded, they had even less room to move around. Piling everything high gave barely enough room to open the door.

"Opening the door," Helix announced and Wynter faded into the background. Helix ignored the gathering of large round eyes and pouty lips as she tossed boxes, boards, and packaging onto the polished wood floor. The pile littered the hall, and some tumbled back into the room. Helix pushed at it with her feet, then hit the security close before any could tumble back in.

Wynter felt sorry for the crew who would have to deal with the mess and pulled down a few older bolts. They should probably use old stock first.

"Oh, don't bother with those," Helix said, "We need to have a dozen cocktail dresses finished before we take off."

"A dozen!" Wynter said, dropping the bolt she was holding.

"We have one chance because I'm certain Captain Ward is not going to allow this many society women on this ship ever again. I bought fast trims too."

Wynter wrinkled her nose at the mention of fast trims. She hated the look of those society jackets, their cuff and bands poorly decorated with long strips of ribbon or flashy sequins.

"Don't look so glum. I'm certain we can con a few of the gentlemen into thinking it's just the thing. Space does things to people who don't travel much," Helix said, pulling out a parcel with extra flare.

"But a dozen?" Wynter asked, focusing on the problem at hand.

"I'll run the quick stitch, and we can put all main seams through the tippler. It's no different from your threaders, and you know it."

"But a dozen—in two days?"

"Less if we can make it. You've had two weeks to relax. What is that?" Helix asked, head turned to the side, taking in the blue confection.

Wynter didn't look up as she continued to pile rows of bolts along the one wall, clearing as much space as possible.

"This better not be another engine design. It's a little, well it's a little different, but I like it," Helix decided.

Wynter smiled to herself. She was wondering if Helix would figure out that the dress she'd planned for Orion was in fact based on sketches of a shuttle engine.

"I had half the room swooning asking for me to design another. You're lucky, if it wasn't a hit, I'd consider adjusting our arrangement. As it was, I cleared my racks, not a single dress brought back up."

"Not one?"

"Not one. Here's your cut, what's left anyway after all this." Helix waved her arms around. It surprised Wynter there had been any profit left after everything they'd just unpacked.

But Helix handed her a stack of thickly plated cards from her bag. They were the size of her hand like disks, two had teal edging while the others flashed gold and silver. Wynter had no idea how much money was on them. Helix had always assured her it was fair and if she ever left, she'd have enough. Funds didn't matter at all on the ship, but it was still nice to be paid. She liked having something she could bring back to Henris.

"I took some out of your funds to purchase this." Helix held up a bolt of yellow fabric. "Isn't it divine? You never wear yellow."

"Thank you," Wynter said a little grim. She wore nothing but her plain black outfit, her crew uniform, and occasionally a simple dress to blend in with passengers. She hadn't worn yellow since the little apron. Henris had told her yellow was dangerous. Maybe it was time to change, but yellow? Probably not.

"How were the parties?" Wynter asked. She didn't want to talk about the yellow fabric.

Helix went into detail for over an hour, barely taking a breath while they pulled basic patterns and measurements from her notes. She explained each dress and designer who had been at the ball, detailing the perfections of *her* gowns compared to the flaws in everyone else's.

She laid out a list of pre-orders including neatly ordered index cards with measurements.

They'd make the ordered dresses first, and then a second set in a few basic sizes with room for quick adjustment.

"I double checked the measurements, and you'll have to let the hips out a little. I don't know why these ladies can't give proper measurements. I tell them a seamstress knows everything and how to hide it all."

They stopped briefly to eat something and drink strong coffee to keep them awake. By the time Wynter's fingers were getting sore, Helix had finally doubled back around to information about the dress and Lady Cristelle who was wearing it, the dress she wished she'd kept.

"She's boarding the ship as we speak. Imagine being commissioned for a Valtine wedding! And, of course, I'd have to attend if there were any problems. She was stunning, although the hips—did you write down about the hips?"

Wynter nodded and rubbed her eyes. Whose hips? Whose wedding? All the dresses looked alike, and the material and bits waved around her. Piles of scraps everywhere, threads stuck in her hair.

"Captain Ward couldn't take his eyes off her, and I heard from a reliable source if the lady offers a proposal, he's finally going to do what his uncle never would and tie the ship to land."

Not any captain, or any ship. Her captain and the Obsidian. She closed her eyes and tried to shake off her tiredness. She should not be thinking about him as *her* captain. She was a stowaway, and the Obsidian was just a hiding place.

"If you can clean up this mess, we'll get a few hours of sleep, then right back at it. We can sleep more when we're famous," Helix said, dumping the half sewn top onto the pile. It was how she usually left, in the middle of a project, with little warning. In less than a day, the clean, organized, workspace was a cluster of mess again.

A Valtine wedding? How much more famous did Helix need to be?

Helix hummed in her room, leaving Wynter to her own thoughts and the unmade dresses.

The bolt of yellow stuck out from under a gigantic pile, taunting her. She let her hand trail over the edge, wondering what it would be like. To own land, to make an offer to a gentleman, to a captain, to fall in love. What she wouldn't give to attend one party….

Looking at the yellow material, she wondered if it would really flatter her?

The room felt smaller, filled with things ready to be made, things she had to make.

She would never marry, or be a captain's wife, or a crew member's wife, or go to those extravagant parties. She would be lucky if no one ever noticed her again.

She would always be alone, on the Obsidian—waiting for Henris to say it was safe—waiting until she was old, or waiting for the darkness in the world to find her.

Twelve

"Captain!" the Ambassador called as he entered the bridge unannounced. His minty green jacket stood out among the black or grey uniforms. "Captain," he said again, coming to stand beside Ward.

Ward was in the middle of briefing Rane and the ship's second mate, Platt. They'd departed from Valtine ten days ago and, so far, had needed constant crew changes.

"I'm moving Fuller to oversee the bridge on the night shift. Platt, you have twelve hours, then I'm putting you onto the day." Ward was trying to complete the details as the Ambassador hovered at his elbow. "That will free me up for other things."

The changes would have been necessary either way, but it relieved him that the bridge was being taken care of. He'd barely slept and although he had experienced none of the other symptoms Dr Moss had mentioned, he'd wondered if he was seeing things. Twice he'd been walking down the halls when he saw *her*. She looked like the temporary cleaner from the pool, maybe it was because he'd almost drowned her. Rane hadn't been able to find a crew member matching the description he had given. Ward could swear it was her he was seeing, but by the time he could get close enough, she would vanish.

If the flux gasses he'd breathed in were causing hallucinations, he'd have to talk to Dr Moss. That was if he could get two minutes without someone demanding his attention.

"Inform Fuller of his temporary promotion," Ward said.

"Yes, sir."

"Ambassador, what can I do for you?" Ward asked, trying to lead him out of the room and down to the passenger decks. He was realizing why the price of transporting an ambassador was so high; they had few rules and didn't follow the basic understanding that passengers were not allowed on the bridge or other restricted areas.

"I heard your head chef was serving cortivels in the dining lounge before dusk——"

"Artificial dusk," Ward corrected, wondering why the late night hors d'oeuvres was causing so much angst.

"I thought a ship as fine as this would pay more attention to these types of details."

"I made it clear to the crew, our guests are their top priority. They are still learning as we haven't had this many passengers on board before."

"But still… cortivels… before dusk?"

"Artificial dusk."

The bright lights turned to a softer glow as they exited the crew areas. He liked what his uncle had done with the passenger decks. One deck had floors with smooth stonework and a polished finish; they looked like a country lane. Another had plush carpets and beautiful paintings hung on the walls. There was a mix of styles and bits of art from each of the planets in the hex-system.

They rounded a corner into an open area with high ceilings and six passenger suites separated by benches.

"Did you know Lady Cristelle was the one who requested the delicacy? She was quite certain her request would be granted. I'm surprised she took such liberties," the Ambassador said, still complaining about the cook's decisions.

Ward was walking in circles, waiting for the Ambassador to get bored and leave him, or for someone else to distract him enough for Ward to make a polite escape. The third time through the passenger entrance where the Idex scans were logged the Ambassador paused, looked at the well concealed Idex scan and tapped the side of it gently.

"Clever," the Ambassador said. It really wasn't clever. Most ships had them at every major point of entry. Crew and passengers could be tracked through the entire ship, it kept everyone where they should be. "Did you know the use of Idex was created by those on Shiloh? It was to track loved ones through the hex-system. Valtinians adopted it for society in the 3700s to track genealogies, a pivotal point for land inheritance laws."

"Yes, very fascinating."

"Do you have much knowledge on the topic?" he inquired. The silence demanded an answer.

"As much as any captain would need to know," Ward replied, wondering if there was any topic more dull they could discuss—perhaps the first use of opening shutters on a spaceship.

Rounding the hallway toward the lounge where he hoped to finally distract and leave the Ambassador, a flushed crew member interrupted them.

"Sorry, sir, but there's a problem with Dr Moss. He won't

come out of his rooms to see patients." The young man was nervous and pale, like he'd been talking to Dr Moss directly.

Ward dismissed him, turned, and headed in the other direction, not doubting for a second the Ambassador would be following.

"I've collected aged medical equipment from all the hex-planets, but you'll find some of the outer planets still use primitive means. I'd love to take this opportunity to speak with the ship's doctor. You know their breed is the heart and humanity of a ship —delicately caring for the intricate needs of space travel."

Captain Ward chose not to warn him of how very wrong he was in this case.

The lights dimmed to dusk, casting a purplish glow on the blue carpets.

"Did you know an astronomer on Calver designed time settings on ships? He determined it reduced stress in space. Using it to adjust to docking time to whatever primary hub arrived at next, did not get suggested until decades later. The technology was there, no one ever used it in such a practical way."

Ward nodded in acknowledgement.

Dr Moss had not barricaded himself in his rooms, but was barrelling down the hallway, reaching them long before they made it to the medical bay.

"I will not administer pain killers, tranquilizers, or mood-altering drugs to women who tip over for not getting an audience with Madame Helix for a tanking dress!" he shouted.

The Ambassador was red-faced, eyes wide at the outburst. He looked at Ward and then back to Dr Moss.

"Ambassador, I'd like to introduce you to Dr Moss. He's the chief medic on the Obsidian."

"I'm not giving him anything for pain either." Dr Moss scowled at the Ambassador, as if to make his point.

"Oh, no doctor. Of course I wouldn't ask for anything. Did you know the council of Torin instituted doctors' rights on board?"

Dr Moss ignored the question and returned his attentions to Ward.

"Those women have been swooning and carrying on. I had one man threaten to report me if I didn't give something to his wife who was in hysterics over a gown. A gown!"

"Did you know gown hysteria—" the Ambassador started, then closed his mouth again when both men glared at him. He swept invisible dust off his mint green jacket, clearly not used to being treated so rudely.

"If you don't do something soon, I'm going to wrap them up in Helix's fabric and push them out the airlock."

"We're on a tight schedule, and I don't have time to stop to open the air locks," Ward said, trying to hide his smile at the way the Ambassador was standing with his mouth open.

A slight nudge at the corner of Dr Moss's mouth was enough for Ward to realize he was enjoying the Ambassador's discomfort just as much.

"I'll have a word with Madame Helix and work something out," Ward said to Dr Moss. "But I'm not making any promises you won't be required to work on this trip. Now, if you don't mind showing the Ambassador to the lounge, it's dusk and I believe they are serving cortivels."

Before either could answer, Ward stepped into a lift to the guild level and headed for Helix's suite.

Upon arrival, he wasn't sure if he'd made the right choice. It might have been better to stay with the Ambassador.

A dozen ladies crowded outside the seamstress's rooms like a prism in a flash of colour. Two of the other guilds had their doors open and were staring at the women. They went back in and closed their doors when they saw Ward coming. The ladies hushed and whispered, moving to the sides as he approached.

He knocked on the door and announced his arrival. The door opened, sliding into the panel. Six more ladies were inside, including Lady Cristelle. She was standing on something to make her taller, being fitted for a red gown. Helix had a set of pins in her mouth, and the lady was smiling sweetly until she saw Ward.

Helix spit the pins into a bowl.

"Everyone out! Out, out, *out*!" Helix rushed the ladies into the corridor; Lady Cristelle stayed where she was on the pedestal.

"Captain, I wasn't expecting you," Helix said.

"I'm sorry to show up unannounced, I wouldn't want to interfere with your business. However, your gowns are causing mass hysteria on my ship, which in any other circumstance would be wonderful, but there are safety concerns, you understand."

"I wouldn't be exclusive if everyone got a dress, where would my value be? Really Captain Ward, you know how to play the cargo game."

"I understand you have a business, but I have a ship to run. I must insist on a certain amount of order."

Ward had no idea what he was going to suggest, how he was going to squash this. He turned and looked at the group of women, all whispering and talking in the hallway.

And then he saw her. Braided hair down her back, fitted grey top. She was moving unnoticed from the Helix rooms through the group, stepping easily between them. His throat caught.

She couldn't be here.... As she reached the exit, she looked back at the room and caught his eye for a moment. Someone moved in front of her, and she vanished.

"Ladies," he said "if you would give Madame Helix and I twenty-four hours to come up with something suitable—"

Ward took off mid-sentence after the vanishing woman, trying to slide through the gathering the way she had, only to have to stop repeatedly to apologize for bumping and jostling the exuberant mass.

In the stairwell, he watched as a bit of grey slipped through the lower-level door and out of sight.

Descending two steps at a time, he called through to Rane on his comm. "I need you to run an Idex scan, second base floor, I'm coming out the port stairwell."

"Yes, sir… not showing any unauthorized personnel sir."

"Scan for *all* personnel."

"There are dozens of crew member down there."

He looked down the grey hallways. This level contained extra cargo and some of the repair rooms. To the other side were the greenhouses and food storage. "Rane, scan only the greenhouses?"

"No one there. Perhaps you should go in for a few quiet minutes?"

Ward walked toward the greenhouse rooms and looked through the narrow, sealed doorway. He could see her, standing halfway down the long row of bedded plants. He watched her walk toward the staircase and disappear from sight.

"Rane, an Idex scan for the greenhouse?"

"There's no one."

"Is it working?"

"Yes, your Idex came through, but you're all alone. Enjoy a

few moments of peace."

"Thank you." He turned off his comm and opened the door to the greenhouses.

Thirteen

The Helix suites were crowded, and Wynter, who needed to stay hidden, had been stuck in the small storage loft. She'd sat with a dress in her lap. Pulling the threads through, she'd cringed, blocking out the chatter below. When the noise level changed, she noticed Captain Ward had entered, and Helix had tried to usher the crowd outside. Wynter had used the distraction to slip through the group of women—like threading a needle—and made her escape.

She was spent. They had completed piles of dresses, but even then, it wasn't enough. The gowns were flying out as soon as they could make them. At this rate, they'd have nothing left when they reached Orion.

The dresses were all similar: above the knee, full of fancy stitches with no meaning. Wynter had tried to give each one a personal flair, as much as Helix would allow before telling her it was good enough and to move on.

They'd never accepted 'good enough' before. All the while Helix dangled her exclusivity, ramping the women into a frenzy. It was exhausting. Everything was geared toward Lady Cristelle, which made it all the more infuriating.

Lady Cristelle who hadn't had a nice thing to say about Captain Ward, or anyone else. Helix lapped up every moment, and Wynter knew a wedding gown was the only thing she had her mind set on. Bitterness took residence in Wynter's chest. They both knew Helix couldn't possibly design a wedding gown of this extravagance, let alone sew one without Wynter.

While some were desperate to get one Helix dress, Cristelle was being fitted for her fourth, counting the two on Valtine. Helix made sure Wynter had set up the colourful display of lush wedding set fabrics. Alongside the displayed fabric, samples of intricate stitches and beaded jewels took up precious space.

She needed a break.

Wynter made her way to the greenhouses, careful to make sure no one was in the hallway when she went in.

It was warm and slightly steamy, blooming flowers in rows of pots, vegetable beds, ivy, and trees. She liked the look of the little green shoots and imagined how she could incorporate them into a design.

She went up the black spiralled stairs to the second-floor balcony. Plants hung from the watering systems, some reaching down to the floor below. All the space was utilized for maximum yields.

The door opened from below and she jumped. There were very few crew members cleared to be in the greenhouses. A guild oversaw it, and no one was ever here in the evening. Her heart was hammering in her chest, but she had nowhere to hide quickly enough. The only way out was back down the stairs she'd just climbed. Trying to formulate a lie in her mind, she squeezed out a breath and turned to face the intruder.

Captain Ward was coming up the stairs, walking toward her. She quelled the fluttering in her stomach. After helping him with his tie, she knew she needed to stay away from him, but following him in the hallways had become habit. She liked watching him interact with the passengers and frazzled crew. He was always so calm and confident.

Now, standing in front of Wynter, he was clean cut and immaculate.

He kept his eyes fixed on her, as his fingers worked to unbutton his jacket. Tossing it over a small pruning stool, he then began unbuttoning the crisp black shirt he wore beneath, taking steps toward her.

Wynter's eyes grew wide. She held a breath when he stopped at the third button and pulled the shirt away from his chest, taking in shallow breaths, as if there wasn't enough air in the room for the two of them. She tried not to stare at the broad chest under the gaping shirt, knowing it was the least important part of her current situation. But what in the world was he doing?

He looked rattled and unsteady, as if he'd just seen a ghost. What could have possibly happened in the minutes she'd seen him outside of Helix's rooms? He couldn't have been more than a few seconds behind her, and yet he looked as if his entire ship had gone sideways. She knew she should come up with some sort of story, why she hadn't got off on Valtine like a day cleaner should have, but he looked so unwell.

"Are you okay?" she asked as he raked a hand through his hair. She instinctively wanted to cross the distance between them and flatten it back down. He didn't look right so dishevelled.

"Oh, you talk too. Okay, this is perfect…" Captain Ward said.

Wynter would have been more offended by the comment, but

the state he was in held off her hurt feelings. He continued walking toward her, and she took a step back. Then, as if he thought better of it, he stopped.

He must know something, or else he would have been asking why she was here and not on Valtine. Did he know? Or had he talked to Dr Moss? She wanted to run, to hide, to bury herself in the plants.

"I was fine—I thought I was fine." He was clearly talking to himself and not to her.

He stared at her like he was trying to see right through her. He closed his eyes tight, and Wynter wondered if he was going to pass out. When he opened his dark eyes, they bored into hers, then he started muttering under his breath like she wasn't there at all.

"Was it the dresses? Did they push me over the edge? Or the Ambassador?"

"The dresses?" Wynter asked. What was he talking about? Her heart felt like it was going to thunder right out of her chest.

She wasn't sure if she was in trouble or if she should try explaining herself. She sat down on one of the little wooden stools and focused on the green shoots beside her.

He let out a strangled kind of laugh, then pulled out a stool and sat down as well.

"The newest problem, the dresses. If I can't come up with anything, I don't suppose you can. I have dozens of upset ladies on the ship. Dr Moss is angry. Madame Helix has a right to her own business…"

"They all want their own dress," Wynter said. She understood the frenzy Helix had caused; it was why she needed to escape to the greenhouses. He looked more upset about the dresses than about her being in the greenhouse, so she went with it.

"Yes, I know. But we both know it's not possible."

They were quiet for a few minutes. He'd calmed down, as if he'd accepted her presence. Maybe the shock of a stowaway had worn off. Wynter played with the bit of ribbon she'd used to tie her braid back. He was watching her hand as it teased the blue silk.

"What about a ribbon?" she suggested.

He looked at the ribbon, then back at her.

"I was thinking the same thing." He frowned. "A ribbon for each of them, something unique, something very *Helix*."

She smiled, something very Helix. A ribbon to thread through their hair, or an armband or belt. Something better than a fast trim. She'd be the one designing them but didn't mind the idea. It would be fun and a break from the dresses and maybe Helix would let her do something more her style again. They couldn't get work done with so many people around.

He was staring at her intently, blinking a little too much. She focused on the flower in front of her. Soft red petals reached down from the hanging vine. They covered the staircase, twisting up the railing to the second floor.

"It's a sky lily, because of the way it hangs. The petals fall away from the sky instead of reaching up, which made sense to whoever names these things. They bloom best in space. Don't I sound just like the Ambassador now," Captain Ward said, letting his hand trail over one of the pretty flowers.

"What else would the Ambassador say?" she asked to keep him talking, noticing his breathing had evened out.

"We've tried to mimic them on every planet in the hex-system, and they don't grow as fast. They need 6 hours of sun, then 3 hours of darkness. We've yet to find a planet to copy these conditions."

He put his head between his knees.

"I knew I'd see you again eventually," he admitted, like it had been a great secret he'd been holding back.

Had he wanted to see her? He knew she was there? She hoped she wasn't visibly blushing and tried to focus on the flowers, the cobbled floor, the small drain ports.

"I don't think it's really a good idea to be talking to you," he murmured more to himself than to her.

"Because of Dr Moss?" she asked. He stiffened at the mention of Dr Moss. He still wasn't making much sense, but she was trying to piece it together. Plucking one of the sky lilies he spun it between his fingers, then placed it on the floor between them. She stared at it and kept her hands folded in her lap.

"Does it remind you of your home?" she asked finally.

"The ship is my home. Valtine is where I grew up," he said, closing his eyes, he shook his head. "Now I sound like my uncle."

"You don't want to sound like your uncle?" she asked cautiously. She liked the way he answered her questions. Dr Moss had been a lot harder to speak to.

"No. I think I did once before I knew him. I wanted the adventures. I wanted to sound like him, to tell stories like he did."

Wynter sympathized, she'd always tried to sound like other people. She hated to admit it, but she wanted to sound like Helix. She wanted to tell stories of the balls and see the dresses swirling across the dance floor.

They sat quietly for a few minutes. It wasn't the same silence as when she was working with Helix. The silence with Dr Moss was something completely other too. This felt like she was with someone and not so alone.

He was staring into the flower when he started talking again. "A man almost died a few weeks ago. It would have been my fault."

Wynter had almost died too saving that crew member. "Did you do something wrong?" she asked instead of admitting her involvement.

"No. It was an accident."

"Then how could it be your fault?"

"Because I allowed it to happen. I should have stood up for myself when my uncle started it all. I thought it would be easier to pretend it didn't bother me. Once he was gone, I didn't want to come down hard on the crew about it."

Years of watching the crew's strange behaviour when they reached Valtine had her itching for more information. The crew never talked, and it wasn't like she could have asked anyone before. She kept her hands still, trying not to look interested, and gently encouraged him to go on.

"How did it start?" she asked.

He took a deep breath, and she almost wondered if he would change the subject again.

"It was my first day as first mate on the ship. I'd finished my education on Orion. My parents had been very clear from the start they didn't like the idea of me being a first mate. I wonder if they thought it a horrible thing to have a captain as a son, or if they knew what kind of man my uncle was. I learned quickly that the way someone acts on solid ground is not always who they are."

He picked at the little green shoots as he continued. "The cargo bay had been mostly unloaded, and I wanted to help, you know, start at the bottom. My uncle ridiculed me. 'A captain doesn't need to do any of it,' he said. Captains are supposed to *give* orders." He paused, and Wynter wondered if he'd continue. Then he said the last thing she'd expected. "I found a body between the last few crates. I went white as a ghost—or so they say."

"On your first day?" Wynter asked, barely a whisper.

"He was laying there, eyes open—poison—but I didn't know it. I was just a kid really, young man, I guess. I insisted on waiting with the man for my uncle to get there, then I made the mistake of asking him if a soul would take longer travelling through space to get to wherever it was going. My uncle laughed, told me he probably didn't die in space, body dumps happened all the time. I was to tag it and store it."

"Store it?"

"Unless we know what happened, we carry him around for 10 years, or until someone claims him. There's paperwork if you want it off sooner, but my uncle said it wasn't worth the trouble if no one was looking for him. I swore to my uncle I'd figure it out by the time we reached Valtine. I told him nothing would stop me. When we reached Valtine and I hadn't even figured out what his name was, my uncle encouraged the crew to *haunt* me. When I accessed the files on Valtine a few weeks ago, I realized he'd made sure it would be difficult for me to figure anything out. I have a name now—so that's something. It would have been decent for him to attach a name to the poor guy."

He leaned back on his hands. "It feels good to say it out loud. I've never told anyone. Not the whole thing. Not like you're really anyone."

She squeezed her fingers tight and stared straight across at the far balcony where a string of orange limes hung. No, she wasn't really anyone. She wondered if he even remembered her from the pool, maybe it was better if he didn't.

"What was his name?" Wynter asked. She didn't want to hear the answer. There was a little voice in the back of her head screaming *no no no*. But she couldn't stop the question.

Before he could say anything else, the lighting changed, bringing a darkness and a heavy mist released from the watering system.

Captain Ward jumped up. The water already drenching them both creating fog between them. He looked at her one more time, a bit of water had collected and run down the side of her cheek. He lifted his hand like he was going to wipe it away, but before he could touch her, he pulled his hand back and shook his head.

Turning to leave, her voice broke through the soft clack of his shoes on the metal grates.

"His name?" she called after him.

He frowned and didn't answer. He didn't say goodbye. Didn't offer to help her leave. Didn't look back. Because she wasn't anyone.

Captain Ward couldn't have known, his first day was her first day. She remembered the announcement on the shuttle welcoming him. It had been cheery, and she'd despised the happy voice. There was no way Captain Ward could have known that what he'd just shared would leave her with questions and a dull ache in her chest.

She wouldn't think of it.

Couldn't.

It couldn't be possible. There'd be no reason for it. She stood with her fingers wrapped around the railing, letting the rain drip down the black metal and onto her slippered feet.

Fourteen

Ward buttoned up his shirt and was shaking off water when he realized he'd left his jacket in the greenhouses. He'd have to send someone back for it, but the Ambassador had already found him.

"Oh, dear!" The Ambassador looked shocked. He pulled out a thin bit of black fabric from his jacket pocket. Reaching out, he dabbed Ward on the arm and shoulder, soaking up little blots of mist. Ward grabbed the handkerchief, balled it up and passed it back, keeping his mouth in a thin line.

"Was there something you needed?" He didn't like the Ambassador just roaming around in the lower decks.

"No. I was just down here looking around. You have a most fascinating ship. I've never seen one constructed quite like this."

As they walked away from the greenhouse, the Ambassador continued to point out various things he thought were unique while glancing at him every few seconds in renewed shock at Ward's lack of jacket and moppy hair.

He commented on the exposed lower deck beams, the various flavours of decor, the cargo holds and shuttle bays in proximity to each other.

"It's a wonder the imagination doesn't get away from oneself in a place like this. Did you know there was a captain from Vesta who believed the souls of his crew would ward off accidents in space? He would kill one on every planet and store their bones in the walls," he said as if it was a suggestion.

Ward tried not to gag. Instead of taking the lifts, they went through the lower deck and up the stairs to avoid passengers seeing him in his current state. The Ambassador had covered over half the ship in the few days since leaving Valtine behind. Ward didn't like it.

"Did you know greenhouses were the first system designed to survive in space? Yes, can you imagine a time when space travel wasn't even a thing? And the primitives were trying to sustain life beyond planets? Time in space was then limited—they worried, you see, about how one would react being off planet for too long."

Ward continued at a steady pace, trying not to show his growing tension.

"I hear you have a unique way of keeping those pesky superstitions at bay," the Ambassador said. He laughed alone and patted Ward on the shoulder, then shook his hand away to dry it.

Taking a deep breath, Ward forced a smile. "I have no idea to what you're referring."

If the Ambassador was fishing for more information on the pranks, he wasn't going to get it. It had nothing to do with superstition.

Ward politely excused himself when they reached his rooms. It was the one area an ambassador didn't have access to—no matter how hard he might try. Before the security slide locked in place, the ridiculous man was down the hall, his disturbingly chipper chatter assaulting the next person who walked past him.

Ward called to Rane on his comm.

"Yes, sir?"

"I'd like the Ambassadors' Idex to be flagged at every security point. I want to know where he is at all times. Also, I want someone with him as much as possible without being too obvious."

"It's against law to tag someone of his status."

"Then let's do our best to not get caught."

"Yes, sir."

Ward wasn't sure if the Ambassador was trying to find out what had happened to Turk or if he was just annoyingly persistent. Either way, he was ready to get the Ambassador off his ship, to get the body off the ship, and to see Dr Moss about another ghost.

* * *

The lighting in the halls sank to the deepest glow level. A traveller could still see easily, but everything felt cloaked in night-time. Patterns of the star systems around various planets glittered on the walls.

Passengers were settling into the new routine and were making their way to their rooms, although more than usual still hung in the hallways and spilled out of the lounges. Ward took a few minutes to talk to some he recognized, then tried to be casual as he made his way to the medical bay.

Dr Moss was riffling through all his drawers, opening and closing them one after the other, then checking the upper cupboards.

"Sneaky little rat," Dr Moss muttered under his breath as Ward entered.

"Doctor?"

Dr Moss stopped his search and glared at him. "Your uncle never would have been dense enough to bring an ambassador on board. It's bad enough you've filled every inch with—"

Two women walked past the half-frosted glass, giggling, and waved at Ward.

He noticed the left corner of Dr Moss's lip turned up in a sideways smirk. "You look more miserable than I am," he said, clearly enjoying the moment.

"I don't think it's possible," Ward replied. There was no way anyone could look as perpetually miserable as Dr Moss.

"What do you need?" He'd gone back to looking in the drawers on the other side of the medical bay.

"I was wondering something about my uncle."

"Sorry to tell you, he's dead," Dr Moss said dryly, not looking up from the drawer as he pulled everything out, then put it back in.

"I know he's dead. I inherited his ship."

"Congrats."

"I was wondering if I could see his file."

"It's confidential." Another drawer emptied and quickly put back in.

"He's dead."

"Sorry for your loss." He left the medical bay to the private rooms, and Ward followed him as he began searching through the other cupboards.

Ward took a breath; he was going to have to come up with a way to ask.

"I'd heard—when I was a boy and a few times before he died —he'd… well, he'd *seen* things."

"You been drinking the haze?"

"No, I never touch the stuff. But you said… with the flux gases, if it triggered—"

Dr Moss stopped what he was doing and leaned against the silver countertop.

"You seeing things in the ship? Or are you seeing them out there?" He motioned toward the hull.

Ward didn't know if he wanted to answer.

"I can't help you if you don't tell me. Can tell you this, twenty years on this ship and I've heard it all. So you're not going to shock me. Man wasn't meant to travel in space for too long— needs to have his feet and his mind on land."

"You haven't left the ship in those twenty years…."

"Yes, makes you wonder why some minds are stronger than others. What's she look like?"

Wards eyes narrowed. He hadn't mentioned he was seeing anyone, or specifically a woman. He didn't trust Dr Moss, but Ward needed him. He was seeing someone who wasn't there. He'd talked to her, had almost reached out and touched her. It wasn't something he felt like discussing with Dr Moss, although he wasn't sure there was anything he'd ever want to discuss with Dr Moss.

But they were out in the darkness of space, and Ward was responsible for an entire ship. This kind of thing was uncommon, but if his uncle had been seeing things and not just rumoured, maybe it was in his blood. Maybe the flux gases he'd breathed in had triggered something.

He had to decide. The safety of his crew or his own pride.

"She's inside the ship, not outside."

Dr Moss stood silent for a moment.

"I'm not willing to put my ship at risk, whatever you think of me."

Ward half expected Dr Moss to call Rane to take over command.

"You talk to her?" Dr Moss asked instead.

Not what Ward was expecting.

"Some, I guess. She always knew what I was thinking, which makes sense, it was my thoughts. Her appearance, she looks exactly like…" He didn't finish his sentence. She looked exactly like a crew member he'd nearly drowned once? Like someone he'd like to see again?

Dr Moss went to his office leaving Ward to wonder what he was doing. He'd basically handed over his fate to a doctor who might not think he was competent to manage the Obsidian.

When Dr Moss came back, he carried a little blue bottle. He poured a little cup and handed it to Ward.

"I said I don't touch the stuff."

"Drink it and go to bed. When was the last time you slept?"

Ward pulled at the bottom of his coat. How long had it been? Had he gotten more than a few hours at a time since leaving Valtine? A brief rest here and there before someone called him away.

"Just go to bed?" Ward asked drinking the small cup full of sour liquid.

"Get some sleep. When you wake up, stick to a routine, don't go wandering about looking for trouble. You'll be fine."

"But my uncle…"

"Your uncle was a greedy liar who was paranoid for good

reason. His 'hallucinations' had more to do with his drink than his time in space."

Ward looked at the bottom of the empty cup.

"Not this stuff." Dr Moss snatched the little cup out of his hand. "Makes you wonder why you drank it without even asking me what it was. Now go to bed and forget you ever saw anything. Stop thinking about it or worrying, and you'll be fine in the morning. And if you see the Ambassador, you can tell him I want my Idex scanner back."

Ward felt dismissed but was feeling drowsier by the second. He needed to sleep, to forget, to wake up in complete control of his mind.

Back in his room, he fell onto his bed, closed his eyes, and tried to forget the woman standing by the sky lilies; the deep green eyes, the soft smile, her body drenched in the greenhouse mist.

He drifted off to sleep, not forgetting.

Fifteen

Wynter's soggy slippers dangled from her fingers. They slid down, threatening to drop and be abandoned in the softly lit stairwell. They'd completely absorbed the misting water and were leaving puddly prints. She'd taken them off, dried her feet as best she could, and made her way back to her room.

Her heart wouldn't slow down enough to let her mind think. Her free hand gripped the railing as she pulled herself up the stairs as quickly as she could.

"Are you alright? Is she alright?" someone asked as she pushed past. She should have been more careful, turned around, taken a different hall. But there were so many passengers no one would really remember her.

Wynter took the stairs two at a time. She needed to think, needed it quiet. Needed the pressing voice in the back of her head to stop.

At the last step, she grabbed the metal railing and propelled herself forward. Through the door and down another hallway, she rounded the corner and ran right into Lady Cristelle.

She was wearing a soft pink day dress. The billows and folds of fabric now carried the smallest hint of water from Wynter's soaked uniform.

"Ugh!" Lady Cristelle squealed, pushing Wynter back. "Look what you've done. I'm soaked! You've ruined my dress. Do you know what this cost?"

For all her work on dresses, Wynter didn't know what it would have cost and her mind felt a blank gap where she used to always have a reason or excuse ready.

The only thing she could think of was the body in the storage room and who it might belong to.

"Oh no you don't," Lady Cristelle said, as Wynter looked back toward the stairwell. She was hoping for an escape, a different route to the Helix suites. A crowd was already gathering, any escape would be just as noticed.

"I will have you fired, sent off this ship, dropped off at the midway station—"

She looked at the floor, maybe Lady Cristelle's rant would stop and everyone would go away. Scanning the crowd, her eye caught another lady's. She'd seen her around before, but never in Helix's rooms.

"Are you hazed? Are you infirm? Stop staring like a sog," Lady Cristelle said.

Wynter looked up as the other lady joined the group. She was wearing a yellow puffed-up jumper suit. It bellowed out around the ankles and wrists while clinging tight at her hips. She walked right up to Wynter, completely ignoring Lady Cristelle, and hugged her tight, leaving splotches of wet fabric all over herself.

Wynter stood stunned.

"OH, THANK YOU!" the other lady sobbed dramatically. Her arms were draped over Wynter's shoulders, "I don't know what I would have done without you finding—" Straightening herself she grabbed the slippers out of Wynter's hands "—my slippers. Oh, my favourite slippers! Thank you!"

Lady Cristelle glared at the woman clinging to Wynter and turned her nose up at them. "Lucy, what are you wearing?"

"Oh, do you like it?" the lady named Lucy asked. "I borrowed it from Lady Bailey, you know she was all the rage."

"Decades ago. Not Valtine decades either," Lady Cristelle sneered.

"I think it's lovely!"

"You do not! You're just wearing it to… to—"

"To show I look better than you, even when I'm wearing this? You know, I might bring it back into fashion. It's terribly comfortable. I don't think you could pull it off," Lucy twirled.

"You do not look better than me. No one here thinks so."

Lucy passed the slippers behind her back to Wynter. Wynter took them. She wanted to say thank you but was aware no one was paying any attention to her now. She slipped through the crowd and down the hallway, the sound of bickering fading behind her as she reached the Helix suites.

Helix looked up from the red dress she had running through the machine. Taking one look at Wynter, she frowned. "Don't touch anything," she said, then focused back on her work.

Wynter climbed up into the loft. She unbraided her hair and combed it through until it fell flat against her back.

She'd been caught. Lady Cristelle would certainly say something to Helix, and then Helix would stuff her in a freeze pod with—

Her mind didn't let her finish the thought.

She peeled off the shirt before it could completely dry to her skin, then hung it on a peg attached to the back wall.

Her mind wandered back to where she knew it would. Back to the day Henris had left her in the crate. When Henris had promised he'd come back for her when it was safe.

But he'd never contacted her. Not once.

Wynter set the slippers beside her mat to dry, her memories flooding back.

Henris had closed the lid and gotten off the shuttle… hadn't he? Except the crate muffled everything. She hadn't actually seen him go.

"Hurry up. I need help with this hem!" Helix called up from the workspace below.

Wynter ignored Helix and pulled the thin blanket out of its box. She was safe, but the thoughts didn't come the way she thought they would.

She didn't have a plan. There was no way to know for sure. She didn't know anything.

Closing her eyes, she tried to block out Captain Ward's words, but they flickered through her brain as she fell asleep. Poison. He'd said that he'd found a poisoned body. On his first day. The same day she'd arrived on the ship.

She squeezed her eyes shut, trying to block out the thought. If he was there, on the ship with her, he was never coming back for her.

* * *

Wynter didn't leave the Helix suites for days. She fixated on her needles.

Helix had been ecstatic with the idea from Captain Ward

about making ribbons, and Wynter had a box ready before the day was out.

The first two days, Helix hadn't noticed the change in pace and speed in which Wynter was spinning out gowns and ribbons.

Sleep came in small chunks. She'd woken up from an afternoon rest and was already stringing an extra round of beads.

Small glass pink beads.

What did it matter if she knew for sure?

Rose bead.

If it wasn't him, nothing changed.

Pink bead.

If it was him… well, nothing changed. She didn't have anywhere else to go.

Pink bead—no rose bead—

"Wynter!" Helix's frustrated voice pierced through her thoughts. "Wynter. Are you listening? I couldn't possibly explain how I'd made all this. I've barely had time to sew!"

"We made more than this when we first left Valtine."

"Yes, but I was in my rooms. Everyone knows I'm out socializing all day, and taking orders, and doing fittings. How do I explain it?"

"Tell them you had a secret pile already finished? Or we could save them for Orion," she shrugged. Helix was contemplating both options when Captain Ward's voice sounded over the ship's comms.

"This is your captain speaking. We'll be docking at the midway station in one hour. We ask passengers to remain within their designated rooms and hallways while we do necessary checks and loading. Once complete, outer panels will open on the first and sixth floors. We set up a special dinner for all passengers and available crew on the port side dining lounges to observe the Carina Nebula."

Completely forgetting about the new pile of finished dresses, Helix hurried to her own rooms to get ready.

Wynter put down the dress. She'd tried to keep working, stay distracted, but the thoughts kept coming like a needle through five layers of twill.

Midway dinners were always an extravagant evening, she'd be able to fit in and go unnoticed throughout the ship. She could go down and check the storage rooms.

She'd only been there once, only for a few minutes, but she knew where to look, and had to know.

In her loft, she took out the patchwork dress and let her fingers slide over each square. The rows of blues, yellows, and greens in succession lined with reds, oranges, and pinks. A bit of each dress she'd wanted to tell Henris about. She'd made them for him, to make him proud.

She had once wondered if he'd altered any of them, touched the same fabric she had. If he'd known and wanted to send a message.

But now he might be here—on the ship—not a single one of her dresses passing by his shop.

Wynter brushed her hair. Instead of a braid, she let it hang down her back. Then put on the dress. The bits of patched colours blended together. It curved up over only one shoulder; a line of translucent silver slid in a narrow line under her arm to the floor. The dress hugged her curves and draped around her legs.

Seven years of dresses. Seven years of waiting.

Maybe it wasn't Henris. Maybe it was someone who'd been dumped like Captain Ward's uncle had suggested. She grasped at hope while she got ready.

The halls were bursting with colour and excited passengers. She avoided the crush and made her way down to the bottom level and the storage room below.

The automatic lights flickered in her presence and flooded the room.

There was nothing but the outer hull between her feet and the infinite darkness below. A shiver went from her toes up her legs, and she stepped lightly.

The room was full but organized with large crates, all perfectly labelled. It was called long storage and contained left behind items, things forgotten by previous passengers, and by law, not yet disposed of.

Wynter inhaled a deep breath. Passing the rows, she scanned the aisles quickly. It would have to be big enough for a person. The light flickered behind her, like a shadow watching her movements.

Then she saw it. A long silver pod crate.

It made sense that it would be at the very back of the storage room, in its own space.

Wynter walked forward until she stood in front of it. A date was stamped clearly on the side, and there was paperwork attached to a clip on the outside.

She read the name three times.

The words never changed, but they felt different each time she read them.

She'd known. Even before coming down, she'd known things would never go back to the way they had been. Everything was different.

Henris Canmore.

His name was in black letters on the clipped paper, like a lost tag waiting for someone to claim him. She stood there, desperate for the air in the room to fill back up. For the space below to swallow them both, for whatever she felt to stop. But it was only her and Henris, meeting again for the last time after seven years.

"Do you remember the dress?" she asked the casket, "I left Orion in it. It didn't look like this then. It was plain. Plain was best." She turned around, making sure the crate could see the front and back.

"I added this patch here first. It was the first dress I worked on. Madame Helix let me have the bit I cut off on the hem. I did hems for weeks before she realized I could do more." Wynter lifted the hem of her dress up and turned it slightly, showing a pale pink strip.

"There wasn't much fabric left from this one, just thin strips. We used every bit, but it was so lovely, like a glass rose. I made sure I didn't finish it until we docked at Orion. I thought you might see it or hear about it, anyway."

Another voice echoed through the bay as the captain announced successful docking and that dinner would start soon.

"I have a few more to add. Ones I wanted to show you. There's a red dress… a lady named Cristelle is wearing it tonight."

Wynter had cried often enough. She'd cried for a week straight when she first arrived on the Obsidian, and Helix had let her. She'd cried the first time Helix had gone off the ship and left her alone until she realized how much freedom she had. She'd cried when she couldn't figure out how to run her stitches backwards. But this time, as the little drops fell from her eyes, they felt different. Like the tears didn't belong to her. They belonged to someone else. They were falling for someone else. The only other someone who had been anything to her, who had treated her like someone.

"Lady Cristelle will look incredible tonight." She sniffled, wanting to reassure the dead of something. "I made her dress look like sky lilies. You would have thought it too fussy, but they're a beautiful flower." Tears fell freely. "They bloom best in space you know."

* * *

Wynter didn't go back to her rooms but made her way up to the greenhouses. She wouldn't be able to explain her presence if she got caught. She didn't care.

Up the stairs and to the second floor, she picked a sky lily and stared at the soft blooming petals, then turned into the little alcove where the stretch of windows provided a space to look out.

The Carina Nebula would be a sight from the other side of the ship. From here, there was only darkness beyond the thick wall of glass.

Placing her hand on it, she looked out to the expanse and let out a breath. She should wonder what had happened to Henris. She should try to remember every sound. Someone had been talking before the ship took off, hadn't they? She should wonder why Henris had been nervous seven years ago, how she hadn't noticed it—not the way she should have. She should wonder what would happen to her now, if she should live on the ship forever, or leave, or hide somewhere else.

All those things were there, like a dull wave in the back of her mind, but all she could feel was the great sea of darkness beyond the glass.

Sixteen

Ward was seeing the effects of Helix's fame ripple through the ship. They were only halfway to Orion and guests had abandoned regular attire for gowns and glamour. Men had attached vibrant fast trims to the lapels of their jackets. Helix ribbons were floating from every wrist and hair piece. Even some of his crew had adopted some of the frill for the dinner. They all tried to cover it when they saw Ward approaching. He just shook his head.

Ward was in the mood to be lenient about the dress code, especially for off-duty staff.

He'd slept properly and followed the doctor's instructions to stick to a routine, as best he could anyway. And he hadn't seen *her* since.

The midway station docking was going well. Guests crowded in the upper dining room, viewing the Carina Nebula. It was a sight he never tired of, the woven colours stretching out and filling the darkness.

They had decorated the dining rooms for the occasion with prisms to catch the rainbows of light and send them dancing. Blue lights twinkled on the glass bottles, leather chairs, and black tablecloths.

He greeted his passengers and shook hands, enjoying a few moments as his upbringing as a Valtine Lord took over.

A tray of glasses passed by, and he grabbed one before approaching Lady Cristelle and those who'd gathered by one of the large lookouts. He was wondering why he was even bothering to try.

She looked stunning in what could only be yet another Helix gown. But he couldn't see himself actually being married to her, no matter how much Rane approved of the match. He took a sip and then almost choked as she drew closer.

Her dress was red. The skirt flowed above her knees and dripped around the edges like red petals dropping down toward the floor. Like a sky lily, exactly like a sky lily.

He'd been congratulating himself on not thinking about *her,* but the dress made it impossible. He was picturing his hallucination, standing in front of the sky lilies, remembering questions she'd asked about his family and about his life. The way the water misted over her. He closed his eyes, trying to shake the image.

"You look terrible," Lady Cristelle snipped, smiling in a thin line her hand still out, waiting for him to greet her properly.

Taking her hand, he recovered himself, brought it up to his lips and kissed the inside of her wrist.

"My apologies, my lady." He would have said more, but she was already not paying any attention to him and was instead scanning the room. If she was planning on making an offer like the rumours confirmed, she hadn't given him any sign of particular approval.

They made their way to the window and looked out at the nebula, ladies coming around them to smile at Ward and coo over

Lady Cristelle's dress. She turned her nose up at Lady Lucy when she came by, making a snide comment. Lady Lucy just smiled, directing her attentions toward Lord Kent.

Rane called Ward, and he let his hand fall unnoticed from Lady Cristelle's arm. He couldn't picture it. The Obsidian wasn't a desperate floundering ship. It was successful with or without land ties. Life with Lady Cristelle would be miserable. He'd been around his uncle enough to know one person was indeed capable of making life misery for everyone.

"Excuse me a moment," he said, clicking the comm. "Go ahead, Rane."

"Something triggered the lights in the cargo hold, sir." Rane hesitated. "We lost track of the Ambassador. He could have been down there also, with loading the cargo we couldn't monitor the Idex. I should also mention that an unauthorized message was sent out from the midway station, but with hundreds of guests we'd have to interview them all to know."

Questioning the guests could prove distasteful, and messages were not uncommon. It was likely they'd just missed logging it. Rane agreed—the missing Ambassador was a more significant concern.

Ward was already heading for the door, leaving his guests to enjoy their dinner. He looked back at Lady Cristelle who hadn't even noticed he'd left, the sky lily dress tugging at the corner of his mind.

"We'll start a sweep of the lower levels first and see who's out of place. Could be the crew requested something and forgot to log it. I can't blame them at this point."

The Ambassador approached the dining hall as Ward was leaving. He was wearing a startling red jacket with fast trims up one side and down the other, and was looking down at an Idex scanner, probably the one Dr Moss had been looking for, and tucked it in his side pocket when Ward approached.

"Captain, good to see you. Did you know the Carina Nebula was first discovered by—"

"Ambassador, I was looking for you," Ward interrupted. The Ambassador looked as though he was going to finish his previous sentence but changed his mind.

"Well, you always know where to find me." The Ambassador's eyes narrowed some and Ward wondered if he'd figured out they'd been trailing him.

"Dr Moss mentioned he needed his scanner back," Ward said, hoping the Ambassador would hand it over. Ward wasn't sure what he would do if he didn't.

"Fascinating thing. Did you know hand scanners carry all the information regarding genealogies, planet of birth, travel records, driving, and space clearance. Not to mention—"

"Well, not to mention medical information, which is required for everyone who boards my ship."

"As an ambassador, I am privy to all Idex accounts on this ship."

"Yes certainly, but not to my chief medic's supplies." Ward held his hand out.

The Ambassador glared, clearly not wanting to give it up, but since he'd already admitted to having it, there was little he could do with the onlooking passengers. He took it out of his pocket and passed it to Ward.

"If you'll excuse me," Ward said

"Of course, you are excused." The Ambassador stepped past him.

Tucking the scanner in his own pocket, Ward contacted Rane again. "I don't care what you have to promise Fuller. I want the Ambassador tracked every second he's on this ship. We're fifteen days from Orion."

Rane agreed and confirmed they had swept the bottom three floors.

Clearing the length of the fourth floor, Ward was walking past the stairs and saw it—saw her. The shimmering of colours like the nebula outside the ship floating up the stairs.

No, not now, not again, he thought. He'd been calm. Everything had been running smoothly. Had the dress triggered it? Or his run in with the Ambassador? Surely he could handle a little stress without hallucinating.

He shouldn't follow her. He knew he should go directly to Dr Moss. But Dr Moss would send him to bed, time he couldn't afford to take. He needed to be alert, at least until they were under way again and moving swiftly toward Orion.

This was what going crazy must feel like. He wondered if his uncle saw things because of the haze, or if he drank the haze because of what he saw. It was starting to feel like a better option.

He entered the greenhouse and breathed in the smell of plants and soil.

She wasn't on the stairs or sitting on the second floor. He caught movement up toward the outer panel where he knew a small section of outer shutters would cross over, showing the space beyond.

He made his way up and stopped. She was blanketed in the low hanging vines, looking out into the blackness at nothing. Her hair fell down her back. She was wrapped in a rainbow swirl, it swept up over one shoulder, leaving the other bare. A thin line of skin shimmered up her leg.

He wanted to keep the moment, pretend he wasn't going crazy, take her all in. His mind had created something fascinating, and he didn't want to let it go. But he needed to. For the safety of everyone on board, he needed to confirm in his own mind that he was hallucinating and hand control of the ship over to Rane. At least until he figured out what was going on. He felt the knots in his stomach. He was going to lose control of his ship. Not lose control, he reminded himself, give up control, temporarily. But it felt the same.

He felt the scanner in his pocket, his fingers wrapping around the metal plating. She turned to face him. Something had changed about the way she was looking at him. Something had changed about her. She looked at him as if she knew this was the end. What a trick for his mind to play on him.

Clicking the scanner beside him, he closed his eyes, waited, then looked down at the blank screen.

She wasn't there. There was no one, no trace of a person. There was only someone his mind had made up. He clicked the scanners buttons again, but still nothing.

He closed his eyes tight, willing her to disappear, for him to be alone in the small alcove. When he opened them, she was still there, staring down at the scanner, a look of terror clouding her eyes.

"Why did you bring that?" she asked, her voice shaking.

"I needed to see it, to convince myself. I've accepted it. I have to get you off this ship. I have to get you out of my head. I need you gone. Why am I keeping you here?" He ran his hand through his hair again. Maybe if he got closer. Maybe if he reached out to touch her and his hand went through, she'd dissipate into thin air.

Her eyes pooled as soft little droplets of collected mist fell from the vines above. One splashed on her cheek, mixed with a tear, and rolled down. She looked pained by his words, and he almost felt guilty.

Guilty for upsetting a hallucination... great. He couldn't stop himself. Reaching up, he brushed the tear away, his hand feathered over a warm cheek.

He pulled his hand back as if it had scalded him.

Reaching out again, he put his hand on her cheek, stepping in close until he felt the warmth coming off her body. Then he let his hand trace down her bare arm from the uncovered shoulder to her fingers.

He held her hand for a moment, turned it so her palm was facing up, then raised it, kissing the inside of her wrist, feeling the pulse beating beneath her skin.

Like the nebula on the other side of the ship, his mind sparked with a burst of light, but all he could say was, "You're real?"

She stood there stunned, but didn't pull her hand back, confusion flashing in her eyes. "Of course, I'm real."

Seventeen

Wynter had been staring out into the vastness of space, waiting for it to reach through the glass and pull her into the darkness.

She didn't want it to. She wanted to take the week back, to be excited about reaching Orion, wondering if this time it was safe to come home, wondering if Henris had seen the dresses.

Henris wouldn't see the dresses this time. He hadn't seen them ever. She pushed the vines from where they stuck to the window. The warm air made the floral scents hang heavy around her.

There had been a plan in the back of her mind. Something she'd held onto, something to keep her content and pushing forward.

Stay ugly, stay hidden, stay alive.

The plan didn't matter anymore.

Lost in her thoughts, she'd looked up to see Captain Ward standing in front of her; he was close, and he was holding the Idex scanner. The scanner Helix and Henris knew would bring trouble. The scanner Dr Moss had told her wouldn't say anything.

"I needed to see it, to convince myself. I've accepted it. I have to get you off this ship. I have to get you out of my head. I need you gone. Why am I keeping you here?"

His words had slammed into her chest with another wave of grief. The Obsidian was the only home she had, and it was going to be torn from her too.

Would he sell her? Dump her on the next planet? What about Henris? She couldn't leave him here alone. The pain tore at her, and another tear had slipped out. He'd caught it on her cheek.

She hadn't understood the change. The hand suddenly touching her cheek, or the shocked look. He'd looked so confused, as if he'd expected it to slip right past her.

Her skin had tingled as his hand ran down her arm, and the feeling of his lips pressed against the inside of her wrist had sent a swirl of flutters into her stomach.

"You're real?" he had asked. Of all the things she'd thought he might say, questioning her existence wasn't one of them.

"Of course, I'm real," she'd replied.

Now, all she could do was stare. Confused.

"You're real!" he repeated, then louder, "YOU'RE REAL." He looked like he was going to throw up. She wanted to step back, but his hand grabbed her shoulder, a little rougher, then let go.

He reached for her wrist, clasped her hand, shook it, then dropped it back down.

"What do you mean I'm real?" she asked, using the back of her freed hand to clear away the forgotten tear.

He straightened his jacket and shook bits of water out of his hair, combing his fingers through it. "I apologize—"

"What do you mean, *real*?"

"Well, you're not… well, you're not—*not*…" he said, looking like he wanted to run. The feeling was mutual.

"Not what?"

"A ghost… not a real ghost… one I made up," he said, closed his eyes and rubbed his chin with one hand.

"Why would I be a ghost?"

She looked down at the scanner at the same time as he did. Both focused on it, collecting their thoughts and not saying anything. He closed some of the distance between them, holding the silver screen in his hand, shook his head, then poked her in the arm.

"Just checking," he mumbled, brows drawn together. "But you don't exist," he added, holding up the scanner.

"I helped you rescue your tie," she argued.

"Well, I knew you were real then."

"And I turned into a ghost?"

"No, I mean there's nothing… there's nothing here. No birthplace, history, record of travel, clearances—you're not here. You're nothing." He let out a sound between a groan and a laugh.

"Nothing?" she whispered his words back to him.

"No, it wasn't. I can explain," he said, looking very much like he didn't want to have to explain. "Dr Moss said the flux gasses could cause all sorts of problems, like seeing things and I thought —well, never mind what I thought. I'm sorry," he said with the same pained look on his face he'd had when she'd first seen him in the greenhouse.

"You don't look surprised by this?" he said, waving the scanner in the air. "It's Dr Moss's."

"Yes, I know," she said, terrified. Now it was her turn to try to explain. She was terrified to find out what they did to stowaways, especially stowaways without an Idex.

He looked at her from head to toe and frowned. She knew her face looked a mess from crying and her long brown hair hanging loose around her shoulders and down her back.

"You were crying before I accused you of being a ghost. Did someone hurt you? Did Dr Moss?" he asked, suddenly examining her too closely.

"No." She realized she sounded confused before she realized what he was implying, "Oh no, I just met Dr Moss—well—no."

He looked relieved. "But you were upset?"

"I'm fine," she lied. He looked down at the scanner's blank screen, shook it, and was going to ask more.

The greenhouse door opened, letting in the cheerful chatter of wandering passengers who were way out of bounds.

Wynter immediately stepped back, pulling the captain with her until her back pressed against the glass and they were hidden behind the vines. They would be out of sight unless someone came right up to them.

But the space was smaller than she'd thought, and his well-fitted suit jacket had hidden just how large his arms and chest were. He slid an arm around her waist so he could press in closer and away from the damp foliage behind them.

She marvelled at what she'd just discovered—what he'd revealed—all while trying to find a way to breathe without pressing further against him.

He'd thought she was a ghost—a real ghost! And she'd thought he was what? A friend? She'd never had a friend before, but they'd both been wrong. He was the captain she'd been hiding from for seven years. She wished she was a ghost.

Damp leaves stuck to her arms. She noticed his height, the citrus smell of soap, the soft line of stubble across his jawline, and the uncomfortable smile he'd plastered on his face. It created the hint of a dimple on his left cheek.

Her stomach flipped again.

Voices filtered up from the first floor. "I told you I could get us in."

Laughter and cheering burst into the greenhouse as a dozen guests poured in. Moving toward Captain Ward, she peeked through the leaves. They were all dressed in their finery, looking as though they had their fill of champagne and sweets.

"Oh it's so delightful."

"Ah, do you smell that? Like home."

"Like Valtine."

"Valtine smells better." Wynter recognized Lady Cristelle's voice and pulled back, shrinking further into the small alcove, trying to disappear.

Lady Cristelle had seen her in the halls once already. Would she recognize her? What if they came up to the second floor?

Captain Ward's body shifted like he was going to leave.

"Someone will see us," she whispered, panic rising.

He smiled full out, as if some weight had finally lifted off him. "I don't hide on my own ship," he said and brushed a hair away from her face.

"You know Dr Moss?" he asked, letting her hair trail through his fingers behind her neck.

She gave the smallest nod, feeling ridiculous. He hadn't moved away, and she had never been this close to another person before. But of course he wouldn't hide on his own ship. She was the only one who needed to hide, and why would he protect her? She was clearly a stowaway.

"Is he safe?" he asked, surprising her again.

Wynter nodded, about as safe as any of this was for her.

Then he clicked his comm and spoke quietly. "Rane, I need you to get ahold of Dr Moss. Tell him… tell him the greenhouse needs a laundry bin and to be grumpy about it, but to be *discreet* and grumpy."

He tucked the scanner into his jacket pocket. "Wait until we're gone." He reached over her head, picked a few of the sky lilies from the vines, and left her standing there alone.

Eighteen

He wasn't going crazy. He was Captain Isaac Ward of the Obsidian, and he wasn't going crazy.

He filtered through what he knew quickly as he picked up the sky lilies.

Somehow, she must have overridden the Idex code, must have done it before boarding on Valtine. How she'd gotten on the ship and who she was hiding from, he'd find out. Whatever her story, it couldn't be a pleasant one. She'd looked so sad standing there. And he'd done nothing but add to her pain. He'd told her she was nothing, and she needed to get off the ship.

He wished he could take it back.

There was one pressing problem he needed to deal with first. He had to get everyone out of the greenhouse without discovering her. If she was hiding, he needed to help her.

He made his shoes echo on the metal grated floor when he came down the stairs. They all looked up at his unexpected approach.

Lord Kent, who was wearing a fantastic violet suit with fast trims around every fold, tried to put some air between himself and

Lady Cristelle, who was draped over his arm. She leaned in more.

The Ambassador was, unfortunately, part of the group. He stood at the back and was picking at some floral bush while trying to get the attention of a slender girl who looked frightened to be caught in the greenhouses. Ten others were in various levels of discomfort.

Cargo ships strictly forbid access to the greenhouses. The plants were a combination of cargo belonging to high paying shippers, as well as provisions necessary for the life of the ship, comfortable life anyway.

Ward overlooked the offence and addressed Lady Cristelle. "Your dress reminded me of sky lilies. I thought I'd come and pick some for you. I forgot they wilt so quickly." He gave her a charming smile. She looked at the wilted flowers with a raised brow.

"Why don't we go see them in bloom? You'd like to, wouldn't you Lord Kent?" Lady Cristelle said, still wrapped over his arm. Lord Kent tried to make at least some space between them, looking hesitantly at Ward.

"You left a formal dinner early to pick a flower?" The lord accused then untangled himself from Lady Cristelle's grasp. He technically outranked Ward, but being a captain made the situation tenuous.

"Of course not. I had other matters to attend to but was walking by."

Lady Cristelle scowled at Lord Kent for throwing her off so easily and changed tactics. "I wonder if sky lilies would make a pleasant addition to the perfumery's registry. You know I've always been interested in the family business." She placed a hand on his damp shoulder and brushed off a clinging leaf. "*If* I stay on," she patted his shoulder, her smile brittle as she looked up toward the balcony, clearly not believing his story.

"If? Oh don't worry, I'll make sure you aren't reprimanded for entering an unauthorized area," Ward said, resisting the urge to follow her gaze.

The Ambassador who had moved himself to the front of the group, was now keenly interested in the sky lilies.

"Did you know," the Ambassador said, trying to step past Ward who was blocking his path. "Sky lilies, I am told, bloom best in space, which is of course an ode to you Lady Cristelle, being gowned in them."

The lady looked less than pleased to be wearing what was now a wilted flower in Ward's hands.

"I'm sure I'd love to see sky lilies in bloom," the Ambassador continued. "Did you know their medicinal purposes on a ship are without compare? In fact, they've eased hallucinogenic moments, like say a yearly ghost." The Ambassador raised his brows and let them dance a little over his eyes. He laughed at his dig toward what he'd already surmised about the Valtine pranks.

The Ambassador's persistent questions were clearly getting him closer to the original source of the ghost pranks. Something Ward wanted to prevent. And there was something else in the way he pressed in. Ward felt like punching him in the face, but kept his hands balled at his side.

Dr Moss arrived quickly, a little out of breath as if he'd run down there. He looked perfectly grumpy, pushing a large laundry cart with a scowl on his face.

The chatter stopped and Ward wondered if bringing Dr Moss into the mix was a great idea. It felt like his only option until he knew more about the mystery stowaway upstairs. He'd already determined Dr Moss had convinced him he was hallucinating in order to keep her a secret. She knew Dr Moss, which made him an ally.

"What is this?" Dr Moss thundered. "A garden party? Get away from those! Do you know what would happen if you touched them?"

One lady pulled her hand back from a black flowering pot and held them tight. Nothing. Ward knew nothing would happen. They were being taken to Corva as a new species to study how they flourished under a different sun pattern.

The doctor drifted the large cart over the rough stoned floor, glaring as each lady tucked their skirts in to shuttle past him. He was effectively herding them one by one toward the door mumbling about passengers and lenient captains the entire time. The larger part of the party took the hint and exited the room.

Ward let the comments slide as Dr Moss was playing his part. A little too well, which helped confirm what he already thought.

The Ambassador was now the only one between Ward and Dr Moss. Lord Kent and Lady Cristelle had been pushed past but had yet to leave.

"What is the bin for?" the Ambassador said, peering at the large metal box. In fact, it was for medical laundry as Ward was sure the Ambassador was well aware.

"Do you really want to know?" Dr Moss stepped close to the Ambassador making him pull uncomfortably at his tails.

"Oh, yes. I'm interested in all things medical, you understand."

"Dead shoots."

"Pardon."

Ward rolled his eyes.

"The shoots of the jasper tree. It's tall and long and best if you get the whole thing, then it's soaked and ground."

"Oh, yes, of course, how fascinating. I'd heard about ships medics resorting to such remedies. Do you dabble for experimentation?"

"You can get in too."

The Ambassador glared at Dr Moss's mocking tone.

"Go ahead, Rane," Ward pretended to connect with his comm. "Of course. Everyone, if you would follow me, we don't want to miss the end of the evening."

The Ambassador looked at the balcony one more time, then squeezed past Dr Moss toward the exit.

Ward placed the wilted red flowers on the laundry bin.

"I was picking sky lilies. I didn't expect them to fade so fast, like holding a ghost."

The doctor looked up toward the balcony. "I'm not doing this favour for you."

"You know, doctor, I don't need favours for myself. I really did only need to get a good night's rest." He patted him on the shoulder and followed the party back to the dining area.

Nineteen

Wynter waited in the small alcove, the conversation drifting up through the leaves she was picking.

The talking finally stopped, she peeked her head out and let out a squeak, throwing the bits of leaves at Dr Moss who now stood just beyond the vines.

He was glaring.

"You talk about staying hidden and no one noticing you and you decide to wear that? When the ship's full of guests? No wonder the captain said to bring a bin."

She looked down at her dress and wondered what was so wrong with it. It hugged her curves, but it flowed all the way to her feet and the swoop across her chest was much higher than what was in fashion, even on Corva.

He turned and started walking back down the narrow stairs, expecting her to follow. She felt numb walking down the steps to where a laundry bin was waiting.

"No," she said firmly. She wasn't getting in. Not this time. She knew it wasn't the same, but Henris had put her in a crate, and now he was gone, and she was stuck on the Obsidian. Wynter stared at the bin—stuck. The word was new to her. She'd never felt like that before, not really. She was waiting, but there had always been a plan. But now?

"I don't care who sees me. They'll think what? Nothing," she said.

"Not nothing. They'll be curious about you. Especially since Captain Ward was just in here. We have a very curious Ambassador and lady waiting to see what comes out of this greenhouse."

He didn't ask again. She climbed into the metal bin. It smelled like laundry soap and damp pudding. Crunching herself up, he dropped the lid down, startling her. She closed her eyes, trying to take in small breaths. He wasn't going to leave her in there alone. Or was he? The space felt like it was shrinking. She couldn't tell if she was being pressed in or if her arms were pushing against the metal walls.

This was not a comfortable way of getting around the ship.

Wynter kept track of the turns as they slid down the halls. She couldn't make out the muffled sounds and felt the cart jolt a few times. She was sure he'd knocked right into someone passing them in the hall. Dr Moss didn't apologize. Up a lift, down another hall. A few minutes later, they turned around, and she was sure they were going back the way they came, then up again.

They stopped. One door slid open, and they went through. She heard it close behind them and then another door. The wheels stopped moving.

He opened the lid. She uncurled herself, arms aching from the one-sided fight and climbed out.

They were in a large bedroom. Thick paned glass reached up three floors where the ceiling peaked and then came down on an angle. Three other walls were lined with drawers, shelves, and cupboards with flat panelled fronts. The bed was off to one side of the room with a small table and lights hanging over it. In the centre of the room was a round table with four black chairs in a semi-circle.

It was the type of room she imagined on a planet, not a ship.

Dr Moss was opening and closing drawers and cupboards, leaving some of them half open as he riffled through. This was clearly not his room. Pulling out black pants with a smooth band and a black knit top, he tossed them to her, then pointed at what she assumed was a bathroom.

"Get changed," he said.

"Why?" she asked. She was wearing the dress for the first time and didn't want to take it off.

"This ship is crawling with crowds of people with more money than brains. They'll get one look at you and wonder where the dress came from, who made it. It looks like a Helix on haze and if you plan on ever leaving this room, I suggest you change. Also, I don't want you distracting Captain Ward while I'm trying to talk to him."

"A Helix on haze?" She looked down at the flash of colours. Would it really distract the captain?

A Helix on haze. It was as if a needle sized bit of laughter punched through the balloon of pain.

A Helix on *haze*. She swallowed the laugh.

"Now," he demanded, but she saw him smile a little.

She scurried to the bathroom. The room was at least three times the size of the one she shared with Helix. She changed quickly. The pants were big. She pulled at the side strings as tight as she could, then rolled it a few times over. The shirt wasn't too bad but hung loose. Baggy was best.

She was carefully folding her dress and could overhear Dr Moss talking to someone else in the other room. She recognized the voice as Rane's and hoped she wasn't in Rane's room, wearing his clothing.

"Is the captain okay?" Rane asked, his voice angry from behind the door. "Where is he?"

"What are you doing here?" Dr Moss asked in return.

"There was a medical emergency override on his room scan," Rane said.

"How else was I supposed to get in?"

"Why are you here at all!" Rane's frustration was palpable.

She blushed and looked down at what she was wearing, hoping again that it wasn't Rane's clothing. Then she opened the door and came out. Dr Moss rubbed his forehead and frowned as if she had done something wrong.

Rane looked at her and then back at Dr Moss, as if some explanation might come out of his mouth. Wynter wondered what the doctor would say too, if she was being honest. She probably should have stayed in the bathroom.

"Captain Ward can explain when he gets here," Dr Moss said, then continued opening cupboards. Rane closed them behind him until the doctor stopped, finding whatever he had been looking for. He took out a little blue bottle and poured two glasses. Then he sat down in one of the oversized chairs and nodded for Wynter to do the same. She took the glass from his hands and took the chair opposite Dr Moss, tucking her feet up under her.

"Moss… what is this?" Rane asked, voice low.

"I don't answer to you," Dr Moss replied.

"Fine," Rane snapped, then turned his attention to Wynter.

His face softened, but she could tell he was aggravated. "Excuse me miss, forgive my surprise at meeting you in the *captain's* rooms, but may I ask what you're doing here with Dr Moss?"

She looked at Dr Moss. Was she there with him? He should have brought her back to Helix, but perhaps that would have been more difficult to explain. He was also looking smug, which was interesting. The last time she saw Dr Moss, he'd told her that he never wanted to see her again, but one call from Captain Ward and he'd shown up.

Regardless of Dr Moss's reasons, she'd been careless. Her first thought was she'd never get back to Henris, but then she remembered Henris was gone. She blinked back the tears, reminding herself that he was still on the ship. She couldn't leave without him….

"Oh, don't cry. What did you do to her?" Rane said, directing his question to Dr Moss.

Dr Moss answered the accusation with a stone-cold glare.

The sound of the black shutters covering the Obsidian reverberated through the large room. Wynter watched as the black panels slid in perfect precision, covering over each other and encasing the ship in a protective layer of darkness.

Rane leaned against the now-covered glass accepting that they would have to wait together. The silence was itchy and made Wynter want to slink away, but there was nowhere to go.

By the time Captain Ward finally arrived, Wynter had pulled a loose thread from the bottom of the pants and was winding it around her fingers.

The man who had, only a short time ago, accused her of being a ghost now looked completely in control.

He let his eyes rest on Wynter. She shifted in her chair, trying not to make eye contact.

"Are those my clothes?" Captain Ward asked, directing the question at Dr Moss, clearly blaming him.

"Convince me it wasn't necessary," Dr Moss responded. Wynter thought of Dr Moss's comment about being a distraction and pulled at the hanging shirt.

"It wasn't necessary," Ward said, but the look he gave Wynter warmed her to her toes.

"Not convinced," Dr Moss said, clearly catching the exchange.

"I thought you would have brought her to the medical bay. I went there first," Captain Ward said, changing the subject. "Why is Rane here?"

Rane went to the cupboard, poured himself a drink, stirred it slowly, then leaned back against the glass. He shrugged indicating he wasn't sure either. Captain Ward stood beside the table in the middle of the room, looking at Dr Moss and then Wynter as if she were a puzzle.

"My medical bay halls aren't exactly quiet anymore," Dr Moss said, one arm resting on the back of the chair.

"Maybe someone can fill me in on what's going on as you all appear to know each other?" Rane said calmly. Sitting down in one of the empty chairs, his glass turning in his hands. "Maybe introduce the lady?"

"Rane this is…" Ward paused for a moment as if he was picking each word out of a hat, "A stowaway from Valtine."

Her eyes widened. Valtine? He thought she'd gotten on at Valtine? She looked at Dr Moss who shook his head. So she held herself quiet. Of course he would think she was from Valtine. The first time he's seen her was in the pools, she'd told him she was just day staff.

"We ran the Idex security scans dozens of times since then, so I don't see how that is possible," Rane said, glaring at Dr Moss as he took a slow drink.

"I... she was... she's been bypassing the scans," Captain Ward said, then pulled out the scanner he'd been carrying and gave it back to Dr Moss. "I recovered this for you."

Dr Moss took it back and tucked it quickly into his jacket pocket. Ward said nothing and paced from one end of the room to the other.

"I ran the scans myself. I don't want to alarm you but tampering with an Idex security system carries significant penalties." Rane was staring intently at Wynter. She wanted to tell him she'd done nothing wrong, but then they would know the truth. She hoped Dr Moss would say something for her, but he let out a sort of mock laugh. It was enough to pull Rane's attention away from her and onto Dr Moss.

"If your technology can work around the Idex it puts the entire hex-system and space travel at risk. Everything is based on it. Tampering with it is illegal and if you helped her—"

"I had nothing to do with this," Dr Moss said, but something flickered in his eyes making Wynter feel like what he was saying wasn't entirely true. He was still keeping secrets, not only from Rane and Captain Ward but from her too.

"Perhaps we leave the threats until we know what we're dealing with." The statement came from Captain Ward, who'd been more or less forgotten on the other side of the room.

His voice was kind and reassuring, but the problem was she didn't have the information they thought she did. She hadn't messed with any security system, and she hadn't got on at Valtine.

Dr Moss shook his head no.

She didn't know what game Dr Moss was playing. He'd brought her here. He had turned it into a spectacle with Rane involved. And now she was supposed to play along, not say anything?

Wynter was tired. She'd just found Henris. She had no hope of a home on Orion. Helix had made it very clear what would happen to her if any of these three men were seen talking to her. There was a party going on a few floors down she would never be a part of. And somehow, the party mattered right now.

Tears threatened again at the side of her eyes, and she blinked them back. Whether she liked it or not, hiding was no longer an option. These men, who were now arguing about Idex uses and scanners, held her fate.

The pressure built in the room, like a copper vat of bubbling soap. All because of her. She wound and unwound the string on her finger until it creased and made little red marks on her skin. And then she found her voice.

"I have a name. It's Wynter. Just Wynter." She heard Dr Moss groan and her resolve faltered a little, but she didn't stop. "I didn't mess with your Idex systems. I… I don't have one."

The room got quiet. Dr Moss finished his drink, and Rane refilled it without being asked.

Captain Ward looked at her. She could see the thoughts tumbling around in his mind. He paced the room and back. Then threw up his arms.

"I don't understand," was all he said and poured himself a drink.

Twenty

Ward let the name roll over in his mind. Wynter, her name was Wynter. It suited her. He stared at her, at his ghost, in disbelief.

Everyone had an Idex code. Maybe this was some craziness Dr Moss had told her.

"Everyone is born with an Idex code, it comes from your mother: traceable, trackable, updatable," Ward said. He sounded like a textbook, but it didn't make sense. "A person can't be born without one."

Ward watched Wynter exchange glances with Dr Moss.

Dr Moss was the first to speak again. "I suggest you all come up with a plan to keep her hidden like she's always been."

"How? We're not rounding back to Valtine for at least eight months," Ward said. He wasn't going to drop her on any planet, not without knowing why she was there.

"She didn't get on at Valtine, you cork."

"Call me a cork again—" he started but then realized what Dr Moss had said.

She hadn't got on at Valtine. Ward stopped pacing. He'd been so thankful he wasn't going crazy he hadn't even thought to ask.

In fact, he hadn't even asked her name before leaving her to Dr Moss.

Wynter had no Idex code. He let the thought run through his mind again, still not able to grasp what it meant.

"How long?" Rane asked Dr Moss.

"She's been on the ship for years," Dr. Moss said, taking a quick drink. "Why don't you ask her?"

"So now you want her to speak for herself?" Rane shot back.

Ward undid his jacket, tossed it onto the end of his bed and walked over to the window, but the shutters had completely closed them in.

Years.

"Over two?" Ward asked. Had she snuck on before he took over the ship? No one said anything. It couldn't be more than two. Turning back to face Dr Moss, he waited. No one moved.

"More than five?" Ward asked.

Dr Moss smiled in confirmation.

She'd been on the ship for over five years. How many? Six? Seven? It did indicate she'd been on the ship when his uncle had been captain. He seriously hoped his uncle wasn't involved in bringing her on board.

Five years at least, he'd been on the ship for only seven. He looked at her closely. Five years ago she would have been a young woman.

He wondered if he had any control over his own ship. She was sitting in the chair, wearing his clothing, and drinking his blue like this was an everyday conversation.

She looked calm, not unlike the calm he knew from Valtine, everything brewing under the surface.

"It doesn't matter how long, having a stowaway on board is a problem," Rane stated the obvious.

A stowaway could compromise his entire reputation, his ship, and his crew. They had time before leaving the midway and could legally get her off the ship. It would be the right thing to do for his ship and those on board. But she didn't have an Idex, certainly the rules didn't apply in this situation, although the look on Rane's face indicated he thought the rule should be followed to the letter. There was no way he would abandon her without even finding out why she was there. Rane had to know that.

"It would be best if we all forgot we ever saw her." Dr Moss leaned forward.

"If you wanted us to forget she's here, then why did you bring me into this?" Rane accused.

Ward had wondered why Rane was there, but it hadn't been the most pressing thing on his mind.

"I didn't realize the captain's nanny would come running the second a medical code was input. Don't blame me."

Ward shook his head, refusing to let Dr Moss get under his skin, although the tactic was working on Rane. Rane was flushed, and he wondered if he'd have to break up a fight.

"Well, so far, you're the only one to blame since you're the only other one who knows she's been here. And for years!" Rane was overstepping, but Ward kept his eye on Wynter.

"If she's been here for years, what possible danger could she pose to us or anyone out in space? Get the ship moving and do your own job," Dr Moss ordered.

"Telling me to get the ship moving is Captain Ward's job, not yours, *medic*," Rane fired back.

Ward watched Wynter take another drink while Rane and Dr Moss bickered back and forth.

No wonder he didn't think she was real. The way she'd reacted when he took her hand, like no one had ever greeted her before. She didn't move, didn't respond. Then he noticed her hands shaking as she brought the cup up to her lips, and she wasn't even drinking anything. She was terrified. She'd announced clearly that she had no Idex and was watching the fallout.

Dr Moss and Rane were now arguing about Turk as pieces fell into place. Of course she'd been there and gotten Turk out. Nothing else made sense. Ward continued to watch her, wondering how scared she must have been. There had been so much blood… He glanced at Dr Moss; he'd known it wasn't a nosebleed. Wynter had saved Turk's life, and in doing so, saved him from losing his ship. But what had it cost her?

He tried to think of all the times he'd seen her. In the pool area for sure, but then in the halls, and outside the Helix suites—the Helix suites. He'd seen her leaving them when he went to talk with Helix. It was the most likely choice for where she'd been hiding all this time. It would explain why she'd known to suggest ribbons—because she'd be the one making them? He wasn't going to learn anything from Wynter with those two arguing. He also knew there was no way he was going to drop her off at a midway station. If she didn't have an Idex the safest place for her to be would be Orion—where guilds had more control and didn't care as much about Idex societal status. He also needed to talk to someone he could trust.

"We'll set out from the midway on schedule," Ward said. "I know the Viceroy on Orion."

"Not Orion," Dr Moss said, no longer looking smug or amused.

"I didn't say I was dropping her there. Wait, why not Orion?

Guild law will be easier to navigate than a planet solely run based on Idex ranks," Ward said.

"I don't recall there being a guild to obtain Idex codes. Why would this be a guild matter?" Rane asked a little too sharply.

"NOT ORION." Dr Moss shouted at the same time.

"Why not on a midway station? We have a perfectly suitable place to leave her right now," Rane continued. Ward had never known him to be so calculating. Perhaps the stress of the past few weeks had gotten to him too, but not enough to treat the poor woman like... well like a stowaway.

"Never mind. Do whatever you want. I'm not getting involved in this. She needs to be left alone. This is the last time I come within two feet of her." Dr Moss looked ready to leave the room, as if he could just remove his obvious involvement, but Ward's attention was still on Wynter.

The string she'd been winding and unwinding snapped.

"You're the doctor, please explain to us how someone doesn't have an Idex in the first place." Rane was clearly getting frustrated with the conversation.

Dr Moss exchanged another look with Wynter. Whatever was between them, Ward didn't like it, but the situation needed some answers.

"Please?" she begged, her eyes wide.

She'd moved up to the edge of her seat like she didn't know either.

So Dr Moss had been keeping information not only from them but from her too?

"Guild law requires secrecy in such matters." Dr Moss pressed his lips tight again, but Ward could tell he was going to give them at least some information.

Ward understood guild law, it was the same with the need for his ship's crew to always keep a tight lid on things.

Wynter was looking down at her hands when Dr Moss spoke again.

"Orion is known for its innovation and experimentation in various guilds. They had medical labs kept in various mining and drilling stations. Some were abandoned. Some were found. Some were hundreds of years old, maybe more. Rumour is they had frozen experiments." He paused and took a breath. "Perhaps frozen embryos. It could have been hard to say how old they would have been, but before Idex coding."

"How do you know this?" Rane scoffed.

"Any doctor who's spent time on Orion knows this, and they wouldn't take well to someone without an Idex—proof of the experiments—showing up and causing trouble." Dr Moss hadn't taken his eyes off Wynter.

It wasn't surprising that Orion would be involved in something like this, and that they would try to cover it up. If Valtine was known for its perfection in etiquette and beauty and elite Idex lords and ladies, Orion was the bastion of law keeping. Aside from the obvious distinctions, it was common knowledge that guild law had a control on Orion that was extending to ships and even other planets. But even Orion had an irremovable dependence on the Idex system and its elites. Regardless of this truth, Ward was having trouble believing the doctor now.

"Maybe they'd have technology old enough to create Idex coding," Rane suggested.

"Does she need an Idex code?" Ward asked. The look he got from Rane and Dr Moss made him feel stupid, but really, what difference did it make? She couldn't own land, maybe there'd be some security issues and who knows what society would think? But did anyone need to know?

"The lab was levelled and for good reason," Dr Moss said, making it very clear Ward wasn't to ask any more questions. Then he leaned back and took another long drink.

Wynter's face was pale, but she sat unmoving.

"Is that where I came from? A lab?" she asked, voice hardly a whisper.

"There are rumours about outer planets and people without an Idex." He shrugged as if it didn't matter.

Ward's heart constricted. Dr Moss had so callously told her where she came from, in front of strangers. At this point, he wondered if Dr Moss was little more than a stranger to her.

"Thank you," Wynter said directly to Dr Moss, confirming whatever he'd divulged was clearly more than she'd ever heard before.

"What I think we need to know is why you brought her on the ship if the captain didn't know." Rane was being equally oblivious of Wynter's discomfort.

"I had nothing to do with her getting on the ship, and if his uncle had known, he would have handed her over to the first person who could profit from someone without an Idex. There are plenty. Or maybe he would have produced his own little brood of children without an Idex—"

Wynter blushed, and Ward had had enough.

"Doctor, Rane—I think it's time you left," Ward said, trying to keep calm. She'd been gripping her own hands for some time now and her knuckles were turning white.

Dr Moss glared. "And what are you going to—"

"Whatever I think is best as captain. If you don't like it, there's about ten minutes before we leave the midway station. I don't mind delaying our departure for you to get off my ship, if you want to question my authority."

"You should keep her hidden… He's going to get you killed," Dr Moss said to Wynter as he stood to leave then stalked out.

"We have a serious security—" Rane started to say once Dr Moss left.

"I agree. Your orders are to get my ship moving toward Orion."

"You're not responsible for her. This could compromise everything," Rane stated plainly.

"I'm the captain. I'm responsible for every person on my ship."

"She's not crew, or a paid passenger, or cargo—"

"Get my ship moving. It's an order, Rane." He'd never pulled his rank on Rane and felt bad, but he needed to get the ship moving. A stowaway could spell danger for a ship in space, the penalty was high, but it was enacted by the captain, and since he was captain, he didn't see why Rane was so concerned.

Rane straightened his shoulders, raising his brow, but didn't push it any further. "Yes, *sir*," he said before leaving.

Ward rubbed his jaw and sat down pulling his chair close to hers. The security slide slid into place, and he knew he'd made a mistake sending them both out. He hadn't thought of how awkward the silence would be.

A smile played on the edge of her mouth. He was pretty sure she shouldn't be smiling. It tweaked up a little, then she inhaled as if she was going to drop another heavy bit of reality onto him and said, "You thought I was a ghost."

"I didn't think you were a ghost," he said, defending himself, then watched her as she finally took a real drink from the cup she was holding. The whole situation was so horrible, it felt like they were both going to crack. "I thought you were a hallucination. There's a difference."

"Because of Dr Moss?" she asked, her brows arched up curiously.

"Yeah, because of Dr Moss. Are you okay?"

She inhaled, and he wished he hadn't taken away the brief moment of reprieve from her. "No, I don't think I am. I don't know."

"Do you believe what he said?"

"It doesn't sound wrong." She shrugged, looking so sad. "It's the only explanation anyone's ever given me. I asked Madame Helix a few times, and she always said, 'it happens' and 'parents wouldn't want to keep a kid without an Idex.' It doesn't just happen though? Does it?"

"No, I don't think it does. I don't trust Dr Moss, but I'd never heard of anyone like you before. I should probably talk to Madame Helix—"

"Please don't," Wynter interrupted. "She doesn't think it's safe for me to be noticed at all. She really wouldn't like you and Rane and Dr Moss knowing about me."

"She's going to know eventually. If I bring you down to Orion, we'd have to tell her something." Ward was trying to sound helpful, but he knew he'd have to deal with Helix at some point. She'd kept a stowaway on his ship, for years. He understood why she may have hidden her when his uncle was in command, but now? What possible reason would she have for hiding Wynter… unless her fame was tied to Wynter. So many questions, but he could only deal with one at a time. He needed to talk with Helix, and find out her involvement in all of this, but it would wait until

Wynter was safe. Her green eyes flicked up quickly. "I won't make you leave the Obsidian, you're safe, but I can't promise we'll be able to keep you as a stowaway after Orion. Is there somewhere else?" He felt guilty the moment he said it. Her face crumpled and she stared into the glass, her chin quivering a little.

"I had someone, but he's gone," she said quietly.

He moved his chair even closer and reached across the distance between them and unknotted her hands. She flinched but didn't pull away from him. Facing her, he sat with one leg crossed under the other, holding both of her hands in his until she turned toward him a little.

"What are you doing?" she asked, looking at her covered hands.

"My mother used to do this. On Valtine, you're not allowed to show certain emotions. And so, she would hold my hands and tell me all the things she couldn't say would travel into my arms and make their way to my heart. I thought it was silly."

She smiled a bit, and his heart constricted. "But you let her hold your hands anyway?"

"I did," he answered.

"Why?"

"Because it made her feel better when she couldn't do anything. I can't change your past, but I can make sure you're safe. Okay?" If Rane had been there, he would have knocked him upside the head. Safety was the one thing a captain couldn't promise a stowaway, but if she didn't have an Idex then whatever she was running from couldn't be documented. How much trouble could it be?

Twenty-One

Wynter's time with Captain Ward was brief. Duty called him back to the bridge to oversee the midway station's departure. Wynter tucked her patchwork dress under her arm and returned to her own room. One foot, then another, up the ladder, she flopped onto her mat, curled up in the borrowed clothing. From her loft, she could hear Helix humming to herself.

Everything had changed. Henris was dead. Captain Ward knew who she was. She'd found out she was likely some hundred or maybe thousand-year-old experiment. Closing her eyes tight, she felt the ship leave the midway station. When they were firmly, irreversibly, back in the space between, she let the midnight of sleep claim her thoughts.

* * *

The following morning Wynter started a new gown, made Helix ribbons, and counted the minutes until she planned to meet Captain Ward in the greenhouse. Helix didn't notice the neatness of her braid, or the blush in her cheeks when she left.

When her slippered feet reached the bottom floor, a hand reached out from beside the door. She screamed then and was pulled toward the shuttle storage area, away from the greenhouses.

"Not that way. He's waiting there. I don't know how he always knows where to find me," Captain Ward whispered in her ear and then tugged her along.

They slunk around into the closed off shuttle bay where dozens of pods were waiting, backs open and empty. A third set of boots clipped on the metal floor moments behind them.

Captain Ward's eyes grew wide in disbelief. Hand in hand, he pulled her along to the back of one shuttle and into the cargo hold. The space was large and empty, with nowhere to hide. Ward shrugged in resignation and sat down on the floor, stretched his legs out, folded his hands behind his head, and waited quietly. Whomever they were hiding from Captain Ward didn't look overly concerned they would be caught. Footsteps walked around the shuttles but turned back before they reached the last one, leaving Wynter and Captain Ward alone.

"I thought you don't hide on your own ship?" Wynter asked, unashamed that she'd just teased him. She sat beside him, mimicking his pose as she stretched her legs.

"I'm not hiding," he said.

"I've spent my whole life hiding. You're not very good at it, but we're definitely hiding."

Captain Ward turned and cast a sympathetic look her way. She knew she'd have to be careful how much she talked about years of hiding. It wasn't like it was all bad.

"Who is it we're not hiding from?" Wynter asked.

"The Ambassador. And I'm not hiding. I just don't want to talk to him for another hour. It takes forever to get away from the man."

"I thought someone like you would want to spend time with an ambassador. It's a really big—"

"Don't say honour. It's not an honour, it's an annoyance. Besides, I'd rather talk to you," he said.

"I don't think a captain is supposed to be talking to a stowaway."

"I think once the stowaway is friends with the captain, they aren't called a stowaway anymore," Captain Ward said as he ran his heel over the grated flooring.

A friend? The word felt so foreign. She took it and let it settle into her heart.

"Well, I'm not a crew member, and I'm not a guild member, and I'm not a paying passenger. And I'm not a ghost." She added the last one in, giving him a teasing smile.

"Maybe I can make it an official position, chief stowaway."

"And what would my duties include?" Wynter asked. She'd never thought in a hundred years would she be sitting with the captain of the Obsidian, joking about being a stowaway. A moment of fear gripped her chest, but she pushed it aside.

"Well, since I'm so terrible at hiding, maybe you could show me?" he suggested.

"If you're trying to hide from the Ambassador, this isn't an excellent place. If he comes back, he'll likely find us."

"I agree, show me some of your hiding places," he said, standing up. He reached down and offered his hand to help pull her up.

They waited a few more minutes, making sure the Ambassador wasn't going to ambush them. Captain Ward went first into the hallway, then motioned for Wynter to follow. She strolled ahead of him, knowing they'd pass passengers and other crew as they went. Purposeful, like she knew exactly where she was going and why. She could sense Captain Ward's eyes on her a few paces behind.

Making their way up one level, she skirted around to where the long corridor led to a room with a little cluster of lift carts.

Checking to see that no one was watching, she put her foot on the metal bracket on the wall, and then propelled herself up to the next one until she could pull herself onto the top of an exposed beam. She crawled across the beam and onto the roof of one of the storage cubes.

Captain Ward followed behind, the space was tight with two people, and his body pressed up against hers. She wiggled to give him a little more room as he joined her.

The edge around the top was high. If anyone came in they'd have to duck their heads down so no one would see them.

"And what do you do in here?" he asked.

"Sometimes I sketch out new dress ideas. It's quiet in here. When it's busy, I watch them bring the carts in and out and gossip about the guests. When it's really quiet, I ride the lift carts."

He laughed loudly, the sound shaking the little interior roof they were laying on. The door opened, and Wynter ducked her head down. Captain Ward was still peeking out over the top, then dropped beside her. Facing each other, noses almost touching.

"How does he know where I am?" he whispered. She brought her finger up to her lips, her heart thudding. Captain Ward wasn't concerned and barely attempting to subside the chuckles. He wasn't afraid. If anyone caught them, nothing would happen. Because he was the captain. A weight lifted off her chest. She was with Captain Ward and if he wasn't afraid, she didn't need to be.

Neither moved, she could feel the heat coming from him, and the brush of his leg against hers every time he moved. A few crew members came in and asked if the Ambassador needed anything and they heard his irritating chatter follow him out.

Captain Ward offered a hand as they crawled down, but she jumped the last section lightly on her own.

As they continued on, the halls felt different. She wasn't trying to come up with a story about where she was or why. She didn't need to. It didn't matter if anyone saw her anymore.

Getting into a lift with Captain Ward sobered her up as three other passengers joined them. One of the ladies she'd seen outside the Helix suites. There was still someone she didn't want knowing about her time with Captain Ward. The conversation was lively, and they didn't look at her, but she knew she didn't belong in their world, or the captain's, or anyone else's.

They left the lift walking side by side, silent when they passed other crew members.

"How do they not notice you?" Captain Ward asked.

"I just, I don't know, walk right past them," Wynter shrugged.

"And if someone asked you what you were doing?"

"I'd say Fuller sent me, or Rane needed something." She liked this, being able to tell someone her secrets. And he looked so impressed with the steps she took. She'd successfully evaded his notice for years, it made sense that he was in awe of it.

Wynter was pretty sure she noticed someone following them again, perhaps the Ambassador, but didn't want to turn around to confirm. Her feet led her to where she knew no one ever followed, past Dr Moss's offices.

She voiced her concern and ducked into the bay, pulling

Captain Ward down the hall, hoping one of the little side rooms was unlocked.

"I don't think anyone would follow us. If it is the Ambassador, he'd be shouting after me," Captain Ward said.

Wynter tried to shush him, but she was too late. Dr Moss opened the door to his rooms. She looked past Dr Moss to the two little glasses sitting out on the stand. He glared at them both, then slammed the door.

"Maybe we should stop hiding," she suggested.

"Maybe, but I do need to meet up with you tomorrow," Ward said, frowning at the closed door.

"Oh, we didn't really talk about anything important, did we?" Wynter replied.

"Other than making you official stowaway."

"I'm sure I already had that title," she said, grinning.

"Tomorrow, I'll meet you in the greenhouses," Ward said, straightening his jacket, and retreating out of Dr Moss's office area.

Wynter watched him go before knocking on Dr Moss's door, but he didn't answer.

Twenty-Two

Wynter continued the new dress she'd been working on. The material was black, like the shuttered windows in Captain Ward's room. A harsh line was cut down the centre where she'd added a long line of black pearls along with dark crystals that danced along the edge.

"What is this?" Helix said, her eyes wide. "I needed a top line dress for Orion. This is depressing. It's horrid!"

"I thought I'd try something different. Orion gives us a chance to use some of the deeper tones and more fabric," Wynter said.

"I'll be the laughingstock of the guild. I can't show this."

"Then you sew something! I made you a dress for Orion and you sold it on Valtine with dozens of other dresses I made for you!" Wynter said, then took a hard look at the dress she was working on. She'd been picturing the Obsidian, the way it had carried her this far, and grimaced. It maybe wasn't the best choice for a dress, but she wasn't starting over now.

Helix narrowed her eyes and glared for a moment. "I think I've made it very clear, not to do anything stupid—"

"Or what?" Wynter asked, throwing the black material down,

"Or people will find out I don't have an Idex and treat me like an outsider? Like I don't matter? Like a ghost?"

Helix set the measuring tape on the desktop, slowly releasing it from her fingers.

"I suggest you come up with something else by the end of the week. I've kept you here because you are useful to me, but don't think for a second that I wouldn't push you out of an airlock. No one would miss you. No one."

Wynter had been all over the ship and hadn't seen a single airlock Helix could push her out of. The threat was getting old, but it still irked her that she'd said it. Wynter never had sisterly or familial feelings for Helix. It was clear why.

Helix didn't care if she lived or died, so long as she was useful.

In over two years, every single dress that had gone out of the shop had been designed by Wynter. Helix had drummed up the basic gowns, but Wynter's expertise had propelled Helix into fame. Wynter wanted to scream, but they still had weeks in the small space, and she didn't want Helix getting suspicious.

"I'm sorry," Wynter said. "There's just so many people on the ship right now."

Helix accepted her apology but took the black dress off the table and tossed it to the side. She placed a vibrant plum and poppy pink print in front of Wynter who rubbed her forehead, then set to work.

* * *

When Wynter met with Captain Ward in the evening, she had one question on her mind.

"Are there airlocks a person can push someone out of?"

Wynter asked. Ward had been waiting inside the greenhouse. He reached out for her hand for a formal greeting, but she pulled it back, and he didn't try again.

"No, it's just something people say on ships. The shutters completely close everything off. The only air lock would be in the shuttle bay, but they're sealed. Even when we're docked somewhere, if you got in there, the security would pick you up and the doors wouldn't open."

"Idex security?" Wynter asked.

"Maybe stay away from the shuttle area. Did Dr Moss threaten to push you out an airlock? Because he's been known to threaten it."

"No, I just wondered," she said.

He gave her a sideways glance but let it go, "Where are we hiding today?"

"I thought we were going to talk about what's going to happen to me?" Wynter asked. She really didn't have too many hiding places she could show him.

"We are, but I figure you still need to earn your place as official stowaway," he parried. She nodded, and they left the greenhouses behind. They went up a floor and down a series of halls.

Opening a small access panel, Wynter crawled in, then stood. Captain Ward followed.

A narrow section of exposed wires and panels ran the length, powering the lighting features, and provided a security tunnel. It was tight, and they had to suck in and squeeze past various places.

"You use these to get around?"

"Not anymore. I used to when I was younger. It was a lot easier back then," Wynter said, ducking down under a low hanging tube.

"Hold on a second," Captain Ward groaned. His shirt had snagged on a small panel door, holding him back. He wiggled and tugged, then she heard a little tear.

"Got it," he said. They made their way down the row, ducking and twisting and having very little conversation. "Okay, this is terrible. How to do we get out of here?"

Wynter grimaced. "Well, we're about halfway, so we can go back or forward, but there's no other way."

Sounds from the hallway beyond the panel froze Wynter in place. Ward raised two fists and pounded on the wall.

"What are you doing?" she whispered to him.

"Years of pranks. Now it's my turn," he mumbled, then hit the wall again for good measure.

"What if it's passengers?" Wynter tried to keep her laugh quiet.

Captain Ward shrugged off her question. "Then maybe they won't come back."

"You don't want passengers?"

Ward took a step in her direction, and she kept moving, a little slower this time, down the narrow space.

"I don't mind having passengers. We always have them. I guess I came on this ship with my uncle to live a different life, away from all those rules, only to find I'm stuck doing the very thing I got away from. I'm not even running my ship right now. Fuller and Rane are. I'm babysitting an ambassador and having dinners."

"And getting an important education in stowaway life," Wynter added.

"Right, an invaluable education. Speaking of education, how

did you get on the ship?" His shirt snagged again, making the hole a little larger.

"In a crate," Wynter said, wondering how much she should tell him. She should trust him, but he was still the captain. He didn't look satisfied with her answer, so she threw a question back. "Would you change it? Not come on the ship with your uncle?"

"No, I love this ship, and I love the cargo. I don't even mind the passengers. What about you?" Captain Ward asked, as they stopped to untangle her braid that had snagged.

"Do I like passengers? Yes, I guess so. It's easy to move around the ship when it's full, it's easy when it's empty too."

"No, what would you do if you were free, if you could do whatever you want?"

Wynter stopped walking. If he had asked her a week ago, she would have wanted to go back to Henris. She'd always wanted to go back to Henris and his shop. She'd been happy there. Now? What would she do?

"I'd go to a ball and see all the dresses. I've spent my whole life making gowns, and I've never seen them in real life. I want to dance and wear gloves and put my hair in something other than braids."

Captain Ward reached up and gave a gentle tug on one of her braids. He was close. Close enough that she could smell the soft citrus soap and feel the air warm around them. The way he was looking at her, with sadness and something else, like if there wasn't a beam to step over, he'd pull her closer.

"Let's do it," Captain Ward said, breaking the moment.

"Do what?"

"When we reach Orion, you can come with me. I've talked to Rane. I probably should have mentioned that before. He agreed

Viceroy Alarik would know what options you might have. And I'll take you to a ball."

They reached the end of the tunnel. Wynter pressed her ear to the panel.

Ward wanted to bring her down to a ball. Off the Obsidian. Her first ball.

She'd leave the ship, and then what? He couldn't just bring a stowaway back up. But she knew she couldn't stay forever; she was going to have to leave eventually, and this way she'd have help.

"We have lots of time before we reach Orion. You don't have to answer right now," Captain Ward said as if unsure of her silence. She liked the way he looked at her concerned, waiting for her to answer. No one had been concerned about her thoughts since Henris.

"Are you sure you can get me into a ball?" she asked, still disbelieving.

His grin assured her. He'd find a way, even if it meant breaking rules.

Wynter ensured no one was in the hall, then slid out of the access panel. Ward followed with a little more difficulty, ripped shirt hanging a little.

"I should probably go fix this. You'll meet me again tomorrow?" he asked.

"I'm running out of hiding places to show you," Wynter confessed, not to mention what they were doing was certainly inappropriate if anyone saw them.

"Well then, I guess I'll have to show you some of mine." He gave her a slight bow like he had the first day in the pools, as if he was in her debt, then took off down the hall, whistling as he went.

A ball with Captain Ward, she loved the idea. She knew he was being kind, but a nagging thought told her not to do it. Because if she left the ship, she was sure there would be no way to bring her back.

***

Wynter let her hands enjoy the simple needlework knowing everything would change. The surety settled into her, undeniably strong. She couldn't keep hiding. What she'd been hoping for was never going to happen, Henris would never come back for her.

Once they reached Orion, she'd leave the Obsidian, and she had to be okay with that.

Wynter crawled into her loft then slept through the morning fittings. When Helix left for a grand lunch, Wynter took stock of all the things she'd collected and what she'd need to bring with her. She had her crew uniform, a few simple dresses, her black pants and shirt, and her patchwork dress. None of it amounted to much. When she finished, she went to the workroom and picked up an orange ruffle to work on.

"It's all but settled!" Helix burst into the room.

"What is?"

"The wedding. What else? Lady Cristelle all but announced it last night at dinner. Just think, we'll make a fortune in fast trims with the people who will be on the ship to be around her and the wedding. She did more than hint I'll be designing the gown. I thought the yellow I bought in Valtine would be perfect."

The wedding. Lady Cristelle's wedding to Captain Ward. The thought tied her stomach into a knot and a tear pricked at the corner of her eye. Maybe spending time with him had been a bad idea.

"My yellow?" she said, hoping Helix hadn't noticed her distress over the subject.

"Well, it's not like you're going to wear it, and lighter colours for a wedding dress are all the fashion right now. How bold, to wear something as light as yellow! They'll talk about us for years."

"They'll talk about you for years," Wynter murmured.

"I want to show her this afternoon."

Wynter hadn't planned to use it, but it was her yellow, and she couldn't stand the thought of Lady Cristelle wearing it for Captain Ward. Designing a wedding gown should have excited her. Instead, she wanted to throw something at Helix's head.

Helix went on for a full twenty minutes about the gowns she'd have to design for all the guests. Something furious bubbled in Wynter's chest. The desire to get off the ship and away from Helix slammed into her.

She knew she should keep her head down and work, but the words tumbled out before she could stop them.

"Since we're passing Orion again, has a message come through from Henris?" She swallowed. She hadn't said his name out loud in years. It felt wrong now to use him in a lie.

"Henris?" Helix looked shocked. She supposed it would be a shock. Wynter held her breath, hoping Helix didn't sense something was wrong.

"If Henris were to contact me—"

Helix's eyes narrowed. "I thought you'd given up on going back years ago."

"I mean, he contacted you before, right? When he left me with you, and he was going to let you know when I could go back, right?"

"I need to get these dresses done. Where's the yellow?"

"But there's a way to contact him?" Wynter pressed.

"No. There's no way to contact him. If he hasn't contacted me, maybe there's a reason. He didn't want you anymore. He gave you away. We have the chance at a wedding. What would you want to go back to Henris for?"

Wynter knew why Helix was flustering. It would be an impossible embarrassment to lose her designer before the grand wedding. There was no way she could pull off half of what Wynter had been designing. She knew she should feel bad she was going to be leaving the ship. She didn't.

"With someone like Lady Cristelle on board, you'll need to get used to more people around and a higher demand."

"Yes, of course," Wynter said.

"The yellow?"

"I coloured the fabric," Wynter lied. "It was too light for me too."

Wynter decided she was going to take the yellow with her.

That night in the greenhouse Wynter agreed to go to Orion with Captain Ward, to a ball, and to talk to Alarik. They would wait until all the passengers were gone, then take his private shuttle. The plan was made hastily. Rane had urged Captain Ward to wait until then to see Wynter again. It made sense but left her with a restlessness. Seven years of waiting and now the days remaining felt insufferably long.

The days leading up to the Orion docking, Helix was completely distracted by dresses and dinners. She hadn't even noticed how little effort Wynter put into sewing. It wasn't like Wynter would be paid for them. Everything she finished would be left behind.

Wynter loaded the crates for Helix, knowing she should say goodbye, at least provide a warning of her upcoming departure. But she didn't want Helix trying to stop her, or worse.

Packing her small sack, she noticed a rip in the very bottom and took some black thread to tie it back up. Then she filled it and made her way to Dr Moss's office.

"You shouldn't be here." Dr Moss's voice sounded slightly slurred. He had a mostly empty bottle beside him, and another unopened at his feet. His usually clean-shaven face was a bristle of peppered grey hairs.

"I think it's time we were on the same side of things," she said, trying to sound confident.

"I've always been on your side."

"No, I think you've been on your side."

"HA!" He let out a laugh, motioned her in and poured her a glass, filling it to the brim and handing it to her. The blue liquid sloshed over the top and onto the floor before she could bring it up to her mouth.

Wynter sat down. She'd been so afraid of him the first time she'd come here, she thought as she looked around the room. She figured she should be more afraid of him now, but she wasn't.

"I wanted to say goodbye. For now anyway," she said.

Dr Moss nodded. "You should wait until Corva—"

"Orion will be fine. I understand guild law, and secrets. And I'm skilled."

"If you leave, you shouldn't ever come back, and never tell anyone you were here."

She leaned back and took another tiny sip off the top careful not to spill anymore. "I'm not coming back."

This would be the last time she'd be sitting here. She'd told herself to let it go, she'd be off the ship and maybe starting the life Henris had thought for her. But she had to know. She knew if she had the chance she'd ask, doubting he'd tell her the truth.

"Was there something else?" He cracked the seal on the second bottle.

"There's a body in the storage…" she started cautiously.

"I don't want to know," he said, closing his eyes.

"Don't want know what? I thought maybe you…" She was having difficulty bringing herself to accuse him of what she'd been thinking. He was the only one who'd known she was there, and he would have been the one to deal with Henris once he'd died.

"You thought I killed him? I thought you killed him," he chuckled. Wynter didn't think it was funny.

"I think Captain Ward mentioned poison?" she asked. Dr Moss hadn't killed Henris. She was relieved. Not that she owed Dr Moss anything, but she'd leave the ship thankful that she could still call him a friend. It had been a ridiculous theory anyway.

"Yeah, the poison is why I always figured it was you. Didn't blame you. It's hard to get your hands on the stuff though. I was going to ask you about it when I was stitching up your leg, but I changed my mind."

"Why didn't you ask me?" she said, and then wondered if it was for the same reasons she'd never asked him. It couldn't just be a coincidence though, that Henris had been so nervous that morning. Someone knew where he was, so why not look harder for her? It wasn't as if she was hard to find, as Dr Moss liked reminding her.

"Secrets are best left kept, and I didn't care either way. Buried files should stay silent."

"He was my friend."

"If I thought you killed him, everyone else will too. Keep it to yourself. Secrets will keep you alive." He took another long drink.

She wanted to thank him. Her hand traced the line up her leg. He'd suspected her of killing someone and hadn't even blinked. His lack of concern was probably a bad thing, but the urge to hug him was still strong. He'd been her first friend even if he was a terrible one.

Instead of doing all those things, she simply said, "I'm sorry you're sad," then got up and left him to his drink.

Twenty-Three

The week leading up to Orion was slow. Ward was excited when Wynter had agreed to accompany him off the Obsidian. She had work to do before leaving unless she wanted Helix to find out, which she didn't, and Ward had a ship to run. Further visits were limited. He missed her. He didn't think it was possible to miss someone he'd just met; he barely missed his own family when he was away from Valtine. But there was something about her, the way she walked and smiled. She had her own secrets, but not the way others did—always looking to either protect or advance their Idex in some way. They'd both decided it was probably best not to expose her until he'd had a chance to talk with Viceroy Alarik. Hiding from the Ambassador had proved to be counter-productive. His time was demanded of him until it felt as if every waking moment was taken by the ridiculous man.

The days dragged. Ward kept waiting for something to happen. Everyone moved around the ship completely unaware. They didn't see what was right in front of them and were happy to believe fabricated rumours regarding an upcoming offer from Lady Cristelle.

A woman never offered unless she was certain of a favourable response. There was no way Lady Cristelle was certain. They'd barely talked, and he wasn't just avoiding her; she'd made no effort to track him down either.

She was more animated talking to the other women or with the other men. Even the Ambassador had got her to laugh. But the rumours continued, and Lady Cristelle never did a thing to dispel them.

It was difficult to persuade Rane that the match wasn't going to happen. Ward wasn't sure if Rane was so insistent because Lady Cristelle would be a good option, or because Wynter wouldn't. Rane had convinced him that time with Wynter on the ship should be limited. For her sake, he'd agreed, but he missed her. It had been a long time since he'd had a friend on the ship that wasn't a crew member, and it was just nice to have someone to talk to.

If the trip between Valtine and Orion had taken its toll on his crew, they didn't show it. They were smiling and polite as Ward watched from the cargo bay deck. Passengers were loading up. He waved at Lady Cristelle and Lady Lucy as they boarded.

They waved back. Lady Lucy smiled.

Once the first group of passengers were safely off his ship, he made his way to his own private shuttle, to Wynter.

Dr Moss met him in the hallway leading up. He was wearing his long medical shawl with blue trim. Ward wasn't even sure he owned one anymore. He was dressed impeccably and walked in a straight line, but the strong smell that rolled off him indicated he wasn't completely in control of himself.

"We're docked, I have passengers and cargo leaving my ship, and you're hazed?" Ward asked.

"I had Landers take over my post. These things always go smoothly." Dr Moss wavered a step from his straight line.

"What if they don't? You are the medical officer on this ship, and as such, I suggest you get yourself cleaned up and back to work by tomorrow."

"Or what little captain?" he said, a half-smile tugging at his lips.

"I don't care who you are or what guild law you have behind you. I will get you off my ship."

"HA! Now you sound like your uncle. Good man!" He clapped Ward on the shoulder. Ward shook it off.

"Seven years," he said, breathing heavily on Ward. "Seven years and then you bump into her, and everything has to change. You're going to get her killed."

"Is there something of importance you're not telling me Moss?"

"*Dr* Moss," he said the slurred correction.

"No, not right now you're not. Get yourself back to your rooms. As far as I can tell, the only danger to Wynter is you."

Twenty-Four

Time was moving too fast. Wynter was in and out of Dr Moss's office so quickly. She wanted to stay and couldn't wait to leave. Everything felt wrong. Like the halls should be longer now, her last time walking down them. Like the lights should be brighter and not the same even glow.

She was leaving.

Now.

In minutes, she'd be flying off into the space that had called to her for so long.

There was no one else in the private shuttle bay, but every little noise and clank made her jump. Ward was late, or she was early. She wasn't really sure, but when he showed up, she had a hard time getting her heart to slow down.

He smiled and took a few minutes to show off his shuttle. Sleek and black on the front, the shutters slid back like a miniature Obsidian. She climbed into the passenger side and wrapped her fingers around the edge of the black seat. It was almost as small as the cargo box she'd arrived in. The space was barely big enough for two people.

He jumped in the other side.

"Lean back," he said. When she did, the straps automatically slipped around her sealing like a ratchet around a cargo box.

Wynter felt a shiver of fear creep up the back of her arms, but she held them still, wishing she had something she could do with her hands, a hem or buttons to sew.

"It runs different from the cargo shuttles. Have you watched them leaving the ship before?"

She nodded her head.

"Well, it's not as smooth a ride, but she's fast." His smile lit up the space beside her. The hatch sealed. She felt the air around them change. The seat rumbled.

He grabbed the controls, confident and focused in every movement. He was so calm, the way he flicked each little light and input what she figured were coordinates.

The shuttle's bay was sealed off from the rest of the ship. The hatch opened, her body sucked into her seat, and her lungs felt like they were going to pop, like she'd never take a breath again.

Then they were out.

He made a wide pass around the ship. The Obsidian's long black hull was massive from the outside. Panels ran in sleek long lines, armoured fins raised up and out.

As they moved away from the Obsidian, the ship shrank, and the planet loomed in front of them.

Captain Ward flicked switches, checked some dials, and turned to her. She wanted to look back at him, but the size of the approaching planet eclipsed the window and held her focus.

"This is normal. Entering the atmosphere is going to make you feel all sorts of things. I've done this hundreds of times. We're perfectly safe."

It felt as though the tiny shuttle would shatter apart as it pierced the atmosphere. Her eyes widened as the ground below came into view.

Vast oceans of azure and amethyst blanketed out beneath them. The islands protruded like misshaped polka dots. The shuttle slid far above the mountain peaks, where she could make out the signs of villages in the valleys below.

"I love Orion," he said, breaking the silence. "It's always been one of my favourite planets. The mountains never melt, but the valleys are warm during the day. There are a few islands down in the tropics. As far as land mass, it's one of the smaller planets. Deep oceans cover a lot, and many of the mining rigs can only run a few months out of the year."

"It's so pretty," she agreed. It had been her home, a home she knew so little about.

They glided over farmland and spotted hills, purple and blue flowered fields were wilted and past bloom. The blue turned into cupped yellow flowers with burnt orange edges and fields with harvested crops and brick faced houses. In the valley, another city sparkled. Captain Ward landed the shuttle on a small snow dusted platform on a mountain edge.

She took a moment to take it in.

She'd made it. She was off the Obsidian with an entire planet before her. And before long she was going to have to say goodbye to Captain Ward.

Twenty-Five

"Just a quick stop before we reach the castle. I think you'll like it," Ward said. After years on a ship, he couldn't imagine what she was thinking, being on land again.

"This feels like a dream," Wynter said, eyes wide as she looked around.

He picked a narrow solar air strip off the side of the mountain. It wasn't the first they'd passed over, but some of the larger ones were quite full. He docked easily and waited for the air to decompress.

When he finally opened the latch, a rush of cold air hit them. He took a deep breath, letting the fresh mountain oxygen settle into his lungs, then jumped out.

"It's a bit of a shock after being on a climate-controlled ship," Ward said, then grimaced, noticing her arms were mostly bare. He doubted she had anything suitable in her small bag and didn't want to ask why she'd brought so little with her.

Walking around to her side, he took his jacket off and wrapped it around her shoulders.

"You won't need it in a minute," he said. Looking down, he

realized she wasn't wearing proper shoes but thin little slippers. He felt like an idiot all over again for not thinking of the most basic things. Even with her obviously cold feet she still looked ecstatic.

"Sorry, I should have picked one with a solar path," he said as she took half a step back.

"I'll lift you over to the cleared walking bridge…." He stepped toward her again.

"I'm fine," Wynter said as she skittered past him and into the snow. Ward watched her feet sink in. Thankfully, it wasn't too deep, but puffed up around her ankles. He noted the sharp intake of breath, then the way she pranced through the snow toward the walking bridge.

Stomping her feet down she lifted them one at a time, shaking off her slippers. His heart picked up a mutinous extra beat.

He followed her onto the bridge, a wave of heat coming up from the warming cables to dry his own shoes.

They stopped midway and looked down toward the valley and across. Houses with blue, red, and purple roofs reached upwards; at the centre was a wheel hub with streets like spokes. Toward the northern mountain extensive gardens hedged in a massive castle.

He watched her face, the soft curve of her jaw, and the way she smiled as loose strands of hair danced around her eyes.

"They designed most of the villages like a wheel hub with the docks in the centre," Ward said, clearing his throat.

"How many are there?" she asked, turning toward him. He took a step closer, blocking the bite of the wind.

"Six, I think. This is the largest and where most ships prefer to dock and trade."

She scrunched her nose and looked up at the shuttles flying.

"Are there always this many ships?"

They littered the sky, ones marked for cargo and smaller personal passenger ships.

"No, not usually, but we're scheduled to be here over the frost festival." There were a lot of ships flying in and out. He wasn't sure if the busyness would make things easier for Wynter to blend in or if it would expose her if someone leaked her lack of identity.

"I didn't think it would sound like this. The ship always has a hum. This is so, it's so something," Wynter said. The warming cables were doing their job creating an abundance of heat. Taking off his jacket, she passed it back to him.

Sunlight danced through the branches turning the flakes into glitter. She turned her face up as a small puff of wind sent a flurry of flakes falling onto her shoulder. He was standing so close he could see the lines melt into her skin.

"I figured this should be at least one of the stops while you're here," he said, feeling like he'd made the right choice. She stilled and looked down at the town.

"I'm not going back to the Obsidian," she said quietly.

"What do you mean not going back?" He sounded shocked, but should he really be? Of course she wouldn't want to stay on the Obsidian when she could have a chance at freedom here. It wasn't as if he could offer her that. No one wanted to be stowaway forever.

"I should have left years ago. I shouldn't have hidden for so long. I don't know why I didn't try sooner," she said, the words tumbling out as if she'd been holding them in confirming what he'd thought. She let her shoulders sag. "I'm sorry, Captain."

"Just Ward is fine. I'm not your captain anymore." He immediately wished he could take it back, the suggestion itself was silly.

"Doesn't everyone call you captain?" Wynter asked, obviously thinking the same thing.

"Well yes, I mean no. On Valtine they prefer to call me Lord Isaac."

She smirked. "You're a lord too?" she asked. "What do your friends call you?"

Ward's brows knit together. Friends weren't something he had many of. Rane would be the closest thing to a friend. He had work contacts, but everyone called him Captain Ward.

When he didn't answer she reached out, her fingers touching the inside of his hand.

Ward looked down. She was on land for the first time in years and she was offering him what? Comfort? Friendship?

"Maybe you can be the only one who calls me Ward."

They had only a few weeks before he'd be out of her life. He wished he'd tried harder to see her this past week. After such a brief acquaintance, he already knew he would do anything to take away the pain she'd been through and keep her smiling. He tucked a stray hair behind her ear, and she looked down.

"Before I leave, I'll make sure you never have to hide again." The promise slipped off his tongue. Time was limited to secure her future, but he felt it as sure as the stone under his feet. He would do what he could for her. Even after he left and was planets away, he'd be thinking about her.

"Captain's promise," he said, trying to lighten the weight he was feeling.

Snow blew in and flurried around them, telling them it was time to go, but he only edged closer.

"You're not my captain anymore," she breathed the words.

The space between them narrowed.

Letting go of every reason he shouldn't, he raised her hand and turned it up to kiss the inside of her wrist. His lips felt her pulse running beneath the skin, but it wasn't enough, it would never be enough. He met her eyes, letting go of her hand, then reached up to brush back another wild strand of her hair. When she didn't flinch away, he leaned in.

His lips found hers, soft and warm. He let the kiss linger, and when her lips responded, brushing against his own, he felt the loneliness in his own soul echo hers.

She leaned in a little more, close enough that he was sure she could feel his pounding heart. But a puff of cool, mountain air blew through them, and they both pulled back.

Her eyes were wide. She pressed the back of her hand to her flushed cheek, then slipped past him and ran across the bridge, back to the shuttle.

His pulse raced, and the touch of her lips lingered on his.

What had he been thinking? She'd just told him she was staying on Orion. He'd wanted to kiss her... probably for longer than he was willing to admit. But he shouldn't have picked *today* to do it. He felt frozen in place, but after a few quick breaths, he followed her. Whatever was ahead for Wynter, saying goodbye to her had just became a lot harder.

Twenty-Six

Wynter tried to quell the flurry in her chest. Ward had kissed her.

Should she have expected it? He was saying goodbye, of course. She told him that she would be leaving. So he'd kissed her, and she kissed him back. She wanted to go back, refuse to let the snow push them apart, wrap her arms around his neck. Instead, she'd run.

The snow drifted around her feet, now freezing. She'd forgotten what the snow felt like, she let her thoughts focus on the light flakes, Henris had loved the snow.

She waited for Ward to open the shuttle, her arms shaking without the warmth of his jacket. The way he looked at her when he got back to the shuttle made her wish she had it to put over her head, utterly embarrassed, and at the same time, wishing she could do it all over again.

The shuttle opened. She didn't look in his direction, not when she climbed in, or when the belts ratcheted around her, or when a blast of heat steamed her toes and warmed her body back up.

He filled the seat beside her and closed the hatch. Instead of powering the engine, he turned his head in her direction.

"I shouldn't have kissed you," he said finally, the words deflating her temporary high.

"You didn't want to?" she asked, then closed her eyes, hoping he wouldn't answer. He probably kissed lots of ladies. What would a lady do? She needed to pretend like she was on the ship, pretending to be crew, pretending to be someone else. But the air around them felt like it was on fire.

"It doesn't matter if I wanted to. As captain—"

"I thought you said I shouldn't call you captain," she said, interrupting him, which was probably *not* something a lady would do.

He tucked a wisp of melty hair behind her ear again. Whatever she'd said, it must have been the right thing because he looked as though he was going to kiss her again.

"You're going to be starting a new life, and I don't want to complicate your plans."

"A kiss complicates things?" she asked, unsure. It was her first kiss, but she didn't expect a kiss to mean much to him. He had a lot of ladies, Lady Cristelle especially, whom he must be kissing. Helix talked often enough about the couples at balls to know a kiss shouldn't mean that much. But it did to her. The thought turned in her head but there was no polite way to ask what she wanted to know.

"No, but wanting to kiss you again might," he said. He turned toward the controls and flicked them on. The engine fired, and the shuttle lifted off the pad.

"Oh," she said, still not understanding.

They glided past the large hub in the centre of town, then swung up and over the northern mountain and came around the side of the castle where a series of docks jutted out of the rock.

The silence stretched on as they docked and disembarked.

A large cavern with other shuttles in tidy rows led to a series of security doors. Ward used a small card to open a door leading into another hall where the bright tunnels turned into the castle walls. She ran her hands over the cold rough edge and dipped her fingers into the smooth mortar lines. The stone walls were cut and jagged. A decorative arch indicated an Idex scan point.

Ward broke the silence, "I think few guests use this wing, so we shouldn't be bothered until I can arrange your own—"

A burst of industrious noise cut Ward's words short.

Instead of the expected, quiet secluded hall, there was a bustle of activity.

Luggage was being pushed around. There were greetings and chatter.

"This can't be right. These halls are reserved for lords." He frowned at the chaos.

An overflow of excitement rippled down the hallways in waves.

"I guess the castle is fuller than I expected." He took her hand, and she didn't pull away as they walked past a large group and had to squeeze between luggage carts. With everyone pushing and moving, Wynter hoped no one took notice as she followed him into his rooms.

He let go of her hand once they were inside and tossed his jacket onto a gold nob by the door.

The front sitting room was large, like space was an endless commodity. It stretched high. A chandelier sparkled over their heads. Chairs, lounges, and little carts with towers of foods awaited them. Instead of the useful things she was used to seeing in a ship's room, there were vases and easels with pictures and little decorative figurines.

A crescent balcony overlooked a hint of the castle gardens with the city beyond.

It smelled fresh. She breathed it in, like citrus but richer. She set down her small bag and noticed the luggage cart piled with travel cases and boxes she assumed were Ward's.

"I think it's best if you stay here for a bit. There's food," he rubbed the back of his neck. "I'll go see Viceroy Alarik."

Wynter nodded, and waited for him to go. He glanced around the room one more time, as if there was something else he should tell her. Staying in the room would be easy, she'd done the same thing her entire life.

When he finally left, she felt like she could breathe normally again.

From the main sitting area, three doors in a row were open. In the first room narrow windows sent sunlight dancing across a gigantic bed. Wood posts reached to the ceiling for no apparent reason. The bed itself was so large it would fit five people across. It didn't fold down into the wall or slide inside. It made Ward's room on the ship look quaint.

The blankets appeared to be more for decoration. She pressed down on the puffy slate grey blanket covering the entire bed. A dozen pillows littered the bed, extra blankets hung off the end. A dark blue cabled one, a black one. She ran her hand across them. So much fabric just for sleeping. She'd imagined these things, but they were always smaller in her mind, more compact. The reality was much grander.

The second room was also a bedroom, but slightly smaller, and more delicate decor. More for a lady. She blushed when she noticed the extra little door opened between the two rooms.

She looked in the bathroom next. A large looking laundry tub was on the floor. It had little dragon heads for feet and a flame shaped tap. The shower was big enough for an entire crew to all wash at once. She stepped in and walked around it, running her hands on the tiles patterned to look like flat scales to match the dragon.

She wished she could start a design, but she didn't have access to material, or anything to sew with, and no idea how she'd be able to acquire those things again. It would probably be too reptilian.

The shower had little round disks along the wall. Running her hand along them, she was instantly soaked by a spray of warm water. She let out a surprised scream, then gave into it and let out a relieved laugh. She leaned back against the wall and let the water rush over her.

She peeled off the soggy day-dress. It hit the stone floor with a flop, but the water collected in a little drain at the centre. She let her hands run across the disks, switching the way the water sprayed.

A line of soaps left her smelling more like the captain than herself, but she felt hot and sudsy and alive.

When she finished, she wrapped the large bathing towel around her body. It curled around her almost twice, and she struggled to tuck in the excess to hold it up. Her hair hung down her back, soaking into the towel folds.

Wynter opened her small bag and pulled out the crew uniform, it would do little good here. Tossing it aside, she pulled on the simple black pants and shirt she usually wore in the Helix suites. She wondered what it would be like to dress however she wanted. To have closets full like Helix.

She tried tying the large towel around her head to keep her wet hair off her back, but it was too large and flopped over her shoulder.

Food was next on her mind, but commotion from down the hallway piqued her curiosity. She opened the door and looked out to see.

She wasn't the only one. The doors to dozens of rooms were open. A small group had gathered two doors down from her. No one was looking her way, and so she watched with the rest of them, part of this new world.

The attention centred around Lady Cristelle and a dressmaker in pink with ribbon and long thin scissors hanging around her neck. She was being pushed into the hall, drawing the attention of all the spectators and anyone who was unfortunate enough to be trying to get down the hallway.

Lady Cristelle was wearing a half-made dress, obviously too tight, causing ripples and bunches. A section was partially covered with burgundy that stressed the ripple effect. The back wouldn't close, and the sleeves puffed out in fluffy arcs. The colour would have been acceptable for her… except it completely bloomed around her, making her look like a giant piece of fruit.

The seamstress was reluctant to leave but noticed the crowd. "If you want a Helix gown, then you'll have to hire Helix," the seamstress said.

Lady Cristelle disappeared and from the open door. A variety of fabrics, ribbons and scissors sailed out collecting in a little pile. The seamstress looked at the mess in disgust.

"I hired you to sew, not give your opinion on my personality. You are completely useless," Lady Cristelle screeched.

The seamstress's face grew red, and she stormed down the hall, leaving it all behind.

Lady Lucy was standing not far off and trying hard to hide her glee.

"A little lost without your Helix?" she taunted. "It's hard when you don't look good in everything."

Lady Cristelle threw down a bin with threads and pins scattering them across the stone floor. She wasted no time unleashing on Lucy.

"I heard it disappointed your father when you returned. You couldn't even offer for anyone because you knew they'd say no. I bet even Madame Helix can't help someone so utterly without fashion. When she shows up, she'll refuse you either way. I wonder, do things just naturally look bad on you?"

Lucy's smile wavered for a moment. Wynter wondered if Lady Cristelle had gone too far. From two doors down, Lady Lucy caught Wynter's eye.

Dread filled Wynter from her dripping hair down to her toes.

"At least I'm not set to offer for a captain who keeps company before the wedding," Lucy retorted, nodding her head toward the end of the hall where Wynter was standing.

All eyes turned to her.

The snowy white towel was hanging around her shoulders, one corner still on the top of her head.

Lady Cristelle looked at Wynter's bare feet, tilted her chin a little, and smiled as if it didn't bother her at all. Wynter didn't know where to look, but directly back at her. She wondered for a moment if Lady Cristelle cared; she looked almost amused.

For a brief second, something else flickered across Lady Cristelle's face. She was staring down Wynter but addressed Lucy, "Everyone keeps company except you, because no one wants you."

Lady Cristelle took a last look at Wynter from head to toe, then went back into her room. Wynter retreated, closed the door, and leaned against it. She could feel the ripple of rumours reverberate around the hallway.

She threw the towel on the floor in the bathroom on top of the soggy clothing, wondering where she'd find the dryer.

The doors opened again. She held her breath expecting Ward, but Lady Lucy filled the frame with the bundle of material and sewing supplies.

"I knew it was you!" Lucy said. "Oh, sew me a dress! Cristelle will be enraged. You should probably learn how to use the door locks. They're on a slide system." Lucy bounced into the main living room, dropping pins and ribbons while she talked.

Wynter felt like Lady Lucy had punched her in the gut. Lucy had just announced to everyone that Ward was keeping company, and now she wanted a dress?

"I don't think I want you in here right now," Wynter said, folding her arms over her chest.

"Oh, you're upset because of what I said? It's not like Cristelle didn't already know about you two."

Wynter paled.

"Don't look so shocked. We've seen you two together on the ship. Oh, I'm sorry! You look really upset. It's not a big deal. Is this enough to make a dress? Although maybe you need a dress more than I do."

Lady Lucy inspected her outfit from head to toe.

"Captain Ward is always so nice. I thought he'd keep his ladies in the finest of everything. Especially with your skills," Lucy commented.

"He didn't... he's not... It's not like that," Wynter said, heat rising again in her cheeks.

"I really am sorry, but you shouldn't be so upset. Lady Cristelle isn't. She told me she thought you're kind of pretty. You have unique features. So delicate."

Wynter knew her blush had turned into full flame. She couldn't believe the two of them would keep each other's confidence, and they'd talked about her.

"So about the dress. I know you work for Madame Helix, but I'll pay double, triple what she pays you."

"How did you know?" Wynter was cautious.

"My aunt, Lady Daye, refused to let me have a Helix, called her a fraud. I knew once I was on the ship there was no way Madame Helix was spinning out so many. Then I saw you, soaking wet, remember? Really, your outfit is pretty ugly."

More things she didn't know. She was so tired of secrets and who knew what.

"Oh, you poor thing, it's not very ugly. No, it is. It's really terrible. You probably have a lovely figure and your hair, well, I know your hair is at least nice," Lucy said, not skipping a beat. "You know what would take your mind off it? Making me a dress for the ball."

"I don't know if sewing for you is a good idea."

"And while you do, I want to hear all about it."

"All about what?"

"You and the captain. Now that we're friends, I get to be the only one who hears all the little details."

"It's not like that," Wynter said again, looking at what Lucy had brought her and what was likely still littering the hallway.

"It never is." Lucy pushed the pile of sewing supplies at Wynter.

Wynter looked at the material on the floor and then at Lucy.

Lucy was her friend? A friend who had helped her slip into her rooms unnoticed on the ship. A friend who had made her a spectacle in front of everyone. She was feeling like maybe having friends was harder than being alone.

Wynter looked at the material, silver and white and pinks. It wasn't right, Lucy needed something else, something unique. Wynter decided she was going to do it because she wanted to, because she could. Pulling the yellow out of her bag she spread it in front of Lucy. Everyone deserved to look beautiful in a gown.

Twenty-Seven

Viceroy Alarik was barrel chested. His large hands looked as though he'd clawed the granite from the mountains himself to build his castle. His jet-black hair was pulled tight into a knot at the back of his head.

Ward entered the formal gathering room. The powerful smell of whiskey, hops, and ancient books greeted him. Shelves stretched to the ceiling. Sunlight crisscrossed through the narrow windows onto the black and green tiled floor.

The Ambassador was, unfortunately, already there. He was puffing up his chest, trying to stand as tall as possible beside Alarik. Ward wondered if he was up on his toes behind the long desk.

Alarik held a polite smile. His eye contact never faltered, an Orion trait so they would not dishonour their guest.

Coming closer, Ward could hear the Ambassador talking about the various stones used to build the castle. He spoke at length about their composition, where to find them within the mountains, and made a grand gesture of offering to allow Viceroy Alarik to take him on a tour.

Ward smiled at the exchange. The title may grant an ambassador on any planet luxuries and free range, but the locals and guilds would be less impressed and unwilling to bend over backwards for him. Guild law unofficially outranked dignitaries on Orion, although they would never say so.

Alarik motioned another man to join the circle.

"Jace, I'd like to introduce you to the Ambassador. He's not been to this part of Orion and wanted a tour of the castle."

The man he called Jace looked pleased. Ward wondered how long before he filed an official complaint with Alarik. The Ambassador must have known he was being dismissed but looked equally pleased with Jace's attention.

"Captain Ward!" Alarik reached his hand out, taking only two strides to cover the distance, and clasped his arm. "You fail to visit on many occasions and now you bring me more 'gifts' than I could possible enjoy."

Ward forced a laugh.

"Sorry for the inconvenience."

"Nonsense. It's nice to hear these old walls echo with youthful vigour again. I hear from our friend you might leave the ranks of bachelor behind?"

"News travels."

"Faster than your ship can."

"If you're speaking of Lady Cristelle, an offer is not something I'm pursuing." Ward shuffled his feet, hoping he wasn't going to get the same lecture Rane had given him.

"Being married isn't bad. She'll hang about the ship for a year, then you'll be able to leave her with these groups of travelling ladies. Last year I had a dozen captain's wives under my roof."

"I'd rather my wife not stay under your roof, whomever she

ends up being."

"You might after a year with her on board." He winked, and Ward shook his head.

They walked over to an open door to the sweep-around balcony where they would have more privacy as guests filtered in and out of the room.

The brisk air came in around them, mixing with the heat coming from the rooms, refreshing him. He missed the change after weeks in space.

"Will you be taking all the ladies with you when you leave or just the bride?"

"Unfortunately for you, no. The ladies plan to be here a full two moons. My cousin's ship will pick *all* of them up for a return journey to Valtine."

He sensed an agitation in Alarik and wondered if the full castle was frustrating the man. He'd never known Alarik to shy from company, and there were at least three ships in Orbit by now.

"I'm sorry there wasn't more notice on the number of guests," Ward said.

"Not to worry. We've plenty of space. I was wondering how my sister was, Lady Daye. You may have seen her. I got some disturbing messages from her." Alarik looked out, puzzling Ward.

"Regarding Lucy?" Ward asked

"Lucy? No, about herself. She sounded off. I know it's history, but I still think I shouldn't have let her marry Lord Daye."

"I doubt you would have had much say in the matter. I saw your sister on Valtine. Lady Daye was fine. She was matchmaking and is the cause of our rumours. Nothing out of the ordinary." Ward thought of his brief time talking with her. She was perhaps more introspective than usual, but Lady Daye had never possessed the same jolly manner her elder brother had.

"No, no, don't think on it. You didn't come here to talk about my family problems. What do you need from me? I already sent the files you requested. I'm surprised your uncle never asked for them. Is the body being brought down?"

"Yes, trying to tie up loose ends my uncle left undone. Thank you." Ward hesitated. "But I had another reason to talk to you right away."

Alarik stood beside him, hands clasped behind his back.

"If someone had an issue with their Idex coding…" he started, trying to feel him out.

Alarik's mood changed immediately. He stiffened and balled his fists. "I don't need to tell a captain what would happen if we caught someone tampering with security scans."

"It's not the scans." Ward thought of the best way to phrase it. "I may have found someone who once belonged here."

"Are you sure this person is from here?" he said, almost dismissively, then appeared to change his mind. "If you know what it is you have, then you know bringing it to me will not gain you any profit. How unlike your uncle are you?"

"No profit. And I'm not certain she's from here. I don't exactly trust the story I was told." Ward realized how little information he really had to go on, and how little he could give Alarik.

"How did she end up on your ship?"

"I still don't know, and I'm not sure she's ever going to tell me," Ward replied honestly.

Alarik flexed his muscles as he pulled back on his clasped hands, raising a brow.

"Are you certain she's your problem, considering she doesn't even trust you?" he asked, echoing Rane's concerns.

"Yes, she is," Ward said, then filled him in on everything else Dr Moss has told him, about the experiments on Orion twenty years ago.

Alarik looked pensive and undecided before speaking again.

"It happened before my time, but your information is generally correct. Anyone directly involved died when the labs exploded, as far as the official report goes. But you know how these secrets work. If anyone *was* left, there is no way I'd know. Information regarding presumed illegal activity wouldn't go on an Idex without proof, and the file is sealed. Even still, I don't know why Dr Moss would think her to be in any danger. It's possible there are some people who could be brought to trial by her existence, but how would they possibly know she was here? It's a highly unusual affair, but after twenty years hardly dangerous."

"Would the guilds reopen the files? If they knew she'd returned?" Ward asked.

"I would think not, but it's for the guilds to decide. I still don't see how it would put her in danger. We wouldn't advertise her involvement in such a trial if it were to happen. Either way, it's a guild matter. You need not worry. No one likes to wake sleeping ghosts. This is part of our history we'd like to forget. However, until I've spoken with some of my colleagues, I suggest we keep this between us."

"She'll be staying with me until it's settled," he said, his voice lowering as they moved back into the main room. Alarik raised a brow but didn't comment further. Guilds would quickly remove Ward's involvement, and he needed to make it clear he had no intention of leaving Wynter until he was satisfied with the arrangement.

Lady Cristelle entered the room, cutting their conversation

short. With her, a ripple of whispers crept around the perimeter. She waved and swayed her hips as she approached them.

Placing her hand over Ward's arm increased the volume of whispers. He could feel the tension, like the entire room was waiting for something.

"She's a pretty thing," Lady Cristelle said, low enough only Alarik and Ward could hear. "But she looked absolutely terrified." She purred against Ward's ear, then she kissed him on the cheek, the room now a buzz. Ward detangled himself from her clutch and introduced her to Alarik as the Ambassador returned from what was clearly a hasty tour.

He pushed into the group, animated, and talking quickly.

"Did you know Viceroy, you have forty-seven outer rooms and also forty-seven unique stones? It is as if each room could have its own stone, although obviously not possible, as they mix all the stones for strength in numbers."

Alarik let his face fall back to a blank mask and nodded politely.

"Thank you, Ward. I think you are due for lunch with the lady here." Alarik turned his attention back to the Ambassador, but Ward could tell he wasn't listening to a thing the ridiculous man was saying.

Ward had no choice but to escort Lady Cristelle out of the room.

He knew he should say something. The surrounding gossip suggested something had happened.

"I don't care," Lady Cristelle said at his silence. "It was pretty hard on the poor thing to be in the hall wrapped in one of your towels. You should pay better attention to her. She doesn't know the first thing about this world."

He looked at Lady Cristelle, who sounded sincere.

"We need to talk about whatever this is," he said, tired of the charade she was playing.

"I have no idea what you're referring to," she said, laughing lightly as she let go of his arm, and went her own way.

He wanted to stop her. To ask her what she was doing spreading rumours about an upcoming wedding when she clearly had no intention of offering for him. But he had left Wynter only moments after their arrival.

No immediate danger, Alarik had said. If the guilds opened the file, then someone could come looking for her.

He returned to his rooms expecting to find Wynter upset or embarrassed from whatever spectacle Lady Cristelle had made of her.

Instead, Wynter had turned his front room into makeshift modiste shop.

Lucy was standing on a small table with a bolt of fabric draped over her. Wynter was underneath, her head and arms covered, but her long legs sticking out.

"Lady Lucy, nice to see you. Umm, Wynter?" He saw the legs stiffen, and she mumbled something.

Lucy's eyes sparkled like she was in the middle of the world's best secret.

"Oh, I should leave you two alone so you can catch up. Here, help me get this off." Lucy undressed right in the middle of the room. Ward averted his gaze, went to the kitchen, back turned, pulling food and drinks out of the cupboard while Lucy changed.

"I want ALL the details." Lucy's loud whisper reached his ears as she reached the door and Wynter ushered her out.

"I tried to tell her a dozen times. She just won't listen," Wynter said as she set to work picking up the pins and bits off the floor. Holding a yellow silky fabric, she sat on the two-seater looking out the windows.

He sat beside her and set the plate of food between them and watched her. There was something comfortable about her being there, in the same room.

Wynter attached long needles to the ends of three of her fingers. They clipped around her knuckles, and she started stringing an intricate design around the edge of the material and up in little darts here and there. Pausing every few minutes, she'd take something off the plate.

The quick precision of the embroidery needles was like an extension of her fingers, quickly pulling threads through and under and weaving a pattern. She wasn't focused; she was driven, as if all the weight depended on every stitch.

He watched the hypnotic movements. She was talented. Talented enough to have gowns in Lady Daye's ballroom.

The sun disappeared and the orbs lit the gardens in a soft glow. He brought out more snacks, made a spiced tea, and she ate, laughed, and asked questions. She'd finished the one row of design and he watched as she started a second over it, layering the thin threads.

"I haven't seen Madame Helix since we arrived, should we try to find her?" he asked, hoping that she'd help him understand what happened on his ship.

"No." Her fingers stopped moving.

"Was she, was it terrible?" he asked.

"No, not at all. I loved the work, and she paid me." Her voice faltered.

There was so much more she wasn't telling him, and he didn't know why.

"Dr Moss, how does he figure in?" Ward asked.

"He saved my life," she answered, then set down the sewing.

Twenty-Eight

The evening was cooling, and Wynter was thankful when Ward tossed a wine-red blanket over them. It was so large it fell over the edges of the couch and hung heavy on them both.

"It was during the ghost pranks," Wynter explained.

"How?" he asked; his brow knit together in concern

"I was in the cargo hold with the silver panelled doors. It's close to where the work was being done, but it's sealed, empty, and most importantly good for dress twirling."

"Dress twirling?" Ward teased, and she was grateful the mood had lightened.

"It's part of the process."

"I'm not arguing. I'm sure it is."

She wrinkled her nose and continued. "I heard them talking on the way down. It's simple right? Find the panel for the signal lights and input a code to make them all a lovely pinkish purple colour. B784A7. I remember it because Turk repeated it over and over. He looked like he was going to be sick if he forgot it. They weren't very nice to him."

"Congratulations, you know the universal code for one colour."

His eyes twinkled

"How many are there?"

"Oh thousands, and don't laugh, it was a terrible prank."

Ward looked down at the bottom of his empty cup. Wynter wondered what that day had been like for him.

"He was stupid to go in there, the signs were posted everywhere. I'm not crew, and I knew not to go down there." Wynter tried to reassure him, then continued. "I opened the manual door easily enough, but I hadn't expected the smell, and when I tried to pull him out, I think my leg caught on something. It's a little fuzzy after I breathed in the gasses. I closed and locked it, tied my dress around my leg, saw you, and ran."

"I knew I saw blood!" His self-satisfied look faded quickly. "How bad was it?"

Wynter pulled the blanket up and lifted her skirt, above the knee. Ward moved closer to her, leaned over, and let out a low whistle. Tentatively, his hand traced the puckered line, stopping at the top of the scar, but the sensation sent heat through her whole body.

"Dr Moss?" Ward asked. His voice sounded raw as he pulled his hand back.

Wynter nodded.

"It was the first time I'd ever talked to him. Not the first time he'd seen me before. What do you know about him?" Wynter asked.

"Not as much as a captain probably should. He was on the ship long before I was. He's brilliant, and kind of terrifying. I should have known you were hurt. He should have told me."

"It wasn't your fault." She quickly pulled the blanket back over her leg.

"My inaction almost cost someone else's life. More than one." His shoulders dropped like the weight of the lives he carried were too heavy.

"I didn't die," she said. Wynter let her hand move toward his letting them rest for a moment.

* * *

The following morning, she woke early, disoriented. She couldn't feel the hum of the ship or noise from the workroom. She was on land, on Orion.

In the kitchen, a pile of boxes cluttered the table. Ward was up and dressed in a thick black jacket with grey woven around the bands and collar. His mug steamed like the misty fog beyond the windows.

He smiled at her and offered her one as well.

"Lucy attacked me in the hallway. She said you needed to borrow some things."

Wynter tried to hide her embarrassment but was thankful for the clothing. Nothing she had would have been suitable.

"I have some things in town to do and thought you'd like to see everything. I ran into Viceroy Alarik this morning as well. He's going to make some inquiries, but no one wants this to go badly for you or anyone else. And I have something you might find interesting."

He wanted to take her into town. She knew she wasn't going to hide the whole time, but to go out? She was going out. Life was starting for her.

The pile from Lucy had a random mixture of tops, skirts, hats, and dresses. She came out wearing a smart navy dress and gloves.

Lucy hadn't leant her shoes, and she wasn't sure how to ask, so she made sure the skirt hung low over her toes. Her hair spun up in a coiled braid, and her silver chain hung around her neck, dipping below the neckline.

Ward stared at her when she came out. She was nervous and fidgeted with her gloves, then looked at herself in the mirror. She was breaking all of Henris's rules. She knew she looked pretty, and this was not hiding. But Ward was with her. Henris couldn't have meant for her to stay hidden forever.

The rest of the castle was still sleeping. Staff wearing a variety of colours passed by. She noted which ones were carrying what and what colour they wore. They didn't have the same stiffness as the crew on the ship but floated through the halls smiling and nodding.

She smiled politely back and wondered what they thought of her.

"I have some business to finish up on the east end of town. It's mostly houses but there are a few sections of shops we can stop at," Ward said oblivious of the attention.

Leaving the protection of the castle, the winds blew down from the mountain, pulling bits of hair out of her braid and into her face. Frost sprinkled the leaves, but the walkways radiated heat from below.

"It's hard to get used to temperatures when you've been on ship for so long. This part of Orion warms quickly. You'll be out of the jacket by high sun," Ward assured her.

"It's so strange."

"The weather?"

"Wearing this much clothing," she replied, tucking her hands into her pockets.

Wynter marked each step and turn. They reached a section with purple cushioned trollies. They had flat fronts and gold trimmed piping. There were smaller trollies with two seats then long fat ones to hold an entire party.

Ward helped her into a trolly for two, and they sped away from the castle and into the city. At the edge of the castle grounds, booths had popped up with lights strung between. Each had guild symbols hanging from decorative posts. Row after row, she wondered which one was Helix's and if she would unpack the dresses into a pop-up shop.

They passed homes with three stories, balconies, and exterior lifts. Some done up in modern style, some looked ancient, but all with coloured roofs, cobbled streets, and floating lights.

Like the patterns she'd stitched into clothing, the homes interlocked and fit together; the larger with the smaller. One of these could be hers. She could live a quiet life.

The first stop was where they made the perfumery bottles at the glass works guild.

A man named Scotts met them at the door and ushered them in. He was round, like the perfume bottle with a bobbly little head. The glassworks smelled of fire and irons. In a side room, she could see exquisite bottles lined in perfectly formed airtight crates.

Wynter watched as men and women blew fantastic colours into long pipes. Ward was talking with Scotts and neither man looked pleased. Glasswork Guilds weren't allowed to travel in space for obvious reasons, but they still had to get cargo from one end of the hex-system to the other.

The glassworks were incredible, and the visit was over far too quickly.

They stopped at a few other places. Wynter kept a respectful distance, complimented the work, and took Ward's arm when he offered it.

The outer jacket was removed long before high sun, letting the cooler air ripple over her skin at the same time as the sun sprinkled a bit of warmth.

In a small restaurant, Ward called for a table. The outside was simple brick. The inside had a circular staircase with landings every six steps. He took her all the way to the top, and they sat on the heated roof. Canopies hung around them, giving an illusion of privacy as figures with plates of food floated in and out past them.

"Captain Ward!" The call came across the roof, Wynter's nerves jittered as a few men came to join them.

"Gentlemen, good to see you. I was headed over to the guild hall next. This is Lady Wynter."

She nodded and tried not to let her shock show. He'd introduced her as a lady.

"So, is this the lady they're all saying will finally land tie the Obsidian?"

"No—I don't want to hear it from you all too," he groaned.

They laughed, patted him on the back, said a few other words about the ship and guild standing. With the activity of the day she'd almost forgotten about Lady Cristelle. She shouldn't have. The little sting brought her back to reality.

She wasn't with Ward, not the way Lady Cristelle would be. He was leaving. She might be safe, but he shouldn't have introduced her as a lady, not having an Idex meant she wasn't a land-titled woman. She wasn't guild, and she could never be more than what she already was. Nothing.

They left the restaurant, and she refused to take his arm.

"One more stop. I know it's been a lot," he said, taking her silence for weariness.

"Are most of your days like this?" she asked.

"Not all of them. It's a lot of boring parties and social gatherings. This next one you'll be interested in though. Maybe you can help me solve a mystery."

The streets were busy. The day getting warmer. The sun caught the windows and sent rainbows dancing along the panes. She didn't realize where they were until they were right in front of it.

"I thought you'd be interested in this," he stated, standing out in front of a shop. The windows were dark, but the freshly painted Laundry and Tailor sign swung gently in the mountain breeze.

Twenty-Nine

Ward was excited. He'd gotten the file from Alarik early in the morning, but knew he had other things to take care of before he could go to the shop. The outside looked clean and well taken care of, as if the owner was out for coffee and not missing for seven years.

If he could find who had kept it, perhaps he'd get lucky enough to find someone who would claim the body, and he wouldn't have to leave it with Alarik. It wouldn't explain what had happened to the poor old man, but he'd at least have it off the ship.

"Don't worry, we're allowed to be here. I got the pass from the guild hall earlier. Their own records are very basic, but I found out a bit about the man who lived here. He was older, no family and no connections, so fits the description of my ghost."

He accessed the security panel and let the door slide open. A soft jingle played as they walked in. He liked the sound. Wynter was still standing on the sidewalk, so he grabbed her hand and pulled her inside.

Unlike the crisp outside, the inside was covered in a thick layer of dust. It collected on the top of the rows of black fabric, turning them grey. The lights flickered and came on.

"What are you hoping to find?" she asked, sounding nervous. He didn't blame her. It was eerie. It looked like the man had got up and walked out. A small basket of orders still had tags. He went over and checked them, none claimed.

"I don't know. Guild law says he had ten years to return and claim his lively hood or for an heir to show up. At the end of ten years, it'll revert to the guild. But now we have a body I don't know what the guilds will do."

The shop would have been charming at one time. He wondered how much the dust would affect the machinery.

The kitchen was metal and stone. Cobwebs hung from the shelves and ceiling like chandeliers.

At the back was an old door. Beside it the crossed needles stamped into the copper.

"You don't see things made like this anymore. I bet it was an original from the Tailor's guild," he said, and watched as she ran her hand over it, wondering what it was like for her to be in the heart of the guilds she'd worked for. He hoped she was enjoying the stop.

He checked the cupboards. Thankfully, all food had been cleared out. A small spot in the back looked almost as if it had been an office or a small room. Maybe the man had slept there from time to time.

"Well, I don't see anything here, no paperwork or files or anything. The guild only protected the shop. The rooms upstairs have been lent out by a dozen people so anything else is long gone."

They wandered around for a few more minutes. He wasn't likely to find what he needed here and might apply to the guild directly for body removal.

"So, there's nothing here," she said.

"Don't you find it strange? He must have people in his life and yet no one was looking for him? The file wasn't lost or hidden; it was just dormant. Dr Moss never recorded his name, even though he must have known it. My uncle never tried to get the body off the ship, and *no one* here went looking for him. It wouldn't have been hard. You wonder what everyone was trying to hide. There's nothing here but a shop."

They were leaving the back room when the sounds of the front door jingle played. And a voice called from the front.

"Excuse me, sir. This store is closed and off limits to the public."

The man was short and stocky and walked with a limp. A small dial hung from his breast pocket. It displayed an intricate circle with small stones representing each planet in the hex-system. It was a quality piece and likely cost the same as one of his shuttle pods.

"Captain Ward," Ward introduced himself, walking toward the man. He put his hand out, and the man grabbed it reluctantly, then pulled his own back quickly. Sensing the man's annoyance, Ward pulled out the screen. "I have security clearance for the day." Ward passed the screen to him, hoping his open manner might gain some trust and maybe get some answers in return.

The man reviewed the screen. Frowned, and then took a long look at Wynter.

"I don't suppose you were around when Mr Canmore used to work here?" Ward asked.

"We spoke very little. I'm part of the clockwork guild." His eyes flicked between Wynter and Ward. "We're private people."

"Are you in charge of the upkeep here?" Ward pushed for more.

"What does your file say?"

"Well, you must be if you could follow us in since I locked the door," Ward said sharply. The man was staring at Wynter, making Ward uncomfortable. "I think we're done here. I don't suppose you know anyone who knew the late owner?"

The man glared. This would make it harder for him to get any other information from the guilds. He was a captain and had rules to follow as well.

He led the way to the door and waited for Wynter to pass out by him; the clockmaker came out too, standing in front of the doorway. They'd taken two steps when he called out to them.

"Oh miss, you dropped this."

Ward tried to grab Wynter's hand to stop her, but she slipped past him. The clockmaker passed her something, and she tucked it into her bag.

"Sorry," she said, and they left the shop and clock-worker behind.

Wynter looked exhausted. He'd wished he'd checked the shop first, then maybe she would have been more interested in it. The ride back to the castle was silent. They were packed into one of the larger trollies. The frost festival would start in two days and the streets were already filling with decorations and people.

There was so much to see. He thought she'd be looking at all the buildings, but her hands were folded in her lap, eyes downcast.

When they got back to the castle, Lady Lucy caught them in the hallway, and Wynter was quick to ask her to come in to do another fitting.

Something had changed during the day, and he had no idea what. Maybe he shouldn't have encouraged Wynter do so much all at once.

He turned as Lucy squealed in delight. The gown fit almost perfectly. It was a soft yellow, certainly out of season, but it made her copper-blond hair look like spun gold. There was a row of white crystals around the neck where the fabric gently gathered. It swooped down, leaving her shoulders bare and came even lower in the back, cascading over her hips. It was elegant and soft, but when she walked, the slits opened, showing off her legs. She looked like she'd stepped right out of a myth. The intricate work on the bottom looked like another world spinning up the sides.

"Cristelle is going to be so jealous, especially since Madame Helix hasn't shown up at all to deliver the dresses," Lucy said spinning around.

Wynter instructed Lucy to not move, and was sitting on the floor, pinning the rolled bottom. Threading a needle, she poked it in and out of the fabric. He'd seen a similar look on her face before, when she was in his rooms with Dr Moss and Rane. She was upset or afraid or something other than the blank calm she was showing.

"Lucy, we still have a few days. It's been busy. Why don't you head back so Wynter can get some rest?" Ward suggested.

"I don't need you telling me what to do," Wynter snapped, flicking the needle in and out, never once striking her own fingers, although it looked close so many times.

Something was wrong. He ran his hand through his hair.

He knelt down beside her. Lucy was gazing at them both. Her hands were clasped at her chest, and she looked like she was going to swoon when Ward placed his hands over Wynter's stopping them.

Wynter froze, her breath coming in slight slips of air, barely causing her chest to rise and fall.

"I'm sorry I pushed you so hard, I thought it was a good idea," he said. She'd lived her whole life in hiding. What did he know of what would hurt her or not? Either way, he meant it. He never wanted to be the one to cause her pain.

She pulled one hand back, then the other. Standing, she turned away from Lucy. "You're right. We have lots of time. I think I'll go to bed."

Then she left Lucy standing there in the gown and Ward kneeling down on the floor.

"Oh, I'll come back tomorrow," Lucy said, glowing. Ward went to the balcony as Lucy unceremoniously stripped off the gown, putting her own day dress back on, leaving the yellow in a puddle on the floor. He could hear Lucy sigh and then slam the door behind her.

The shower ran in the bathroom, then the soft click as Wynter closed the door to her room. Whatever had upset her, she wasn't going to tell him tonight.

He went to his own room. He knew he needed to sleep but he could hear her get up. He wanted to go out, sit with her, almost did a few times, but held back.

The next morning, Ward went to Alarik before the castle woke. He needed to ensure her safety, to make sure she wouldn't be lost in this world when he was gone.

Thirty

Wynter had been home, her real home. The place she'd dreamed of returning to for years. Henris's shop looked the same, but she remembered it all being so much larger. She wished she'd been prepared, wished she'd known they would go there. But how could she have been? Ward still didn't know her connection to Henris. She'd been home. A dull ache pulled in her chest, a feeling she couldn't quite place or put away.

That night she slept fitfully for a few hours, then woke in middle of the night and went out to the living room. She picked the yellow silk up off the floor and finished the dress for Lucy. Once completed she was finally able to sleep, and by the time she woke again it was midday. Ward had left without waking her.

Wynter traced the small clock medallion from the watchmaker, letting all the questions in. It was like the one Henris had given her but had the symbols for a clock with dials and moons and planets in small gemstones. The clockmaker had known who she was, she was sure of it.

She knew she should have told Ward about her connection to Henris the moment they stepped into the shop. She should have told him her knowledge of the ghost weeks ago, but hiding secrets was all she'd ever known.

Ward would be leaving on the Obsidian in only a few weeks, she reminded herself. It was better to say nothing. Dr Moss had warned her that others might think she'd killed Henris. She doubted Ward would think so, but what if he did? What if the watchmaker did? She needed to find out if the watchmaker knew what had happened the day she'd disappeared before she told Ward anything.

After going through the rest of the clothing Lucy had loaned her, she made a short list of things she was going to need. Instead of the outfit she'd worn the day before, she put on a simple day dress with long warm sleeves, a black band laced in the back, and a skirt that hung down to her feet. She'd fit in more with the others she'd watched the day before. She put on her simple black slippers. Her feet were sore from the day before. Walking down cobbled roads was not the same as the plush hallways on the ship. They'd all but worn through; and so shoes would be needed if she was going to make it back to the watchmaker.

Checking the stack of cards she'd made from sewing for Helix, she tucked a handful of them in her pocket. It would be important to have at least an idea of what was on them. If she was going to meet with Alarik, she wanted to have a plan.

Wynter set out into the hall on her own to Lucy's room and was relieved when she answered her door. Wynter held up the dress; Lucy grabbed it with one hand and used the other to pull Wynter into her room.

"Oh, it's perfect! Everyone will be so jealous. Just think, I'll have the first Wynter gown."

"I don't know what the plan is yet. Maybe for now you can

keep it a secret?" Wynter asked.

"Oh, I'm great with secrets," Lucy said. Wynter highly doubted it.

"I have a favour to ask. Can you take me shopping? I need a few things, and I don't know where to—" Wynter's words squeezed out of her as Lucy hugged her tightly.

"I just knew we were friends! Oh, let me grab my bag," she exclaimed.

Wynter wasn't sure what she'd say to Ward if she ran into him in the hallway, or Helix, but they made it out of the castle without incident. There was faint hope in talking Lucy into going all the way down to the watchmaker. Wynter remembered the way easily enough, but there was little to entice Lucy to shop around there. If she could just see him for a minute, say hello, leave him a note.

She stepped into the back of the open day trolly. Lucy input the first location, and they sped off, covering the grounds with tall trees, past a pond, then through the gates. Wynter wondered how long it would take to get used to the feeling. She made sure Lucy explained how the carts worked. If her plan failed, trying again on her own was an option. She swallowed her nerves and convinced herself that it would be no different than walking around unnoticed on the ship.

There were long rows of shops and men and women walking through the streets with packages or deliveries. Cafes had windows open. Light globes hung suspended in midair.

Wynter made it clear the need for new shoes, and Lucy excitedly rambled on about all the places they could stop.

They went into the first shop. Around the outside of the narrow room were rows and rows of glass cases, each with a shoe on display. When pressed, the entire row popped out with all the sizes hidden behind. In the centre, pedestals reached up throughout the room displaying dazzling shoes with stones, crystals, colours, and painted heels.

Lucy abandoned Wynter quickly to try on yellow heels. The toes were open with little straps. She passed them to the clerk.

"What happened after I left last night?" Lucy asked in a loud whisper. The staff and other shoppers pretended like they couldn't hear the conversation.

"Nothing. I went to bed."

"But the way he was looking at you!" Lucy coo'd.

"I'm really not in any sort of relationship with Ward."

"Ward, you call him Ward? *Of course* there's nothing there," Lucy patted Wynter's hand and went looking for another pair.

Wynter rolled her eyes. Lucy had a small stack before Wynter had found what she was looking for. They were on one of the centre pedestals, a price listed underneath. If Lucy was buying six pairs, surely this one pair was affordable.

They were simple black shoes with no heel. The outside was shiny and smooth and had a hint of blue and deep plum. They reminded her of the Obsidian and felt soft and sturdy when she walked around the shop in them.

She was going to make her first purchase and realized she didn't really know what to do.

"You've never shopped on Orion. No, of course not. It's different from on a ship or Valtine or Corva. A guild wants to inspect the item before it goes out. Mr Prinvel is the best. He won't let you take them unless they're perfect."

She nodded at Lucy and walked to the back of the store.

"May I see?" he said sternly, holding out his hand. She placed the shoes in his palms and waited while he inspected them. He wasn't looking at them so much as looking at her over the top.

She didn't remember Henris acting like this, but he was a tailor. Maybe shoes were different?

He wrapped them in a thin paper and placed them in a box. She wanted to reach out and touch the coloured paper. Excitement bubbled up inside her. She was out on her own buying shoes, the feeling of independence was so utterly foreign to her.

He told her the amount, and she pulled out the stack of little cards. They all had markings on the back. One was blue and shiny, the green one with the gold rim looked the costliest. She remembered getting it from Helix after a round on Corva where she'd designed three decadent cake-like gowns. They'd been a hit and had launched Helix's career, eventually getting them into Valtine ballrooms. She held it out proudly, her heart pounding so loud.

He looked at the card, then back at Wynter.

Something was wrong.

Was it too much, wasn't there a machine to check? Had she made a mistake? She pulled the card back and flicked through them. A golden one had to be enough. Maybe this wasn't the best idea if she had to live off these for a while.

Holding it out, she waited for him to take it, to say something. Colour crept up his neck.

Lucy came up beside her. "Oh Wynter, no. They don't accept that kind of payment here. I wouldn't think Captain Ward would want to share either."

"Captain Ward?" The cobbler raised a brow, interested despite his obvious discomfort.

Wynter had done something wrong, but she didn't know what.

She wanted the shoes but didn't think another card would make a difference.

Lucy took the chips out of Wynter's hands and then exclaimed, "Oh my goodness, I can't believe you did it with a straight face. You got him so good! All right, the shoes are on me, but it's my turn in the next store. Send it to my dad with mine."

The man nodded and let out a breath he'd been holding. He chuckled uncomfortably, but with the sale of seven pairs of shoes from Lucy, he was overlooking whatever Wynter had done. His thin hair looked like it was perspiring and stuck to his forehead.

"How fun for you and the miss. Perhaps you do not try this at Revells. His wife has passed recently, and he might not be so amused."

"Thanks for the warning. You're such a doll," Lucy gushed. "Have mine sent to the castle."

"I'd like to have mine if I can." Wynter's feet ached, and she wanted to put them on before going any further.

"Of course." He handed her the package, and she held it to her chest.

Lucy waved and smiled at everyone as they left. Wynter felt like she'd done something terribly wrong.

Leaving the store, Lucy marched Wynter into a small garden alcove. Wynter sat down on a small stone bench and pulled the black shoes out.

"You're changing those out here?" Lucy balked, but then noted the thin slippers. "Wynter, you can't try to pay like that here, and I don't think the captain would like it."

"I don't know what you mean."

"You might not be exclusive, but people do talk, and if my father found out... well he doesn't mind someone staying at the castle, but the guilds don't allow it."

Wynter stood. The shoes felt perfect, but the rest of her body felt off, like everything was spinning as the trollies sung past them. She fought down the frustrated tears.

"I don't know what you're talking about. How do I get the money off the cards?"

"Money? There's no money on these." It was Lucy's turn to look confused

"Well funds? Trades? I don't know. What are they?"

Lucy looked like she wasn't sure if she should answer then blurted out, "Room keys. You didn't know you were offering him a room key, to, you know, a room?"

Wynter looked away from Lucy, watching the trollies— watching anything else. She bit the top of her lip and blinked quickly against the sun. Helix had given her room keys.

"Was someone paying you? WAS THE CAPTAIN PAYING YOU with room cards? Oh don't cry, it's okay I have oodles of money," she kept talking, then squeezed her again.

Wynter had nothing. Seven years and she hadn't been paid for a single dress.

"Who did this to you? Oh Wynter, I wish you'd tell me what was going on."

"I can't." Wynter looked at her shoes. She should bring them back. "I don't know how to pay you for these."

"Don't be silly. I have a gown from the real Madame Helix for the ball. I owe you a dozen pair of shoes." Lucy was holding Wynter's arm and gently rubbing it. "In fact, I owe you a ton, so why don't we go spend all your hard-earned money."

"Can we just go back?"

"Sure," said Lucy sadly. "Don't worry, I'll help you fit in."

Thirty-One

Wynter and Lucy walked arm in arm until they reached the castle. Lucy looked reluctant to leave, but Wynter insisted everything was alright. After Lucy had gone, she'd made a cup of tea and wondered what Ward was doing, hoping he wouldn't be back soon. Breathing in the spicy aroma, she relished the moment of privacy. How was she going to tell Ward that she had no funds? Maybe it would be better if he left without being told.

She wanted to hate Helix, but hated herself more. Why hadn't she tried to use the cards? Demand to know how much was on them? She'd never needed them. Food and clothing were never a concern, it all felt like a lie now.

Wynter walked toward the balcony. The door was ajar, and a cool breeze was sliding in through the panelling, cooling the room. Reaching to close it, she jumped. She wasn't alone.

The woman was tall and wore a long silver coat. The fabric looked like it should shimmer, but it was flat. Wynter thought it was Lady Cristelle until she turned around.

She was beautiful. Wynter backed up a little, spilled some of her tea on the floor. Looking down, she mopped the droplets up with her toe.

The lady came inside. The cool breeze she carried with her dissipated once the door closed.

"Alarm is unnecessary," she said, her voice like honey.

Wynter wasn't sure what she should do. A lady required a formal greeting, but Wynter wasn't a lady. Whoever this woman was, she was clearly someone important. But how had she gotten into the rooms without Wynter's knowledge? She didn't imagine Ward would have let her in without at least warning her first.

The stranger motioned to the chair but didn't sit, and so neither did Wynter.

"Lady Daye," she said, holding out her hand palm down, then dropped it and shrugged. "Lucy is my niece. And you are Madame Helix—essentially."

Wynter bristled at the mention of Helix.

"Yes. I thought I should introduce myself since I vouched for you at the guild meetings today. You are quite the topic of conversation."

Wynter set the cup of tea on the counter and pulled one out for Lady Daye. Questions dancing in her mind, why would Lady Daye speak on her behalf?

Lady Daye stood on the far side of the small table. The boiled water hit the spicy leaves, filling the room with a fragrant steam.

"You talked to the guilds? About me? Why?" Wynter asked.

"Why is not as important as what. But I won't bore you with trying to get it out of me. You should know, we discussed your situation without your captain, he was quite upset to be left out, but since he's just a captain it was to be expected." She waved her hand as if Wynter knew what she was talking about. "What will interest you the most, however, is that I convinced the guilds to take what was Madame Helix's and give it to you. Not her place on the ship obviously, it will revert back to the guild or be empty, but you'll own any goods she acquired."

"Why?" Wynter asked in disbelief. She'd gone from having a plan, to having nothing, to being given so much in such a short amount of time it was making her head hurt.

"I would have done it simply out of spite of Helix, something easily accomplished without helping you, but I need you to do something for me."

"You're asking for a dress?"

"No, no dear." She laughed, but it didn't sound like a laugh. "It's simple. There's something I need, and you're the only one qualified to get it."

"What could possibly qualify me if not a dress?" Wynter asked.

"Freedom," she said, smiling, taking a quick sip from her cup. "We have little time, so I'll get right down to it."

Lady Daye spent the next few minutes explaining her plan—a plan Wynter didn't like, but she felt somewhat indebted to her, if Lady Daye's influence had actually acquired the life she spoke of. What Lady Daye was asking wasn't difficult. Not for her. Wynter knew she could refuse, should refuse, but there was something else. She recognized the blank face as Lady Daye spoke. How many times had she worn it?

"What if I say no? Do you go back to the guild and take away everything you've given me?"

"No, I wouldn't take anything from you. I would ruin your captain. If you cross me, if you tell him or anyone what I've asked you to do, I'll spill the secrets of every guild and half the crew his uncle had working on that monstrosity of a ship. I'll make sure it's ripped from his hands. Although if you aren't as taken with

Captain Ward as Lady Cristelle tells me, then perhaps it won't matter."

"He's not my captain," Winter murmured considering her limited options.

Eventually Wynter agreed, even though they would be going their different ways, she couldn't sit by and watch Lady Daye hurt Ward or his ship.

Lady Daye talked easily about what would happen if either or both got caught, as if they were planning a breakfast tea together. Then she got up and left, leaving Wynter with a thousand questions and a ball to plan for.

Thirty-Two

Cargo meetings kept Ward tied up for most of the day. He had a strong feeling someone had selectively herded him from one place to the next, making it impossible to attend the one conversation he wanted to be a part of. The guild leaders had gathered to discuss Wynter, and how best to handle the situation.

When he finally arrived back at the castle, he had only a few minutes to talk to Alarik.

"Your friend will have a place on Orion," Alarik said, shaking his hand as if he was congratulating him.

"There's already been a decision?" Ward asked, not believing it would be that simple.

"Lady Daye arrived this morning," Alarik offered as an explanation. Despite guild control, a landowner as significant as Lady Daye would have incredible sway. "She had little concern for your Wynter but was determined to see justice done as far as Madame Helix and her use of a stowaway for free labour were concerned."

Ward's eyes narrowed. He was happy for Wynter, but Lady Daye must have taken a dart in order to arrive so quickly behind them. A lady didn't travel via darts, and how could she possibly have known?

"No files will be opened," Alarik continued. "Only those in the meeting will know her unique situation. As far as society goes, we'll need to be careful not to draw any attention and keep the circle small, but it'll be done easily enough."

In one meeting, they decided unilaterally to pretend as if Wynter's life and existence were normal. Secrets. Typical guild behaviour.

"She's coming with me to the ball. I promised her," Ward stated, leaving no room for negotiation. The guilds had decided her fate without input; at least he could do this for her.

Alarik thought for a moment, then nodded. "Fair enough, with the festival in full swing and multiple ships docked I don't see why not, but perhaps she should enter with Lucy. Your little situation with Lady Cristelle has caused some gossip."

Ward was hoping the rumours would have dissipated, but it seemed the less they talked to each other, the more everyone talked about them.

* * *

When he reached the rooms, he caught almost a hint of something, the perfume reminded him of Valtine, like the smell of songbird flowers only softer. He shook his head and went in.

Strolling into the room, he passed a new pair of black shoes. They were simple and pretty. He was eager to ask Wynter what she'd done with her day and to share what Alarik had told him.

Wynter was out on the deck, a thick brown wrap over her shoulders. The cool breeze split the air between them.

"You got shoes," he said.

"Lucy helped me," she replied. "It's so pretty here." There was a hint of resignation in her voice.

"I think you'll be happy here, and safe. Viceroy Alarik met with the guilds. They don't want to open the files. If no one knows you're here, then there's no risk after twenty years," Ward said. He knew it was a lot to take in, but she looked more concerned than relieved. "And there's a ball to get ready for, do you know how to dance? Aside from dress twirling of course."

She shook her head and looked down at her feet.

"As a Valtine Lord," he said, holding out his hand, "that is something I know I can help you with."

She placed her hand in his, the furrow in her brow deepening.

"The steps are similar for all the dances. If you know the basics you can use them for almost any song, but Orion loves their fast reels. If you hear the tempo pick up, get off the dance floor!"

They spent the next hour doing something that was sort of like dancing, using the chairs as other couples to move around. It was all footwork and stumbling, and she'd stepped on his feet at least a dozen times. But he didn't mind because at least she was smiling now.

"Let's pick it up a little," he suggested, hoping the increase in tempo might make the movements more natural.

"I thought you said to get off the dance floor if it got fast?" Her green eyes went wide, but she laughed. He liked the sound, even if she was teasing him, especially because she was teasing him.

"This isn't fast, trust me."

He moved his feet quickly, and she kept up, until she didn't—instead falling into one of the chairs.

"I give up! Stowaways shouldn't dance," she said, laughing and breathless. His chest felt tight watching her, and he knew then he didn't want to let her go, couldn't let her go.

"Come back to the Obsidian with me," he said.

She stiffened and stopped laughing.

"I can't."

"Why not?" he asked.

She didn't answer, but he knew there were a hundred reasons. She didn't have to say any of them. Wynter had been on the Obsidian hiding for seven years. She had a chance at a somewhat normal life, with friends and a home, here on Orion, on land.

"I'm sorry. I shouldn't have suggested it. You have a future here," Ward said, embarrassed, but still hoping she'd contradict him. He knew, if she gave him even the slightest hope, he'd give up anything to bring her back to the Obsidian.

"It's okay," she said in response, and he felt that hope deflate. "Dancing is making me a little light-headed."

She placed the back of her hand on her cheek and retreated to the safety of her room, leaving him staring at a closed door.

Thirty-Three

Wynter had been trying to pay attention to her feet, not on where Ward had his hand on her waist. She'd fallen into the chair laughing and making a terrible mess of the dance when Ward had asked her to come back to the Obsidian.

She couldn't consider it. What would she be? A seamstress? A friend? She'd made a ridiculous excuse about dancing and headaches and retreated to her room.

There was still so much she didn't know, and it was all moving too fast. She couldn't agree to go back up, not until her business with Lady Daye was finished. If she was going to have control over her own life, she needed one thing everyone else seemed to have: information.

Wynter waited until she was certain Ward was asleep and snuck out of the room, down the hallway, and out into the courtyard where she and Lucy had walked before. She wore an ink black jacket and her new shoes. They hugged her feet and kept them protected from the night air.

Holding the small clockwork pendant in her hand, she turned it over between her fingers, refusing to let her resolve falter.

The city met the edge of the castle; the streets were quiet but not empty. Music floated into the street from various open houses and taverns, the noise crisscrossing over the darkened, closed up shops. She boarded one of the free trollies to take her to the other end of town. A woman sat on the seat across from her; she looked tired heading home for the night. A few more joined from one tavern. They were loud and laughing with each other. No one looked her way.

Getting off two blocks early, she walked down the shop streets.

The clockmaker's shop was dark. She tried the door and was surprised to find it unlocked. It swung easily, but the jingle didn't sound. Maybe he didn't have a jingle. When she closed the door, the lights flickered back on outside as if they were waiting for her, keeping her cloaked in darkness until she was inside.

"Hello?" she called out. The tick of clocks all set to the same second filled the room. Clocks lined the walls. There were long counters and, toward the back, glass cabinets. Maps and charts hung between the clocks, displaying the hex-system planets, all with their solar systems, moons, and calendars.

A small screen opened, and a small beam of light poured into the shop front. She followed it. The door swished opened and closed quickly as she stepped through.

"OHHHHH," she was greeted by a large woman who squeezed her tight. "You came! You finally came! We've waited and waited. He said he saw you. I didn't believe him. It is you, isn't it?"

"You know me?" Wynter asked, confused. Henris was always careful to keep her hidden from everyone.

"Of course, we know you! Wynter, we'd know you anywhere."

"Let her sit down," the clockmaker said. She sat and he put a large mug of steaming grog in front of her. She took a long drink, letting the liquid sit on her tongue before swallowing. The cheese lady was beaming.

Wynter looked at them both, then down at her mug. She wasn't sure what she was supposed to say.

"How did you get here?" the woman asked.

"I took a trolly, but I got off a few blocks back."

"No, not here, Orion. How are you alive? What... what happened?" She looked pained and as confused as Wynter felt.

"I was hoping you'd be able to tell me." Wynter looked down at the wood table and pushed her fingers over the small rivets. "I didn't kill him," she added quickly.

"Never thought you did. How could you?" the clockmaker said. "We'd hoped, but never believed you were alive. We thought they got you, we thought they—we thought we'd failed again." His eyes were shining.

"We got a notice a few weeks ago informing us Henris died. There was no word of a girl at all. We... we feared the worst for you."

"A few weeks ago? Ward mentioned he'd opened the files a few weeks back, but Henris died over seven years ago. He put me onto a ship and gave me this," she said. Her hands trembled as she took out the medallion, letting it hang from her neck for them to see. Then she took the clockmakers out of her pocket and put it on the table sliding it back to him. "Henris said I'd be safe with Madame Helix. I thought he was going to come get me when it was safe. I didn't know until recently that he was gone."

She noticed the look between the two. They didn't look happy.

"He's been gone this whole time?" Tears welled up in the lady's eyes, her hand balled into round fists and shook as she spoke. "Why would he go to Helix, he knew what she was capable of, and what she'd do."

The clockmaker shook his head. "She kept Wynter."

"Of course she did, but keeping a young girl doesn't mean she wouldn't—"

The cheese lady released her fists and blew her nose into a lacy cloth, it didn't look like it would hold much.

"It's too much, I can't... I can't live this again," the cheesemaker said, standing.

"Why don't you go make us some tea?" the clockmaker suggested. She nodded and walked out of the room leaving Wynter alone with the clockmaker.

Wynter didn't want tea, she didn't want anything. The grog stuck in her throat.

"What about Madame Helix?" Wynter asked.

"How much do you know?" The clockmaker pinched his lips together.

Wynter told him the bits Dr Moss had said, leaving out who she'd heard it from.

"We thought we were doing good," the clockmaker said, shaking his head. He held his hands, working his rough looking fingers over his wrists. "We'd heard about the medical labs in the foothills. It was just rumours, really."

"They were doing experiments to try to change their Idex coding, right?" Wynter asked. He picked up his mug. She waited for him to keep going, feeling her throat constrict in funny ways.

More secrets, always more secrets, Wynter thought.

"Yes, they saw an opportunity. If they could change or trick the Idex system, guilds could have control. Proper control—not having to tie every bit of land to a family Idex line. We all wanted that, until we found out how they wanted to go about it."

"Were there more like me?" she asked.

"There were," he nodded. "A group of six joined together. Myself and a few others. We planned to get you all out. It was a decent enough plan, but we didn't know what we were doing—not really. We were going to clear the labs and then blow them up. But it all went terribly wrong, we blew it up for sure, but not everyone made it out. We still don't know why. If someone tipped them off, we'll never know."

"Henris was part of your group?"

"Yes, he was so reluctant. He wanted us to take it to the Viceroy, but we didn't know who was involved. Three of our group died. Domo was inside when it blew. He's the one who carried you out, but he didn't—he didn't make it. Henris found you both in the snow. So many people died because of what we did." The clockmaker buried his face in his hands.

Wynter tried processing all the information. The clockmaker reached out, putting his left hand over his medallion, which Wynter had put on the table. He tapped it absently as he talked.

"Henris kept you. He was the least likely out of the three of us. If anyone got wise, they'd check a woman's shop first. She'd be able to tip us off. Then the world went on as if nothing had happened. No one spoke of it. If they suspected, no one looked too closely at you. The day you left, Henris had been acting antsy, but had said nothing. He must have been tipped off, but there were always rumours. Then you were both gone."

"Madame Helix was a safe place, no one knew I was there," Wynter said. It was safe, but it had cost her. Helix had paid her in room keys and fake promises. She must have wondered why Henris hadn't tried to contact her. "Why do you think Henris wouldn't have thought Madame Helix was safe?"

"Madame Helix is not all she appears to be, and we know she blamed Henris for Domo's death. It wouldn't be the first person she'd poisoned, not that anyone could prove anything," he said, looking bleak.

Then it clicked in. The missing pieces, what the clockmaker was telling her. He thought Helix had killed Henris. It couldn't be.

Wynter had spent seven years making Helix famous and trying to be grateful for the little chip cards, waiting for Henris to come back. Wynter remembered the little box of green syringes she'd seen in the bottom of the bathroom cupboard. Could they have been poison? Helix was somewhat selfish, but murder?

Wynter questioned every moment on the ship, wondering if it had all been fake.

"Why didn't you report him as missing?" Wynter asked, keeping her face calm and voice even.

"We weren't involved in the experiments, but a lot of people died that night, and our names are on that. If you being here opens the files, we're all at risk."

The woman came in with the tea, but Wynter stood. Her existence put them at risk. They had as much reason to want her gone as someone who'd been doing the experiments.

"This is the last time we can meet. You can't know me." Her head swam with the news. So many lies, so many lives hurt.

"It's enough," the watchmaker said, putting his hand on the cheese lady. "To know we saved one life alone."

"I'm not alone." She knew it was true, but it felt like a lie saying it. Ward had been so kind and patient, and she'd kept secrets. She hadn't told him about Henris or how she'd gotten on the ship.

Silly things to hold back, she saw that now.

"We never imagined what kind of life you'd have. We took you without even thinking." The woman broke into sobs again. Wynter wanted to comfort her, but she needed to leave. The watchmaker picked the chain back up from the table and squeezed it in his palm. She ran from the shop and into the artificially lit night.

She sat on the trolly her arms tucked into her sides letting the sting of the night and the misting frost hit her cheek. The entire way back, she felt as if she was being followed, watched, but no one was there.

In the castle, her cheeks warmed and burned from the change in temperature. For a moment, she thought she saw a shadow slide past the door behind her, but when she looked, it was just empty space.

Wynter felt like she was going crazy, like her mind was walking on the top of a wall and if she could tip one way or the other, she'd fall into a darkness and never come out of it again. She wanted to wake Ward, talk to him, tell him everything, but it was safer for him if he didn't know, safer for her and for them if she stayed hidden.

Wynter slipped silently into the rooms but couldn't sleep. She grabbed the patchwork dress and brought it out. Her fingers ran over every square. Hundreds of them, all the work she'd done, the plans she made, stitched together.

Nothing on the Obsidian had been real. She felt like she should be able to connect all the pieces, but it felt like the truth hidden in the stars, out where the Obsidian was looking down on them. She'd waited for Henris, wondered what had happened to him. All the time the truth was right with her on the ship.

Picking up the dress she'd so lovingly made, she took the thin sheers and started taking out the long seams piece by piece.

All of it lies. The dresses she didn't get paid for. The dresses that had been used to propel a murderer into fame. The dresses Henris would never see. She wanted to go back, to tell Henris to hand her over to the guilds, to open those files and make everyone pay for what they did. She wanted to go back and take back every stitch she'd made for Helix. She wanted to undo every buttonhole and pull away every word between them.

She pulled another string, as small squares fell to the floor in ribboned strands. There was no going back, but forward felt like an impossible spiral.

.

Thirty-Four

Only a few days had passed since Wynter had left the Obsidian, and already her life had unravelled. Now she had to stitch it back together.

She'd stayed up most of the night working on her dress for the ball. Her eyes heavy, she startled with every noise, wishing Ward would come out, so she could tell him everything, and knowing if he did come out, she wouldn't say anything—couldn't say anything.

The rumours had continued for the past few days, Ward was going to marry Lady Cristelle. Even if she went back up to the Obsidian, she wouldn't be with him, not in the way she knew she wanted to be, and she couldn't bear that.

It was all too much, so she focused on the only thing she could. She had a ball to prepare for, and something she needed to do for Lady Daye so Ward could keep his ship.

Wynter fell into a restless sleep on the couch and woke to the smell of rich coffee. Bits of dress and material covered her, along with a heavy blanket she didn't remember getting.

Ward set a steaming cup and plate beside her, and then went to eat his own breakfast, or maybe it was lunch.

He said nothing, but she could feel his eyes on her as she lifted the blanket and picked at the bits of material littered around her. She let the hot coffee cool beside her and ignored the plate of food. He asked her something, and she nodded absently, focused on the threads she was now weaving together. She didn't want to talk, she just needed to finish the dress.

Threads in and out. She had to pull it all together.

He left again, and she breathed a sigh of relief, but he returned after only a few minutes, and had brought Lucy with him.

"Wynter? Are you alright?" Lucy asked. "Maybe you should move into my rooms until the ball is over?"

"I'm fine here," Wynter said, letting the silver dart up and down in rapid succession.

"Oh good, I really didn't want to share my rooms. I mean there would be enough room, but after living on such a small ship, for over a month I really need…"

They both heard Ward clear his throat from across the room.

"I have some more clothing you can borrow. The weather here can change quickly, so here's a coze," Lucy said as she dumped an armload onto Wynter's lap, covering her sewing, then topped it off with a soft wrap. It was sky blue with tightly woven threads layered into a thick bunch.

Ward cleared his throat again, and Wynter looked up, no longer able to sew with her arms covered. She was no longer able to ignore her friends.

"I know you're working on your dress," said Lucy. "But I want to show you the castle."

She looked at Ward, who smiled reassuringly.

Wynter got up, tucked the material under the blanket. She

straightened her legs and shook out the cramps from sitting on them for too long.

"I guess I could use a walk," Wynter admitted to Lucy, feeling the weight of everything crashing against her without the fabric and threads running between her fingers.

"Maybe you should shower and change first. New clothes, see?" Lucy said. Wynter realized she'd spent the night on the couch and probably looked terrible. Her stomach rumbled as she made her way to the shower.

The water was hot, and it felt good to clean up. She couldn't help but wonder what Lucy and Ward were saying about her in the other room.

She must have looked a little crazy sitting and sewing all night. It felt nice to be noticed; not nice to be talked about.

She tried on soft brown pants. A long top wrapped around her and partially covered the top of her legs. She dried her hair as quickly as she could, braiding it into a knot at the back of her neck.

Ward had left, probably on captain business, but had set out another plate of snacks and a fresh coffee. She picked at the plate, took a sip of the coffee, and then followed Lucy into the hall.

The castle was larger than Wynter had originally thought. There were people everywhere. From the windows they could see everyone in the courtyards below.

Lucy showed her the family houses. An extensive field with stone archways and cobbled paths separated the castle from the houses. It boasted five tall towers with a black gate, and the mountain crept up behind.

"I'll go back there once everyone is gone. I don't always stay at the castle, but I didn't want to miss a thing." She winked at

Wynter.

When they finally reached the ballrooms Wynter stopped, her knees felt weak looking at the size of the room.

"Have you ever been to a ball?" Lucy asked. Thankfully Lucy didn't ask too many questions of Wynter unless it involved the captain.

"No, well, once I watched one. There was a group from Corva. They did a dance that was so fast."

"Oh, I just love the way they dance. It's easy," Lucy said, leading her onto the floor before Wynter could protest.

The strings at the end were practising and gave them a look of annoyance. Lucy hollered at them from across the ballroom, they murmured, and then started the song for her.

"It's quite simple," Lucy said, returning to her. "When the music starts, we take three steps to the right then three to the left. It's a dance made for friends, so there's no lead or follow. You stomp fast here."

It was easier taking lessons from Lucy, who wasn't making Wynter's heart beat faster. Her feet still couldn't keep up.

They stepped and stomped around the room. Every so often, Lucy would yell something like, "No, you have to stomp harder with your left foot!"

They were out of breath and laughing when the music stopped. It felt good, like she was stomping and shaking off all the lies and secrets and doing something new. She'd finish her dress, and go to a ball, and help Lady Daye, and bury her secrets in her new life. The secrets that were so old they didn't matter anymore.

A large man stepped out from behind the pillars. Wynter stiffened when he came over, but he took Lucy's hands.

"You look like your mother. She used to love to dance." And

he kissed Lucy on her cheek.

"Dad, I'd like you to meet my friend. This is Wynter."

Ward had told her Alarik was Lucy's father, but she hadn't expected such a formidable-looking man for how sweet and silly Lucy was. She wished she knew what the proper greeting for a viceroy would be. He did a half bow. Wynter stared.

"I am honoured to finally welcome you to my home. Be at ease and after the ball, we will have much to discuss."

Wynter nodded, her fate was held in this man's very large hands.

"Can we try this one at the ball? You and me?" Lady Lucy asked Alarik, ignoring the interchange between the two.

He laughed, shook his head, and promised to take her to Corva one day.

His voice was rich and deep. The ball wasn't only for dancing; she reminded herself. If this man was Lucy's father, he was also Lady Daye's brother. She liked the idea of him protecting her; she did not like the idea of getting caught.

Thirty-Five

The ballroom was already bursting with guests in their finest when Ward arrived.

Stone pillars with glittering rocks and polished crystals created mosaic artwork that wound its way like a colourful story through the main room. Wide open hallways led to side rooms to provide acoustical breaks so conversations could be private while still seen by everyone else in attendance. There were gaming tables, food and drinks, lounges with open windows, and balconies leading to the back where the gardens resided below.

From the front rooms, you could watch who was coming in, in all their glittery finery, and from the back you could watch people weave their way in and out of the lightly frosted gardens.

It was less formal in manners, and even those accustomed to Valtine felt more comfortable at an Orion soiree. It was also open to those who claimed guild level status without special invitation.

Ward had taken the last few days to secure the rest of his cargo and had been back and forth to the ship. Everything was feeling easy and unimportant. He'd informed the crew the pranks were ending and if they were unhappy, they could get off the ship. No one left. Too many of them looked relieved at his announcement, proving he wasn't the only one who disliked the regular disruptions.

He liked Orion. There was an ease that hard work brought on. Making his way through the crowd, he greeted his suppliers and Guild Lords. They found confidence in shaking hands with the one who would take their cargo off world.

Ward had been apprehensive the whole day. He scanned the room, anxious to see Wynter, but caught Lady Daye's attention instead. She blended in with the sizeable crowd. It was the first time he'd seen her where she didn't specifically stand out.

"Lady Daye?" Ward said when he reached her. She turned toward him and let his hand take hers. He bowed over it, as was done in Orion.

"Too bad," she smiled, taking her hand back. "Valtine greetings are more delicious, don't you think?"

"I didn't realize there was another ship coming this way from Valtine," he stated, trying to confirm his suspicions.

"I took a dart," she said as if it was a common thing for a lady to do.

"Is Lord Daye with you?" He couldn't remember the last time he saw her without having Lord Daye close at hand.

"No, he was too busy to make the travel. I wanted to see my niece settled. I felt we parted on bad terms with dresses and all the drama. It's a lovely party." She smiled absently.

"Yes, it is." He stopped talking as Lady Lucy walked toward them. She was wearing the gown Wynter had designed, her skill and style on every fold and sweep.

"Aunt Daye?" Lucy asked, her eyes wide and brows raised. "When did you get here?"

Lady Daye was eyeing Lucy's dress. He noticed what was almost a smile at the corners of Lady Daye's mouth.

"It's not a Helix," Lucy said.

"Of course, not dear. You wouldn't have tried to get one of those after I specifically told you not to. How have you been?" Her tone softened but fell short of a motherly tone.

Ward looked past Lady Daye and Lucy as they talked. Lucy was animated and loud, while Lady Daye barely said anything, merely nodding along. Where was Wynter? She was supposed to come with Lucy, so she couldn't be far behind.

Then he saw her. Her dark hair looked almost black, curled up, tied back with silver ribbons looping in and out and around her hair. The gown was silver; it pulled up over her shoulder like her patchwork dress had and fit her to perfection, then flared out at the bottom. She'd been caught by a few women complimenting her dress. When she turned, he could see the back. The fabric scooped low, it was silver and then it wasn't. It cascaded down and around to her toes in a flood of colours all strung together. When she faced him, the line of colour ran its way in a sliver up her shoulder before arcing down. If Lucy was made to look like a sunshine then Wynter was a bow breaking through the storm.

Ward's view of Wynter was blocked when Lady Cristelle stepped in front of him. She placed a hand on Ward's arm, drawing his attention for a moment. She glared at Lucy.

"It's not a Helix." Lucy bounced up and down in a fit of absolute glee. The other guests moved about the small group as if it was a normal occurrence to hear them bickering at a ball.

"So, you finally decided you needed to look half decent to catch a man. A little secret, they don't go for blubbering dolts either." Lady Cristelle rubbed her nose with the back of her hand and

244

tugged Ward. He tried to gently brush her off, but her nails dug into his jacket.

"Is that why you're still single?" Lucy said, after a disapproving look from Lady Daye.

"Am I?" Lady Cristelle responded. Taking Ward's arm, she pulled him toward the dance floor.

Ward kept his feet steady to avoid further embarrassment to either of them. He allowed Lady Cristelle to lead him out, hoping it would be a short song. He'd put off speaking to her and as far as he could tell the rumours were still in full swing.

The Ambassador had shown up, his voice carried across the room in a wave of chatter, and to Wards horror, was leading Wynter onto the dance floor. Ward remembered dancing with Wynter and was certain this wasn't a good idea. Even a common lady would know more steps than Wynter did.

"You need to stop staring at her. People are whispering," Lady Cristelle said.

"I thought you wanted people to whisper?" he replied. He felt bad that he was dancing with Lady Cristelle instead of Wynter. He'd promised her she'd feel safe at the ball, but now he was stuck on the floor with someone else.

Lady Cristelle stepped on his foot. Hard. He winced at the pinch under her heel. He was being horrible. Even if he had no intentions toward Lady Cristelle his behaviour didn't need to match hers.

"I'm sorry, you look lovely," he said dryly, catching whispers of them as a couple. How anyone believed it, he had no idea. Lady Cristelle must be feeding into the ridiculous rumours.

Her face soured at his compliment.

He made it through the dance and for Wynter's sake, tried not to watch her too closely. As the music slowed, he looked for Wynter again, but Lady Cristelle demanded more of his attention.

"We should talk outside and don't be so concerned. She's a grown woman. Nothing is going to happen to her in a room full of people while we talk."

He agreed. It had been a minor annoyance on his ship, but clearly everyone was watching them now. It was time to put an end to the gossip.

The music stopped, and he offered his arm, thankful he wouldn't have to have the conversation in front of the entire ballroom. They walked through the crowd, and he resisted the urge to look behind him. They must look like the most miserable couple, at least no one would be surprised when they found out the truth.

Thirty-Six

"I only know the three steps," Wynter told the Ambassador. She had refused, but somehow ended up on the dance floor with him anyway.

"It's easy. If I need you to step a foot back, I'll tap it like this." He brushed his hand against her leg, which startled her a little and it instinctively moved away from his touch.

"Lovely, and if I want you to turn, I'll just push you a little this way." He did, she turned. He was a superb dancer and walked around her feet, making it look like she knew what she was doing.

The Ambassador was cheerful. He stared at her intently and asked what ship she arrived on. When she didn't answer, he asked if she was from Orion. She murmured something about trying to focus on the steps, which he took as an invitation to talk more.

He commented three times on the beauty of her gown, and said that her hair looked like coal diamonds. Then he compared her dress to the fissure on the north point of Corva. She made the mistake of saying she didn't know what a fissure was, and he went to lengths to explain it.

The Ambassador had muscular arms under the layers of silk

and lifted her a few times so her toes were gliding above the floor. His hand pressed gently against her side, guiding her.

She blocked out the constant chatter so she could enjoy the moment as she'd promised herself she would. She was dancing at a ball. Only months ago, it was a dream, and now she was here.

She looked at the women, the dresses, and the gentlemen in their fine clothes as they moved around her. Everyone was just as she imagined, with long scarves and jewel-tipped head pieces.

They turned, and she could see Ward dancing with Lady Cristelle. Their heads were almost touching. Wynter looked away. They were beautiful together.

Wynter tried not to think about what it had been like dancing with him. Much clumsier.

At the end of the dance, she said she needed a refreshment and left the Ambassador, who was telling everyone within earshot he had danced with the stars and was eternally burned with the moment.

Lady Daye caught her eye and joined her at the drink table.

"Wait until they are out of sight, then take my arm. We'll grab some air together."

Lady Daye led Wynter across the gardens, away from the crowds and around the side of the castle. Off the heated paths, the air was still and ice cold and smelled like frost tickling the inside of her nose. Tucked behind a wall, they were out of sight.

"What if I hadn't been here? If I wasn't who you hoped I was?" Wynter asked as she increased the slits in her dress so that her legs could move freely.

"If you hadn't been here, then neither would I. I would be home on Valtine. If I could have done this any other way, I would have years ago." Lady Daye was standing in the shadow of one of the tall evergreen trees.

Wynter didn't like being used, but she heard the pain in Lady Daye's voice. So far, she hadn't lied to her. Wynter appreciated the honesty.

Wynter looked up the eight floors and was thankful her destination was only on the second floor. She gripped her fingers around large stones jutting out of the castle wall and started climbing up the jagged stonework. It wasn't far up, and the footholds were sturdy, but Wynter's fingers ached against the sharp edges of the stone. Hitting the ledge, she fumbled a bit as she pulled herself in through the open window.

The hall was empty, with a low glow of lights along the edge of the runners. Large pictures hung in the gallery like ghostly figures watching her.

She glided down the hall. At the end was a set of double doors. They were exactly as Lady Daye had described them; the curved iron handles looked like a warning, not an invitation. It was unlocked. Everything here was unlocked because if anyone came into this room, it would immediately trigger the Idex security.

She had the one thing Lady Daye needed: a way in undetected.

Wynter slipped into the room, lit only by the moonlight and decorative glowing orbs floating outside the windows, dancing in the gardens below. She'd prepared in her head what she would say if someone found her; she'd been overwhelmed or she'd gotten lost. Any number of excuses might work, as long as they didn't scan her for an Idex.

The room looked to be dusted regularly and cleaned, but vacant. There were no decorations on the desk, no sign of regular use.

Like Lady Daye said, there was a false bottom on the desk.

Wynter ran her fingers along it until she felt it click and something drop. The tray that had been the bottom of the drawer held a silver box the size of the old books in Dr Moss's office, but heavier. She turned it over in her hand, then tucked it under her arm and pushed the false bottom back into place.

Wynter held the box to her chest and hurried out of the room. She raced down the hall like a shadow and slipped back out the window. This was what made her dangerous. No one was even patrolling, no one suspecting anything. Because everyone had an Idex. She'd just confirmed everything Dr Moss had said she could be.

She didn't start breathing again until she was surrounded by the night air—feet planted firmly on the ground.

Wynter waited for Lady Daye to come out from her hiding place in the shadows.

"You could come with me," Lady Daye said, taking the package from Wynter, her voice shaking a little. "You could make quite the thief."

"No, thank you. Can I ask you a question?" Wynter asked. Lady Daye tilted her head to the side, "How did you know about Madame Helix and about me?"

Lady Daye wrapped her arms around her chest. The box she was holding was clearly very important to her, although Wynter still didn't know why.

"I knew Helix when we were girls. She went into the guilds while I was studying on Orion. We were young ladies and in love with the same man who was too old for either of us, not that it mattered." Lady Daye waved a hand around, as if the memories were fluttering around her. "I never would have given Helix enough creative credit to come up with those designs. When I looked closely, I saw a very distinct needles crest with a blue thread stitched into the gown. Something I knew she would never sew."

"You were both in love with Henris?" Wynter asked, confused, thinking about his fluffy white toes.

"No, no, dear, not Henris. A man named Domo." She ran her hands over the silver box she was holding.

"I've heard his name before. He died, didn't he?"

"Yes, he died saving you." There was ice in her voice. "But not right away. Henris brought him back to the shop but refused to call for help. Because they would take you away and they didn't know who to trust."

"Madame Helix blamed Henris." She'd heard as much of the story from the clockmaker.

"Yes, she blamed him for that and other things. And I blamed her. She was with Domo at Henris's shop when he died."

"Is there anyone who doesn't know I'm here?" Wynter threw her hands up in the air. What had been the point in all the hiding? It seemed like the only person she was hiding from was herself.

"Think for a moment, of all the people who do, and who aren't doing a damn thing to harm you. I never agreed with what they did, but you're here, and you've given me this." Tears pooled in the corner of Lady Daye's eye as she looked down at the box.

Wynter wanted to ask what was in it but knew she wouldn't tell. Just like she'd never told Ward about Henris. People who were used to hiding didn't know how to share secrets.

Lady Daye looked up from the box, her face like marble once again.

"I wouldn't have ruined your captain's career," she stated.

"I would have helped you either way," Wynter replied.

"Trust is funny, isn't it? Once broken, we're doomed to make the wrong choices," Lady Daye said, then turned and disappeared into the night.

Wynter let her skirts down, knowing she'd trusted all the wrong people and had failed to trust the one person she should have. She needed to tell Ward about Henris and about Helix. She hoped he would understand why she'd kept it a secret for so long.

Thirty-Seven

Ward and Lady Cristelle walked into the chilly evening air. She held her head high and smiled at other couples who walked by. The gardens were lush with low hedges on the main part, growing slowly taller as they walked on. Rose and pink dahlias bloomed in greenhouse globes. The heated path wound its way through ponds with blackened water.

Lady Cristelle sat down on a bench and patted the seat beside her, inviting him over like a child. The bench was warm with a half-moon cover. Unseasonal blooms grew up beside and around them, the ones on the edges turning brown from the frost.

"You are very unlike your uncle," she said, picking at the flowers. They had curled over the armrest and clung to the sides. She plucked one off and tossed it in front of her, then pressed it down with her toe.

"You knew my uncle?" Ward asked, thinking it was a strange way to start the conversation. There would have been very few occasions where a woman as young as her would have seen him.

"Yes, he loved to tell grand stories of the Obsidian and its freedom in space; not tied to woman or land," she said. "I was at the dinner the night he died. He was delightfully rude."

Lady Cristelle plucked another flower a little higher up, tossing it down as quickly as she'd spat out the information.

"When Lady Daye asked me to join you on your ship, I assumed you were like your uncle."

"Why did Lady Daye ask you to come on my ship?" Ward wasn't surprised, he knew there was something wrong with the whole thing.

"Bad blood with Madame Helix, I guess. She wanted me to get close by pretending I wanted a wedding gown. I don't know, it's all boring, but she promised me something in return. I just had to send her a message at the midway if her concerns were valid. It didn't turn out so bad. I got some fancy dresses out of it."

She picked another flower and added to the pile.

"So, you're pretending to be interested in order to spend time with Madame Helix? This whole farce was for a few dresses?" Ward felt the agitation in him growing. He knew Lady Cristelle hadn't been very interested in him, but she'd turned his ship into a gossip puddle. "Well whatever the reason for Lady Daye's involvement, Madame Helix won't be sewing anymore."

Lady Cristelle shrugged. "She's not the one who made my dresses. I spent weeks with Madame Helix; her and that Wynter are about as dense as rabbits. I know that ninny isn't sewing the dresses. Don't look at me like that, I won't tell anyone your precious secret."

Ward wondered just how much Lady Cristelle knew.

"I went to Inktons guild suppliers yesterday," she said changing the subject abruptly.

"It's quite extraordinary. I see why you'd taken an interest in it," Ward responded, hoping that his calm tone would draw out more information. But Lady Cristelle was being quite forthcoming all on her own.

"They were excited about the upcoming wedding," she said.

"Wedding?" he asked, she couldn't be serious about the rumours.

"They received notice from my father. It pleased him his eldest was making a match. You know I have four younger sisters. There's no reason for me to marry a captain, but for you it would tie your ship to a land insurance and would increase its value tenfold. If you weren't a lord with a mother with an Idex unlike many on Valtine, he never would have considered me to be a captain's wife." She shook her head, the curled ringlets bouncing.

"I'll take the fault for the miscommunication and advise the perfumery in the morning," Ward said. With all the rumours, he knew it would be a letdown for everyone on the ship, especially Rane, but they couldn't have expected it to happen.

"You didn't even try to get a proposal from me," Lady Cristelle pouted.

"I tried… or I really thought about trying." He shrugged. He really had thought about it.

"Lord Isaac—"

"Captain Ward," he corrected her. And then he realized what she was doing. He wanted to stop it before it happened, but she said the words.

"I was wondering if you'd do me the honour of marrying me and joining the perfume empire and give me daughters to inherit all of it."

He sat stunned for a moment, feeling a little like the petals under her shoe.

"Is it because your father thinks it a good idea? Is marriage what you want?" he asked, hoping she'd say no.

She faltered for a moment and looked up to the stars.

"Yes?" she suggested, like she was expecting something, but there was a look of sadness behind her smile. "We won't do unwell together. We could mostly leave each other alone, and I think *that* would suit me very well." She pulled another flower off and crumpled it in her hands, letting the petals fall beside them.

He picked up the crushed petal and smoothed it out, causing little pieces to break off, then pressed it flat on the seat.

"If you were free, what would you do?" he asked instead of answering.

"What do you mean? I'm heiress to vast land on Valtine, and our guild investments rival all other exports," she said, her back straight and her tone sharp.

"If you weren't? If you could do whatever you wanted, not what your Idex coding said you were born to do? What would you do with your freedom?"

"Those kinds of questions are meant for dreamers. Don't tell me you're a dreamer *Captain* Ward."

He took her hand, feeling a moment of pity for her.

"Will you answer the question?"

She looked at the hand holding hers, then up at Ward staring him straight in the eyes.

"No, because I know what answer you'd give me if I asked the same question. If you were free, you'd take her."

She pulled her hand back from his.

"It's not what you think—" he started, but she scoffed.

"I know it's not what everyone thinks. I saw you. I saw you in the greenhouse. I saw you when she came to your rooms. I saw you watching her tonight. I know it's not what everyone thinks, but it is what I think, isn't it? It's love. But love doesn't exist for us. You can't marry a seamstress, so talk of freedom is useless, and I know what else she is. If you did this, your mother would disown you, and you'd never be allowed to set foot on Valtine again without risking marring the Idex of everyone you love. You might think her unique or special, but I promise you the rest of the world will see her as worthless."

He leaned back and ran his hand through his hair. It was the same warning Rane had given. It was one thing to delay tying a ship to land but having Wynter in his life meant giving up his status as lord in order to protect his families Idex.

The night was getting cooler. All other couples had made their way back inside.

"You're not going to marry me, are you? Won't my father be so pleased with me. Perhaps you are a little like your uncle." And then she got up, stepping on all the delicate flowers, and left him sitting there alone.

He took a few minutes to process everything she'd said. Lady Daye had put her on the ship, knowing Helix wasn't the one sewing dresses. Bad blood? What would she gain from Lady Cristelle's presence in the Helix suites? It probably had something to do with Lady Daye's fast trip to Orion, but the truth was hidden underneath a pile of secrets.

As Lady Cristelle walked away from him, he realized one thing. Tying his ship to land would give one more person control. He knew then he was not nothing like his uncle; he was exactly like his uncle. No one was going to tell him what he needed to do with his ship.

When he finally returned to the ball, whispers followed him at every turn. And for the first time in his life, he didn't care.

Thirty-Eight

Wynter returned to the party, careful to take small steps so her skin wouldn't show too far up her bare leg. She watched the dancers spin around the room, picked some sweets from the table and something she thought should be sweet but was actually quite tart. She washed it down with a bit of light rose. The Ambassador hadn't asked her to dance again, and she'd successfully said no to all the other men. It was enough to just be here. To be a part of it.

Ripples of gossip ran through the ballroom. She caught bits of it, but whatever it was, it was about Lady Cristelle and Ward. They had been out in the garden. Lady Daye had assured her he'd be distracted and not looking for her, but had failed to mention what that distraction would be.

The looks and the whispers meant something else had happened. Had they finally announced the engagement then? She knew eyes were on her, speculating.

The words *engagement* slid around her, and she tried to smile and pretend like she didn't know what was happening, which she really didn't.

Lady Cristelle had already made her way around the room,

looking radiant and whispering in anyone's ear who would listen. Ward came in a few minutes later, a pained smile on his lips.

She slunk around the side of the room as the orchestra started another set. It was her first ball, but she wanted to leave, to be invisible again.

Before she could clear the pillared arches at the edge of the ballroom, Helix entered, taking long strides right in her direction.

A lump rose in Wynter's throat, and all bravery left her.

"There she is!" Helix said to the two guards beside her, who were quickly joined by Alarik.

"Explain yourself!" Alarik said in a hushed tone to Helix. "We were informed of the guild decision to strip you of your standing. Being here is a direct breach of that order."

Helix stood confidently, unconcerned with Alarik's warning.

"I think you'll reconsider your stance. The woman you've been keeping in the castle is a murderer," she accused.

The room stilled, and the music halted with the commotion of everyone trying to get close enough to see what was going on.

"And I can prove it." Helix stepped forward, pulling hard on the chain around Wynter's neck causing it to pull her hair and snap. Helix held it between her fingers and let it dangle. The crowd took in an audible gasp even though none of them knew what it meant.

"Alarik, what's going on?" Ward stepped in front of Wynter, blocking her from the guards at the door.

"We need to move this out of the ballroom now," Alarik started, walking toward them. "I need Wynter to come with us."

Her heart was pounding and her hands sweaty.

"I haven't hurt anyone." She tried to defend herself, but everyone was talking at once.

Alarik was trying to move them out of the ballroom and cued the musicians to start up again, which did very little to disperse the growing crowd.

"She killed one of your most respected guild members and wore his chain as a trophy!" Helix said louder. "I only found out when the body was being taken off the Obsidian and put it together. I've been lied to all these years."

"Captain, do you recognize the necklace?" Alarik asked, still trying to move the whole mess out of the ballroom. Ward shook his head, but Wynter could tell he was lying. He'd seen it at the Tailor shop.

Ward's face changed. Not angry or confused, just sad. Like everything was coming together in his head, but in all the wrong ways.

"The lady was seen down at his shops," the guard beside Helix said.

"Henris's shop? I know, I brought her!" Ward defended her, but she knew the time she went with Ward was not what they were talking about. She wished she'd told him everything, she wished now she'd had him accompany her to talk with the clockmaker.

"You brought her in the middle of the night?" The guard asked again. Alarik had pushed two of the guards out into the halls, trying to make the rest follow.

"No. I…" Ward was rooted in place and looked devastated. Wynter fought to find the words to say.

"I wanted to tell you." Wynter reached out for his hands, the way he'd always reached out for hers.

"You were going to tell me you killed Henris? You knew who he was the whole time?" He swallowed down the last words.

260

"No, I didn't! It was Madame Helix. She—"

"We need to move this out now," Alarik said, refusing to allow the scene to continue. His voice bellowed in the room, no longer trying to be quiet. Everyone moved at the same time. He nodded to his guards, who escorted Helix out. She smiled smugly at Wynter.

She'd designed the dress Helix was wearing. She'd done it for nothing.

Wynter felt numb.

A guard came over and gently took her arm to escort her from the ballroom. If she could get past him and run... but she was being ushered out, accused of murder.

They were in the hallway when Lucy caught up to them. She pushed past the guard, who stopped as she blocked the way.

"What is going on?"

"Lucy, you need to go back to your room," Alarik said sternly.

"I don't care what she's done," Lucy said. Alarik ignored her and continued to usher Wynter away from the prying eyes in the hallway. She wanted to call out to Lucy, but the words wouldn't form. All the practising what she would say in a bad situation, if she ever got caught, and none of them came to her.

Looking from one to the other, hope fled, leaving a vast space. Alarik said something to a guard, and they split her from the rest of the group.

Her heart was hammering. She hadn't killed Henris, but it would be impossible to prove.

Without an Idex code, she didn't have any way to prove it wasn't her.

Thirty-Nine

Ward took his coat off and crumpled it over his arm, holding it close to his side. His hands were balled into tight fists. Ward had remembered the crest and the look on her face. She'd known. Had she been running away? She would have only been a young girl, maybe twelve years old?

He ran his hand through his hair. He wasn't sure where Alarik was taking them. He noticed when Wynter was led down another hall. She didn't struggle against the guards, which was good. He wanted to follow her but knew his best chance of helping her was to stay with Alarik.

They reached a large office room at the end of a long hallway on the main floor. Tall black pillars lined the outside of the room. The back wall was stone, ground down and polished flat. The air felt thin and un-lived in. A long desk with three chairs was in the middle of the room, additional seats in pairs circled the outside.

Helix pulled one of the chairs and sat down, a smug smile on her face, tapping her foot on the floor.

The room slowly filled with various guests he'd seen during the ball. Alarik called Ward over to the desk.

"Helix said this was in Wynter's personal items on the ship." Alarik pushed a small metal tin toward Ward. He opened it and inside were two very small vials with a green translucent liquid. He closed the lid and looked at Helix. Something was incredibly off about the entire story. Wynter had only said she'd been put on the ship in a crate, not how she'd ended up with Helix. Wynter couldn't have done it on her own, if she'd been involved at all. What had she been trying to say about Helix before they took her away?

Alarik was talking quietly to two other men, three more joined them, each from the ball wearing long tasseled scarves in various colours. Guild heads and those married to landowners, by the looks of it. They whispered in the corner while Ward paced from one end of the room to the other. He knew they had a way of dealing with things on Orion, but he didn't like it.

They should involve him in the conversation, but he didn't have a solid reason to give them why.

Alarik looked at Ward a few times, then came over to him while the others continued their private conversation.

"She's just a seamstress," Ward said to Alarik. Alarik's face showed no emotion, like stone.

"The guilds have unilaterally decided *your* innocence in the matter, having recently inherited the ship. However, a captain is required to have full command. We suggest you finish loading the Obsidian and leave Orion as soon as possible."

"No." The word came out of his mouth before he could stop it. He pressed down on each knuckle, trying to calm himself.

"It wasn't a request. I'm doing you a favour by letting you get out of here with your Idex and your ship contracts intact. This is a guild matter. We don't need a captain's interference." Alarik was still calm and even.

"Ship contracts? She's not coming back on my ship." He pointed at Helix. He had no idea where she'd been for the week and why she'd chosen to show up, at a ball and accuse Wynter.

"Also a guild matter, and one you have little control over unless you want to break contracts with every guild on Orion."

"Maybe I do." He knew he was being irrational. "Wynter's just a seamstress," he said again. His seamstress. He knew he shouldn't think that way, but he felt responsible. Dr Moss had warned him that he was a danger to Wynter, he just hadn't believed that he was.

"And we intend to treat her as such. We feel there is no one but innocent people left in the matter from twenty years ago, and there is nothing to gain from dragging anything out."

"You're going to bury it then? Keep your secrets? What happens to Wynter? Does she even get a fair trial?" Ward's voice was wavering. They would bury it, so that those with superior Idex codes wouldn't have a reason to question the strength of the guild. Always the same battle.

"She'll be kept safe," Alarik assured him.

"What? Safe and hidden, like she always has been. Hiding is not living."

"She killed a man," Alarik stated.

"Says who? The very woman who's been hiding her for years? She shows up just as she's about to lose everything. She doesn't even look concerned. You're not even going to look into it, are you?"

"Inktons has agreed for your silence in this matter, they could write a contract," Alarik said.

Ward knew it wasn't meant as an insult, but he couldn't help but take it like a low payoff. He was being paid to look the other way. He took one last look around the room and left.

The party had ended, but guests had moved the conversation into halls and private rooms.

He thought of going back to Henris's shop, or to find Lucy, who might know where they were keeping Wynter. But there was one person who had information he hadn't shared. He needed to talk to Dr Moss. The only way to meet with Dr Moss was to go back up to his ship.

Taking his private shuttle back up, he docked on the Obsidian where he was met by Rane. He looked like he'd slept as little as Ward had.

"I don't want a single shipment from Inktons brought onto the Obsidian."

"Sir?" Rane asked. "They forwarded up a contract."

"Cancel it."

"Are you certain? You won't get another opportunity."

"You might not want to stay on after this. We might not have many opportunities." He needed Rane, but it wasn't fair to ask him to stay on with a sinking ship.

"I'm with you," Rane said and patted him on the back.

"I thought you were set on me securing the ship to land?" Ward questioned.

"Forgive me, I thought it was best, and that you might need a certain level of credibility for your ship," Rane said.

"You don't think I need that now?" Ward asked, knowing Rane had every reason to believe he wouldn't have been able to manage the ship on his own.

"I think you'll do just fine. Hopefully you're prepared for what's next."

"Wait, what's next?" He turned around, right into Dr Moss's fist.

"You let her go to a ball! You paraded her in front of all of them? I told you to keep her on the ship." Dr Moss had Ward by the shirt and looked like he was going to punch him again. Ward winced at the sore jaw but felt he hadn't taken the full brunt of Dr Moss's strength. At least, not yet.

"Where is she?" he growled.

"She's in holding right now, but I'm going to figure out—"

Rane cleared his throat. Dr Moss swore at him. "While you were on your way up, a notice came to the ship's security. Wynter has disappeared. You were only cleared because you'd left before."

"She's gone?" Ward asked.

This time, Ward swore and rubbed his face. He wondered if Alarik would still refuse to do anything or if he was involved in the timely disappearance. He wasn't going to wait to find out.

"She'll be impossible to track, no one knows who even took her," Rane said.

"I might be able to help with that, but this is *your* fault. I told you to leave her alone," Dr Moss said to Ward. "If I help, I want immunity on your ship when this is all done."

Ward stood toe-to-toe with Dr Moss, his heart beating in a thundering rhythm. Dr Moss knew who would have Wynter, knew why Orion hadn't been a safe place to send her. He had no idea what he was granting immunity from, but it didn't matter— not if he could help get Wynter back.

"You help us now, and I'll give you immunity on my ship," Ward confirmed.

"But, sir—" Rane protested, Ward held up a hand silencing

him.

"To be clear, I'm helping her, not you," Dr Moss said, then told Ward why he'd never left the ship.

Forty

The room they gave her was small for the castle but large to Wynter. The narrow bed was covered with a striped silver and red blanket. Pretty lights hung from high ceilings. There was a separate bathroom and a little desk with a few books stacked on it. It was more than she had on the Obsidian.

There was no window, but a secured door locked from the outside. Feeling the cold of the stone beneath her feet and the mountain closing in, she knew she preferred the emptiness of space.

It was too quiet.

* * *

Without a window, she had no idea what time it was or how much had passed. There were three rapid knocks on the door. Wynter waited for it to open, wishing it was Ward and knowing it would be unlikely.

Instead, it was the Ambassador with a wide smile on his face. He had a black cape draped over his arm.

"We need to hurry. Did you know guards are required to answer specific calls no matter their position? It was easy to get them away, but I fear they're going to be back," he said.

He didn't step inside but motioned her forward.

"It's okay, let's go." He looked down the hall and back again.

"Why are you here?" she asked, slipping on the silver shoes Lucy had loaned her. They only had the slightest hint of a heal and had been fine for dancing, but now they were too tight and rubbed against her ankles.

"A little jail break. Your friend Lucy is waiting for you." He hurried her out and put the black cloak over her shoulders. A lot of good it would do. The halls were well lit, even without windows, but she was thankful for something other than just her dress.

"Lucy? But she thinks I killed someone."

"She also thinks you had a good reason. She knew, as an ambassador, she could trust me with these things."

She looked down the hall, wishing she could leave a note for Ward, tell him she hadn't done it.

They were in the lower part of the castle. Down three stone steps with black carpets lining each step. The halls were clean and well lit, but no windows to help her get her bearings. At the end of the hall was a single door. The Ambassador put in another code, and it opened for them, closing quickly behind. It was cooler, and she tucked the cloak around her. It felt as if they were going down as the rocks changed in colour the farther they went. She wished she had her black shoes.

"They used these tunnels for years as a way for people to escape. There were wars at one time on Orion. Can you imagine a place like this being at war?" He laughed to himself.

They went through another door and another set of halls looking more and more like tunnels.

"Why would Lucy be down here?" she asked, stopping. They'd travelled quite far.

"She's waiting on the other side of the mountain, just a little further. But I'm going to take you away—save you." He grabbed her wrist and pulled on it, tugging her close.

"I want to go back. I didn't do anything wrong. I should go back." Panic gripped the back of her throat.

"Like a dance, did you know the viceroy would hold balls back in the day to dance with his enemies, to look them in the eye—"

"Enemies? I'm not…" But something in the way he was looking at her changed, or maybe she was finally seeing it.

"Did you know when you talk all the time people stop listening to what you're saying? They will say things they never would have meant to otherwise."

She turned around, but right into two other men who'd come out of a tunnel behind her.

One reached out to grab her arm, but she spun and slid under him. Trying to fit between the other and the side of the wall, she was blocked. Going back the other way, she was grabbed around the waist and pulled back.

"Shhh, you're too pretty to be so upset, dear. Did you know women who hold land or other qualities are highly revered? I'm not going to hurt you, so come with us, won't you? No more fighting. Jac you might want to watch—"

Wynter bit down hard on the man's arm. He yelled and released her, but the Ambassador grabbed a pile of her curls and pulled hard. She screamed, the pain bringing tears to her eyes. One hand holding her curls to her head, she reached out with the other trying to push him away, but without much control she skidded and slipped until a large arm around her waist lifted her feet off the ground. She tried kicking but had nothing to push off.

The last door opened, and fresh air hit them. Sunlight crept over the trees and was spilling into the small clearing. She was dropped onto the rocky ground. Her head hurt, her side hurt, her wrists hurt. She wanted to run, but they were closed in as far as she could see.

There was a small shuttle, similar to the one she'd been on when Ward brought her down. A side panel opened with four seats along the edge. One of the other men who the Ambassador had been calling Rubio had opened it and was already inside.

Jac was rubbing his arm where she'd bitten down and glaring at her. The group of three men became four as they were joined by another. She heard his voice and tried not to look up, tried not to react.

"You three are worse than Captain Ward," he laughed, his voice deep and rumbled around the rocks.

"Somes? Is that you, old man? What are you doing here?" Jac said. Reaching out they clasped hands, Jac winced and covered the bite mark.

"Watch the bite," he said, pulling his hand back. "Wow, you haven't aged a day. Well, not as bad as Rubio has."

She heard a grumble and some cusses from inside the shuttle.

"Good to see you, old friend. When did you pick up an Ambassador?" Dr Moss looked at the Ambassador, the two of them stared each other down.

"You weren't much of a friend on the Obsidian." The Ambassador had narrowed his eyes and was staring at Dr Moss.

"I haven't had much contact with these two in the past twenty years. How would I know? Didn't even know who she was until it was almost too late. Now that we have her, what's the plan?"

They looked between them, hesitating. The Ambassador shook his head, clearly not trusting Dr Moss.

"Don't forget, gentlemen," Dr Moss spat the word. "I lost twenty years because this one got away."

Wynter realized they hadn't called him Moss. It was something else. Somes?

"She was under your nose half the time, and you never knew."

"She's good at hiding." Dr Moss looked at her for the first time.

She wasn't good at hiding; they were just terrible at seeing. Sitting up, she looked around the clearing, but the trees were still. He'd known she'd been there since the first day. "Besides, it's a good life up on the Obsidian."

"But you came down."

"Sent her down to you. Left all the breadcrumbs you needed. I only came to get my share. You don't think you're going to take her without giving me my cut? She wouldn't even exist without me."

Wynter had wondered... pushed the thought down, didn't want to think about it... but he'd just confirmed it. Dr Moss had been involved in the experiments, the ones that had given her life.

"Fine. I assume you're still skimming past the Idex coding?" Jac said.

"I am," the man she knew as Dr Moss confirmed.

"How did you find us?" the Ambassador asked.

"I knew who I was looking for."

Wynter looked from Dr Moss to Jac, who shrugged. "Doesn't matter much either way where we're going," he said, making his way to the shuttle.

"We don't have time for this. Bring him along and we'll sort it out after," Rubio called from the ship.

"Ready for boarding," Dr Moss said as he jumped onto the shuttle. The Ambassador had an iron grip on her arm. If Dr Moss was there to help her, he hadn't done a very good job of helping her get away.

The morning light lit up the sky behind them in a blaze of red. They took off from behind the mountain that hid the castle and into the morning sky.

Forty-One

After crossing an endless amount of water with loops and double backs, they'd finally reached an oil rig. Dr Moss had said nothing. Arms folded, he leaned back against the metal hull. The Ambassador hadn't stopped talking and prattled on about shuttle technology, the speed, the types of shuttles, how many have malfunctioned in the past six years.

Jac and Rubio whispered from the cockpit and looked back at them from time to time until they'd reached the oil rig.

Wynter tried to wrap the black cloak and slits of fabric around her. They walked across the oil rig platform, the icy brush of wind like needles through the cloth.

The outer shell was painted light blue, its low lights cast shadows and blinked against the setting sun. Above the platform was a series of cabins all stacked on top of each other with little doors, thin railed balconies, and stairs. She looked down into one of the open hatches. The spiral stairs descended into the depths below.

"They shut this one down last year. There was a potential leak at the base, and it needed to be inspected. How fortunate for us it never got done," the Ambassador yelled over the wind, unable to stop talking even when they could barely hear him.

Wynter was grateful when they stepped through a heavy metal door away from the cold. The exterior had looked weather beaten, once inside, out of the wind, it wasn't much better. Hallways looked like they'd been repainted a hundred times, with chips of paint peeling off in small chunks. The air felt damp and smelled like the salty sea and frozen metal.

The hallway opened to a large room that reminded her of the lounges on the Obsidian; except it was nearly empty. There were white tables bolted to the floor and red chairs scattered around, and clustered together in little groupings.

Wynter sat on one of the red chairs and folded her hands to keep them from shaking.

She kept herself quiet. Not looking anyone in the eye or down at the floor.

Blank.

A ghost.

Inside, her blood felt thick as it pumped through her heart, each beat heavier than the last. She was trying not to panic, wondering how many more she had.

I'm not alone, she reminded herself without looking up.

Dr Moss was there. She didn't look at him. If she did, she knew her face would display what she was feeling.

Betrayed, hurt, confused, hopeful.

If he was there, then maybe Ward wasn't far off, or maybe he'd always planned this.

Jac and Rubio were talking in hushed tones by one of the dirty windows. Then they left, leaving the three of them in the room alone.

"So, are we going to sit here for the next two years?" Dr Moss asked.

"No, Jac and Rubio are securing the platform. We hadn't counted on another member in our little party. I don't think they like you. And if you were wondering, there are no Idex scans on this platform. No one will find us out here."

"No one likes me. I don't think they like you either. If you were wondering, I've been bypassing the Idex systems for twenty years —not worried about it now."

Wynter pushed her toe against the peeling paint. Twenty years he'd stayed on the ship. So maybe he hadn't bypassed all of them, only the ones on the ship. But it wouldn't matter much. If Ward was tracking Dr Moss's Idex, it wouldn't do them any good.

"I heard they called you Dr Somes. You're in my files, you know, the ones I could get. The closed ones. You are supposed to be dead." The Ambassador licked his bottom lip like he'd tasted something a little too sweet.

"Yup, buried under a mountain with the medical labs and everything in them. How'd you get those files? You couldn't have been more than a boy when it happened."

"I was young, not as young as you might think. Jac and Rubio, you see, were there and didn't have the luxury of disappearing. If one ounce of evidence shows up, which I think includes you, Dr Somes, those files open and everyone knows who they are. But since it was all turned to rubble…"

"So they had you just watching some files hoping something would turn up? A bit tedious for an ambassador don't you think?" Dr Moss had gotten up and was looking out the window. His shoulders were relaxed and calm, but Wynter could see the way he was scanning the platform as the Ambassador talked.

The Ambassador pulled up a chair across from Wynter, staring at her downcast eyes.

"Oh yes, but I'm good at digging." He spoke to her directly. "Rubio really didn't expect me to find you after all these years. I don't think they know what to do with you. But I was watching for a file on a Mr Henris Canmore. Jac thought he was getting close to something seven years ago, to you, to him, and then Henris disappeared, practically into thin air."

"How did you find me?" Wynter asked. The Ambassador clapped his hands together and smiled cruelly.

"Your captain, of course. What a useless man. On Valtine, he opened a file on a person of interest. Very interesting. It sat dormant for seven years, never filed properly, floating out in space with no name. All it took was for your captain to attach the ID in our Idex system. Funny, a ship's doctor should have tagged it years ago."

"Not the first body I didn't tag properly," Dr Moss responded to the insinuation.

The ghost pranks had triggered Ward to look into getting the body off his ship. Not just a body, Henris.

Wynter thought of the morning she'd arrived on the Obsidian. The Helix crates were the first unloaded along with the other guild crates. Helix didn't know what she'd started when she'd killed Henris, and Dr Moss didn't know what he'd stopped by not properly tagging the body. Both had kept her safe.

She watched the wind churn up the waters beyond the rigging.

Wynter wanted to rewrite history. If Henris had turned her in to the Viceroy when she was a baby, or if he'd just confronted these men back then, he might be alive. If he hadn't kept her hidden, all of these men would have been punished for their crimes.

She didn't want to hide anymore.

She wanted to fight.

"What do you get out of this? You weren't there," Dr Moss said lazily, as if it didn't even matter.

The Ambassador leaned in close. Wynter shuddered at the way he looked at her and went back to picking at the paint, trying to figure out how she was going to get out of there, but her mind swam and jumped from thought to thought.

"I get to keep her. I came all the way to Orion to guarantee it." He moistened his lips and Wynter shuddered. "Did you know your children won't have an Idex code?" he asked. He reached out to put a hand on her leg. "I can't imagine the freedom. I have places like this on every planet. And yet I can't get into where I want without detection because of some little coding I was born with. I didn't ask for it. And yet there it all is." He drew a blade across his hand and bits of blood sprinkled out. He shook it on the floor. "All of it. Every place I've been. I can look up my ancestors' Idex. Everything is there. Every time I walk through one of those doors, my life is there. I love seeing mine displayed. It's impeccable. But my perfection can't be passed on. My deeds are basically useless. But what about you? You are nothing. You are less than me in every way. Do you know what people would pay to be nothing?"

He stared down at his red hand watching the blood pool a little then closed his fist. "Do you think it would work if I took out your blood and put it in mine? I heard it doesn't, but I want to try. Maybe we can try the blood first."

"You think Jac and Rubio are going to let you keep the one piece of evidence who could put them away for life? I doubt it."

Dr Moss sounded so calm. Wynter wanted to scream at him to do something.

"I've paid them very well. So if you want her dead, they won't help you."

"Oh no, I don't want her dead. I could have killed her myself. I want her, same as you. You clearly don't know the first thing about medical Idex other than what you've read in your reports, which I imagine are very sparse since it's illegal. I'm the only one who's been able to effectively manipulate it. No Ambassador, I want to be your partner. I think it odd you trust those two. Where are they anyway? Do you hear a ship?"

The Ambassador looked between Wynter and Dr Moss. She stared straight across, trying to look frozen in fear, which she was.

"I'll prove to you my wealth is worth more than my death." The Ambassador got up, showing no signs he was concerned about being double crossed.

"Aren't you worried I'll kill her?" Dr Moss called after him.

"No, because then you'd be dead. There's nothing but metal and lights on this rig for a thousand miles."

He left, closing the door behind him.

Metal and lights.

A single thought cleared out all the others.

Blinking lights. The oiling rig couldn't be much different from a ship. It had to have a control room and a way of signalling to anyone out on the water. She let out a gasp and jumped to her feet.

"Where would a control room be?" Wynter asked, pushing any doubts about Dr Moss aside. If he'd wanted her dead, he would have killed her years ago and left the ship.

Lady Daye's words came back to her, once trust is broken, we always make the wrong choices. Dr Moss was probably the wrong choice, but it was the only one she had.

"Control room?" he asked, his brows knit together "It wasn't supposed to go like this. Your captain was supposed to show up with Alarik or someone before we got on a shuttle. I wasn't expecting them to move you so fast."

"Why didn't you do more to stall? Never mind. The control room—can you get me there?"

"It would be one of the highest rooms overlooking the whole rig. I can't get you there, but I can make a path for you. You sure you know what you're doing?"

She nodded. He went to the door, opened it, but Jac and Rubio were already waiting. Dr Moss barrelled into both men, knocking them down. She could hear the fight behind her, but she didn't look back. She ran, her feet scraping on the cold metal floor.

Up the metal stairs, a blast of cold air hit her from an opening. She ran past it and into another hallway, then continued her climb. At the end of the hallway was an open door, she could see the long control tables overlooking the lower decks of the rig, like the Obsidian towering over the hull of the ship.

She knew she didn't have long. Sprinting to the control panel, she searched for the lighting codes. It wasn't exactly like the ship. She closed her eyes, remembering the conversation in the hallway. The crew planning the prank. Finding the right panel, she typed in #B784A7.

The rig lit up a glorious mauve.

Winter heard footsteps in the hall and turned just as Jac appeared in the opening. She had never learned to fight, Henris was not much of a fighter. She couldn't let him turn off the lights, not yet. Without thinking, she ran at him and swung wildly, her fist making contact with his jaw. She staggered back as blinding pain flashed through her fingers; it felt as if every bone was broken, and tears stung her eyes. The punch had stunned Jac enough to knock him off balance. She rushed at him again dropping her shoulder into his chest while cradling her hand. The impact knocked her assailant off his feet but not before he had pulled out a long knife and swung it at her, catching her leg as she passed.

She screamed, reaching to stop the blade as it ripped into her leg catching her scar and pulling down. Her head swam as she kicked wildly. She could tell it wasn't super deep but deep enough. She lost balance and fell to her knees. She desperately kicked behind with her good leg, catching Jac in the side of the head. He went down again. She struggled to her feet and limped out of the room leaving a trail of blood behind her. Stopping to lean against the wall, she stretched her bruised hand to make sure her fingers would work and tore a strip from her dress to tie around her leg to stop the bleeding. The red was already seeping into the coloured bit of fabric but at least it wasn't dripping or leaving a trail.

She limped down the hall, turning the corner she ducked into what looked like a galley kitchen. There was nothing but long tables, ovens, and cupboards. She silently tried to pull on one drawer after the other, but they were all locked. No knives or pots or utensils of any kind were accessible to her. She limped around the room, then sat on the floor behind the long island. Pulling open the end door, she was relieved to find the cupboard under the sink was unlocked. She squeezed her body into the space, trying to not think of how small it was. She tucked the cloak around herself and closed her eyes.

If she could just stay hidden, just long enough for Ward to find her. The minutes ticked by. Every second she felt hope Ward might find her and fear that Jac would first.

After what felt like forever, footsteps clicked on the kitchen floor, coming towards her. The cupboard door opened, and a cold hand grabbed her arm. She screamed as Jac pulled her out, trying to kick, he dragged her back down the hallway. She let her body go limp, surprising him, and he lost his grip for a moment. Before she could get away, he grabbed her by the calf, the makeshift bandage coming off.

Back in the control room, he threw her against the desk, her ribs and side taking the impact. She dropped to her knees, screaming for the pain to stop. She curled up on the floor waiting for the next blow to come, but it didn't. She looked around for Dr Moss and Rubio, but it was only Jac and the Ambassador.

"You idiot!" Jac shouted at the Ambassador, rubbing his bruised cheek. "We hired you to keep our secrets. It was a simple arrangement. Turn these lights off!"

"I don't know how," said the Ambassador. "Did you know there are over sixteen million colour combinations and—"

Wynter screamed as Jac took out his long blade and ran it across the Ambassador's neck. His eyes grew wide as his hand reached up, soaked with blood. The blood ran between his fingers as the life left his body, and he fell to the floor. She closed her eyes. She needed to fight; she needed to do something.

He pulled her body up to standing, the metal blade tip set gently on her neck.

"Turn the lights off," Jac said to her, just above a whisper.

She reached for the panel and took a breath. She knew the moment she turned them off she'd be dead, but if she didn't...

Forty-Two

"We should keep Alarik informed." Rane wouldn't look up from the screens he was flipping through. They stood on the bridge, looking out over the front of the Obsidian. The ship's sleek exterior melted into the surrounding blackness.

"I already contacted Alarik," Ward replied. He knew Rane was still hoping to get the Inkton cargo, but that ship had already sailed. What they were doing went directly against what Alarik and the guilds had told him to do. He didn't care. He had to find her.

Rane stood still, mouth open, then he closed it.

"If you tell me she's not my responsibility, you can get off the Obsidian."

"No, sir. Yes, sir." Rane went back to flipping through the screens.

There simply wasn't enough time. Waiting for the guilds was like waiting for the mountains to thaw, and so Dr Moss went down to Orion on the hunch that he knew two of the men who might be involved. It was a long shot and so Ward had stayed with the Obsidian.

Dr Moss sent up vital information before he also disappeared. Wynter had been found, along with two other men and the Ambassador, which was surprising. Ward didn't know what the Ambassador could be doing there and thought back to the Idex scanner and conversations. Had the Ambassador been looking for Wynter the whole time?

"Sir, Viceroy Alarik just responded, the shuttles up to outer ships have been flagged, they won't be able to get off the planet." Rane informed him.

"Great, only an entire planet of mountains and deserts and frozen poles...." Grumbling came from the front of the room where crew had gathered to run land scans and Idex tracking. It was like finding a speck of dust in a meteor shower.

With three ships in orbit, all carrying cargo and passengers plus Orion guilds who'd travelled from other islands on the planet, there were just too many ships.

His ship locked on and scanned each one, but it was likely they were already docked somewhere, hiding.

Negative reports were coming in from every area.

"There are mountain tunnels and oil rigs in every part of the ocean. There's no way we can narrow it down." Rane was saying what everyone on the bridge was already thinking, what Alarik had told him. It was impossible. Alarik said he'd send out some shuttles and watch for the Idex for Dr Moss-Somes.

"Sir? I don't even know what we're looking for," said one of the younger engineers. There was a nod of heads.

"Anything unusual. If it looks like a good hiding place or—"

"Or an oil rig glowing purple?" One of the engineers from the front stood up and passed Rane the screen.

"That's her! Rane, tell Alarik... tell him anything—I don't

care," Ward said then he addressed the bridge. "Rane has control of the ship until I return. Primary crew is required to stay. Come with me if you can. It's not an order."

He had no idea if he would be going in alone, but as his own shuttle dropped into space, he took an arc around the Obsidian and saw the other shuttles dropping beside him.

He broke through the planet's atmosphere feeling as though everything inside him was going to explode.

When they got to the rig it was still lit in various shades of purple. The long deck was abandoned. His crew were fast behind him. They formed in groups of three and fanned out over the deck.

Ward didn't know if he should go down into the opening that sunk into the sea or to check the tower of rooms on the far end.

"Over here!" Ward heard one of his crew members call from through the icy wind from the living quarters. Ward ran toward them.

Dr Moss was slumped against the wall, pushing the crew member away from him and trying to stand. "She went to the control rooms!" he shouted at Ward. "She hasn't come back down."

Ward rushed past him taking the metal stairs two at a time, quickly scanning abandoned rooms as he went.

A scream sliced through the empty hall, echoing off the walls. He was on the top floor when he saw the trail of blood from the kitchens to the control room and sprinted toward the open door.

Wynter, he had to find her. He had told her she'd be safe, and he'd failed her. He followed the blood to the control room.

Ward could see Wynter leaning over the desk, a man as big as Alarik coming at her with a bloodied knife. Ward ignored the body of the Ambassador and charged the man, hitting his hand and dislodging the weapon. It fell to the ground. He kicked it away as a strong arm came around his neck. Bits of stars and darkness crept into the corner of his eyes, he tried to look for Wynter, to tell her to run. Shouts from his crew distracted the man and he loosened his grip. Ward slipped out of the big man's arm as a dozen of his crew joined the fight. It took enough of them to restrain his attacker.

Ward crawled over to where Wynter had crouched under the control desk, her eyes wide and body shaking. She was holding her leg, her hands covered in blood. He slid under the desk, wrapped his arms around her and let her rest her head on his shoulder.

"I'm sorry. I should have told you, but I didn't do—"

"It's okay," Ward said. "Hold still. We're going to get some help."

Ward helped move her onto the medical float gurney when it arrived, holding onto her leg where the blood was coming from. It had soaked through the thin strips of material and covered his hands. Her eyes had closed, her face pale, and her breathing slowed.

One of the medical crew that had arrived took over for Ward.

Ward wiped his hands on his pants trying to clean the blood off and followed her out.

* * *

Ward was showered and cleaned up when Alarik met him on the bridge of his ship.

"You have quite a mess down there," Ward said,

unsympathetically. "Thankfully for you it was just an Ambassador who died, and not Wynter."

Alarik cleared his throat, Ward hoped he was feeling the weight of the threat.

"The guilds have decided that this unfortunate accident should remain an Orion incident."

"You're going to cover the whole thing up?" Ward asked, not surprised. The incident would mar every Idex code involved, including the Viceroy's. A murdered Ambassador would be a hard thing to explain. "In your grand cover-up, what is going to happen to Jac and Rubio?"

Alarik's hard gaze told him what he'd suspected. If anyone did come looking, there would be a convenient trail of clues that would lead back to those two.

"And Helix?" Ward asked, hoping for at least some justice.

"The guilds will decide. I know you live in a world where your Idex grants you liberties and a ship that allows you a certain sense of ownership, but on Orion we have laws." Alarik puffed out his chest and Ward knew he was trying to intimidate him.

"Sadly for you, I don't live under your rule on Orion."

"A secret is a powerful thing, what do you want?" Alarik was grasping.

"I'll guarantee my crews silence, in exchange for Wynter's freedom. The freedom she should have always had."

"That's it?" Alarik said, sounding relieved.

"It's the only thing that matters."

Forty-Three

The sounds of instruments clanging and people talking hurt her head. There was a light buzz and soft dings like pots being thrown into the copper steam vats.

"What did you give her? She's completely out of it!" Ward's strained voice grated through the fog. It felt like a cold blanket had been put across her chest, and she was struggling to breathe.

"I don't know what I'm doing." The voice sounded panicked, angry. "Without an Idex code to give me more information…"

She tried to open her eyes, tried to remember. She was on the oil rig; there was blood and light and then there was Ward.

"Aren't you a doctor?" Ward asked. She could hear them bickering, wanted to tell them she was fine, but her mouth wouldn't form the words.

"I told you I don't know how much to give her. I have no idea how her body will react to any of this medication."

She wanted to see who the other man was, but there was another rush of noises splitting through her ears, a cold cloth placed over her eyes.

She reached her hand down, felt for the pain.

.

There was swearing, yelling. Someone grabbed her hand and gripped it. Something coursed through her like ice, then black.

Floating, adrift like ink darkness beyond the hull. Nothing.

When Wynter woke again, the room was quiet. An ache in her leg made her reach her hand down and run her fingers across the lines.

She hadn't dreamed it.

"Need to check your leg," Dr Moss's gruff voice agitated her ears.

"What happened?" she asked. She looked up, eyes clearing. There were guards at the door, and she remembered they had arrested her for Henris's murder. He poked at the stitches making them sting.

"Don't worry, they're here for me, not you." He didn't sound too upset by that. "You've been cleared of all suspicion. I traced the poison used for Henris back to a stolen vial from my medical bay. It dates back to before you boarded the ship."

"Really?" she asked.

He shrugged, and she realized he was lying. There had never been any proof, but the story would be enough to keep her safe.

He bent over her, poked at her stitches again, and slipped something into her hand. The smooth pouch with beadwork he'd thrown out. Inside, she felt a long chain with the guild crest and gently closed her fingers over it.

"I took it from Alarik's office when they were questioning me." He smiled the same way he did when he'd been aggravating Ward. She wondered if he'd done it for her, or to upset them. She didn't care which.

"Thank you," she whispered, and squeezed the small medallion.

"Don't. Never thank me." His eyes were downcast.

"Dr. Moss." Ward arrived at the medical bay. He was standing at the door, wearing his navy captain's coat and not a hair out of place. Wynter felt her heart pick up.

"It's time to go," Ward said to Dr Moss and nodded toward the guards.

"So much for immunity on your ship," Dr Moss said.

"We both know the promise wasn't really an option."

"Well, you know where to find me. I left a basic document if she should ever need medical treatment, but if it's serious, there's little hope of someone knowing what to do with her." Dr Moss walked toward the guards, then turned back to Wynter.

"Stop hiding. You were never any good at it."

Then he was gone.

"Did you have to turn him in?" Wynter asked. She knew there were a hundred reasons, but Dr Moss, or whatever his name was, had saved her life. He'd left the Obsidian for her.

"The matter with the Idex labs is closed, you don't have to worry about that. He's being held for other reasons." Ward didn't tell her what, and she wasn't sure she wanted to know.

"He kept me safe," she defended him.

"No, he kept you hidden to keep himself safe. He didn't know who Henris was, but a formal investigation on the ship could have revealed him."

Wynter knew she should hate Dr Moss, but the feeling never came the way it should.

"And who knows why my uncle never properly tagged Henris's body? Maybe he thought mocking me was more fun than solving a murder. Maybe he did it to protect Dr Moss? Or maybe he did it to protect Madame Helix? She's being sent to a small island factory, or so I'm told. It doesn't feel like justice."

"So… I'm safe?"

"For now. The guilds met. They've agreed to give you his shop. You're safe, at least for now."

"Henris's shop? My own shop?" she asked. She was finally going home.

"It's a friendly offer." He held her hand. "And Inktons still wants me to carry their cargo, so I guess no one loses."

"I'm truly free then." Wynter sighed. But going to the shop meant she was saying goodbye to Ward. Wasn't that the plan all along? And with Ward telling her about Inktons, that must be his way of telling her that he'd agreed to marry Lady Cristelle after all? She knew it was inevitable, but her heart ached at the thought. "I'm happy to be staying here. I have a whole life in front of me."

"Of course," he said, then let go of her hand.

At least she didn't have to worry about sewing a wedding gown.

"Thank you for everything you've done." She wanted to say more, to say how she felt about him. He was her first friend, her first kiss. He'd set her free. So why did she feel so bound?

Forty-Four

Lucy was sitting on the long stone counter. One foot swung back and forth as Wynter let the sudsy citrus smelling soap swirl from the copper vat down the drain with a pile of grime.

"I still don't understand why you're not coming tonight," Lucy said, frowning as she stirred a cup of tea mixed with blunut.

"I told you, I have a lot of work to do here." She had a lot of work, it was true, but an endless amount of time. She had years ahead, decades in Henris's shop.

She looked at the sign on the wall. It confirmed the shop was hers. She had a piece of paper with her name on it.

Wynter Canmore. Henris hadn't been her father, hadn't brought her into the world. But he'd been her father in all the ways that mattered, and he'd given up his life, so she could have one. Knowing that truth made him something.

She spent the last few days wondering how many people knew. Wynter Canmore.

The guilds decided it was best that she was a beloved daughter, he'd taken her through the Hex-system to learn the trade and had passed away of natural causes. They all remembered a little girl in the shop, didn't they? Wasn't it wonderful the shop was open again? Did you hear, she specializes in gowns?

It was a good story, as believable as any other.

However many knew the truth, Alarik assured her they'd never talk. Guild folk were good at keeping secrets. The clockmaker had no problem keeping his distance, perhaps she'd get a chance to find out what he was doing in his shop that made so much noise. The cheese lady thought perhaps, it was time to move on, retire, move into the mountains with her sister.

Lucy clicked her heels together, bringing Wynter back to the moment.

"But it's the last ball. The ships all leave tomorrow. There won't be another for months. You don't know how dreary it is to go so long between balls. This stuff is terrible." Lucy put the sticky cup onto the counter and hopped down.

"I can't dance. My leg hasn't fully healed," Wynter threw back, hoping Lucy wouldn't pry any further.

"Don't you want to say goodbye to him?"

Lucy picked up the lace dress she'd brought and waved it back and forth, trying to entice her.

"It's not going to fit me. I barely fit in the clothing you'd loaned me before," she said.

"It's not mine. I stole it from Lady Cristelle. It's too plain for her."

Wynter definitely didn't want to show up wearing a dress belonging to Lady Cristelle.

Evening crept through the streets, setting the glowing orbs ablaze with light. "Well, I should go, but you're going to miss everything. Poor Captain Ward, all the heroics and having all those ladies on his ship, only to sail away alone."

"Alone? I thought Lady Cristelle was going with him."

"No, why would she? You wouldn't believe the horrible things she's saying about him. It was just dreadful at the ball. Well not as horrible as Helix, but you know."

Ward wasn't going to marry Lady Cristelle.

Her heart beat faster, but it was too late. She'd already told him she wanted to stay, and truly she did. She was home, in Henris's shop. It's what she'd been waiting for, hoping for. She wanted to make Henris proud. But Ward wasn't going to marry Lady Cristelle.

Lucy left Wynter to her thoughts, smiling and promising she'd tell her everything the next day.

* * *

The jingle sang as the door opened again. She looked to see what Lucy had forgotten, but it wasn't Lucy.

Ward was dressed perfectly, wearing his formal captain's jacket with silver buttons.

She'd been bent over a steaming scrub pot, her face dewy and her hair tumbling down her neck.

She hated the way she felt the blush rush up her cheeks. She smoothed down the apron covering her soft yellow dress, then reached up and tucked a stray strand of hair behind her ear.

"It's a nice shop," he said, looking around. "I'm going to the ball, and I thought I'd stop by on my way. I ran into Lucy. She said you weren't coming."

"It's not on your way," Wynter replied. There were so many things she wanted to say to him, but the words weren't coming out right. She was going to mess it up, and he was going to walk

294

away and leave.

"I know it's not on my way. The buttons on my jacket are loose." He changed subject, his voice catching as he spoke.

She didn't know what to do. She felt like she was wading through syrup.

"Are you going to the ball tonight?"

"No," she said, knowing it was pretty obvious from her appearance. "I wasn't planning on it."

She moved toward the counter where Lucy had slopped blunut. She rinsed the cup, shaking the bits of water to the floor, then set it on the counter.

He'd been fiddling one button on his sleeve while he spoke. It popped off and clattered to the floor.

She picked it up, wincing as her scar pulled. His hand was under her elbow as she straightened.

"I'll fix it," she said.

He took off his jacket and handed it to her. A needle between two fingers she pressed the thread between her lips, she wet it and slid it through the eye of the needle, then passed it through the little holes.

"I should have come sooner, but we've been loading cargo. It's as full as it's ever been. I guess everyone's heard what no one is talking about. I know I have no right to say this, after everything everyone has put you through, but I can't leave without you knowing…" His voice caught. "The Obsidian always has a place for you, if you need it, or want it."

"I'm finally home—" she said, that's what she'd been telling herself the past few days.

"I wouldn't ask you to give up the shop. It's yours. It will always be yours. But the Obsidian will always be your home too.

You could make your gowns. We have an unused guild shop fully stocked. The Obsidian has plenty of cargo options between Valtine and Orion. We could be here as often as you wanted. Sorry, never mind, it was a silly idea. I was just thinking…" He let the silence fall between them. What was he saying? That she could have both? Have everything?

"You're saying I could work on the ship? That I'd stay in the Helix suites?" Wynter asked.

"No." He stepped closer, lifted her wrist to his lips and held it there for a moment. "In mine."

A warmth flooded her; a sweet giddiness travelled from her toes to her fingers.

"I can't offer you anything. I'm nothing. I have no Idex, and no past and no land. I may as well be a ghost." Her voice trembled.

"I fell in love with a ghost once. I'm sure I can do it again." He smiled. "You're the only freedom I want."

Forty-Five

Captain Ward and Wynter were late arriving at the ball.

Wynter's stolen dress almost fit. It hung a little loose around the middle, layers of lace flowed down to her feet. Her braided hair had to be redone three times.

Alarik looked as though he didn't have a care in the world, except for the pleasure of a ball. Wynter wondered how he hid so much behind that smile.

Ward took a moment to talk to Alarik, letting him know the change in plans, and he agreed to suggest a few safe prospects for who might oversee the shop while they were away.

Lucy skipped toward them and hugged Wynter tightly.

"I'm so happy you made it. Everything is going to be so boring for the next few months, and you know Lady Cristelle isn't planning on staying."

"I'm sorry, Lucy. I'll be leaving on the Obsidian." Wynter blushed, she knew it reached to her ears. "And it's exactly what you think," she added.

Lucy squealed and spun her around. Dizzy, she regained her balance, watching the dancers spin around the room in a glorious flurry of colour.

Lady Cristelle approached Lucy and Wynter. Her glittery bright green dress drew attention in not quite the right way. Her eyes flicked to the dress Wynter was wearing.

"Don't you love it?" Lady Cristelle asked, pulling Wynter aside so only she could hear.

"Love what?" Wynter asked, her heart racing, wondering what Lady Cristelle was thinking.

"The way the whole room hums like a bed of roaches. Waiting to see what I'm going to do next. And it doesn't even matter. I could hug you and they'd swoon. I could slap you and they'd cheer me on, or if I take it too far, they'd feel for you, but they all just want to know. It doesn't matter what I do next, they all need to know. I don't understand why Lady Daye wanted to leave all of this."

At the mention of Lady Daye, Wynter stiffened. There was one more secret she'd been keeping.

"Did you hear? She's disappeared. No one knows what happened to her after the ball." Lady Cristelle's eyes narrowed. She took another step closer. "Lady Daye is my friend, probably the only one I've ever had and if you so much as breathe a word about what was in the chest—"

"I never opened it," Wynter said. She'd thought about telling Ward, or Alarik. She knew she should. But there were some secrets that weren't hers to tell.

Lady Cristelle smiled, and Wynter realized her mistake. "I'm happy to hear she got it then. She deserves to find what she's looking for. And for that reason only, you can keep the dress. Lucy can pay for it."

She turned on her heel and left Wynter standing staring after her. Within seconds Ward was back at her side.

"I'm sorry. I was busy dispelling more rumours," Ward said leading Wynter away from the wide-eyed Lucy onto the dance floor as the orchestra started a slow song.

"About us?"

"And the future of my ship—the future I'm choosing."

"It could be dangerous *Captain* Ward, keeping me hidden in the stars," she said as he pulled her close.

"Not hidden." His faced dipped close to hers. "But I'm okay with dangerous."

Orion 7827

"Dr Somes."

The cell door was opened. Six guards stood outside along with an elderly gentleman in a long black robe. Dr Moss felt it was a little overkill. He'd willingly left the Obsidian to help Wynter. He knew what it would lead to. The guards looked frightened to be in the eerily quiet prison with him—all of them except the elderly man. Dr Moss reached his arms over his head and, feigning a yawn, he flexed his muscles. The man in the robe rolled his eyes and motioned for Dr Moss to follow.

"Dr Somes, if you would come this way please."

"I prefer to be called Dr Moss," he said and gave the guards a wicked grin as he exited his small cell.

"About that… Moss has shown up on each of the hex-system planets Idex logs in the past number of years."

Dr Moss kept his face neutral. If that's all they knew, this would be easier than he'd thought. He kept his pace slow, his feet heavy on the stone floor.

"For the last twenty years it's been well known that you—Dr Moss—have not left the Obsidian," the man continued. Whoever he was, Moss thought to himself, he was stupid to be giving so much information.

"It's a nice ship." Dr Moss said, suppressing a smile.

"Jac and Rubio are not co-operating."

"Who?" Dr Moss asked, just to be annoying, not that it

mattered. Jac and Rubio didn't know anything of use. The fact that they were holding them would work in his favour though.

"The two men who were with you on the oil rig."

"Sorry, don't recall any oil rig." Dr Moss picked up the pace, exiting the first set of cells and ascending the grey stone stairs.

"I was assured, that in exchange for the girl's safety, you would give us what we want." The man stopped walking, subtly suggesting he was willing to turn around and walk Dr Moss back to his cell.

"Of course, of course. No need to worry." Dr Moss cajoled him. It wasn't precisely what the deal had been, but he could play along for now.

As they made their way down the hall, the guards followed, and Dr Moss breathed in the fresh mountain air. Getting back onto the Obsidian was going to be easier than he'd thought.

LOST
BETWEEN THE
STARS

BOOK TWO OF THE
STAR STITCH CHRONICLES

2023

Follow Hazel Vale and get exclusive content at
www.hazelvalebooks.com

HAZEL VALE BOOKS

Manufactured by Amazon.ca
Bolton, ON

29468885R00185